MYSTERY ON THE MIDWAY

VERA DODGE

Guideposts
New York

Guideposts.org
(800) 932-2145
Guideposts Books & Inspirational Media

Cover design by Wendy Bass
Cover illustration by Joyce Patti
Interior design by Lorie Pagnozzi
Typeset by Aptara

Printed and bound in the United States of America
10 9 8 7 6 5 4 3 2

For my father and brother—Sarah's biggest fans.

PATCHWORK MYSTERIES

 CHAPTER ONE

S arah laid her hand on the doorknob of the fairgrounds exhibition barn, and paused to take in the scene. To her right, the carnival workers were a blur of activity, setting up the midway for the fair opening tomorrow. Hammers clanged as workers brought giant pieces of metal together to form familiar rides: the Tilt-A-Whirl, the Ring of Fire, the Ferris wheel. Generators hummed as vendors set up booths where they would sell elephant ears and candy apples. A young boy in a bright turquoise shirt busily blew up balloons and stapled them to a wooden background in the dart game trailer.

In the Maple Hill fairgrounds, the exhibition barns that ran just parallel to the midway were alive with activity as well. A towheaded teenager in a flannel shirt led a clumsy calf past Sarah to the faucets between the buildings where owners had been hosing down their livestock all day, the first step in grooming them for show tomorrow. Sarah smiled. The baby animal display, with calves, lambs, and tiny newborn chicks warmed by incubator lamps, had always been one of her favorite corners of the fair.

This year, though, it couldn't compare to what waited inside the door. *I've had this dream for so long,* she prayed. *Thank you for letting me see it come true.*

She pulled her keys from her pocket and fitted one into the lock, but to her surprise, the door opened easily under her hand before she turned the key. Sarah's brows drew together in puzzlement. She had come early, expecting to have a little time alone to collect her thoughts. Who had opened the hall before she arrived?

As the door swung open, a small sea of faces turned to look at her, surrounded by the dozens of quilts Sarah had spent the last several months collecting for the landmark historical display. Sarah recognized Abby McCormick, reporter for the *Maple Hill Monitor,* and a few members of the fair board. Several more were complete strangers, probably from far-flung papers. And heading them all up was Allie Turnquist.

As Sarah stepped into the room, Allie turned and gave her a thousand-watt smile. Sarah smiled back wanly.

"Sarah!" Allie said. "I'm so glad you made it."

Made it? Sarah thought. She had done all the work to put this historical display together. All Allie had done was donate the funding. But that, of course, was no small feat. Allie's generosity had allowed Sarah to rent equipment to turn the normally humid and drafty exhibition hall into a safe environment for the delicate quilts and hire extra security to watch over them. The annual quilt competition had new life this year too, thanks to Allie: an increase in the size of the prize had changed it from a sleepy small-town competition into a buzzed-about regional event.

But so far, Allie hadn't done anything else—except insist that Sarah lead what Allie described as a "publicity tour" through the exhibition the night before the fair opened. Sarah hadn't been crazy about the idea. She knew through her own contacts in the quilting world that excitement had been building for months by word of mouth. And she had already spent a long day supervising the hanging of the exhibit. What she really wanted to do was relax in her favorite chair with a good book and a cup of hot chai. But Allie had done so much for the quilt exhibit that Sarah hadn't been able to refuse, so after the finishing touches were put on the quilt display, she had hurried back home, rinsed the fair dust off with a quick shower, and returned to give the tour.

"I thought we were planning to meet at 7:30," Sarah said, checking her watch. "It's 7:15."

"Oh, I asked everyone else to get here at seven o'clock," Allie said with a nonchalant wave. The gaudy bracelets on her wrist clanked as her hand dropped back to her side. "I thought it might be nice for us all to have a chance to get to know each other before the tour."

Sarah took a deep breath and forced a smile.

"This is such a beautiful display, Mrs. Hart," a teenage girl in the front of the little cluster said. She wore one of the cheap ribbon sashes that designated contestants in the Junior Homemaker competition over her blue sundress, with the words "Maple Hill Fair" picked out in sparkly letters. Sarah recognized her as Lily, Allie Turnquist's daughter. Lily shared her mother's blonde hair and soft brown eyes, but that was where the resemblance stopped. Allie had a habit of walking around town as if she owned the place—which in some cases was true. But Lily's gestures were more hesitant, as if she wasn't quite sure how her hands and feet worked, but she desperately wanted to do everything right. "I can't wait to hear all about it."

Sarah smiled at her.

"From what I can see already, it's quite impressive," said a man beside Lily. His white collared shirt was rumpled, but his eyes were sharp. He shifted a notebook under his elbow and extended his hand. "Peter Wimber," he said. "*Patchwork Magazine.*"

Sarah shook it. She hadn't invited him, so he must have come at Allie's invitation. But she had to give Allie credit—*Patchwork Magazine* was such an influential publication that Sarah would never have thought they would send a reporter out to Maple Hill. It was exciting and frightening at the same time to realize that the exhibition she had worked so hard to put together might get some attention in the national quilting press. "Peter," she said, "I've read so much of your work."

"I'm looking forward to seeing yours," he said, and smiled back.

"Well," Allie said, clapping her hands together. Her jewelry clinked again. "Shall we?"

A dozen pairs of eyes turned to Sarah.

Sarah took a deep breath. "Why not?"

As soon as she looked up at the first quilt in the exhibit, her nervousness vanished, replaced by enthusiasm for the beautiful and unusual pieces she had collected from around the state. "As some of you may know, Massachusetts is one of the oldest settlements in the United States," she said. "The first English settlers in North America landed at Jamestown, in Virginia. But the next two groups landed in Massachusetts—the Pilgrims at Plymouth Rock, and ten years later, at Massachusetts Bay."

"Near where Boston is today," Lily chimed in.

"That's right," Sarah said. "Somebody's been paying attention in history class." Lily beamed. "And they came over a hundred years before the country was founded," Sarah went on. "Starting in 1620."

"Are these quilts that old?" asked Carolyn Johnson. Sarah was glad to see Carolyn, one of the fair board members. Over the past month, she had seen her around town several times with Sarah's pastor John, one of the kindest men Sarah knew.

Sarah shook her head. "Not quite," she said. "Until recently, we believed that the original Pilgrims must have made quilts from their discarded clothing and textiles, since they were so far from home and had to make the most of everything they'd brought from England. But research hasn't supported that idea. Quilts don't really appear in large numbers in Massachusetts until the second half of the eighteenth century. And when they do, they're not always bedcovers. They're often cradle quilts, or quilted petticoats, like these."

The group looked up as Sarah gestured. Side by side on the wall hung a pair of intricately quilted petticoats. One was still pristine with details of shining white ribbon, while the other was deep yellow with age. "Can you see the difference between these?" Sarah asked. "This first," she said, pointing to the whiter one, "was owned by a wealthy woman. The fabric was likely imported from Europe, along with the ribbons and the lace. But the well-to-do weren't the only people who cared about fashion. This one," she said, pointing to the age-darkened muslin, "was made from simple muslin, likely woven right here in Massachusetts. What I love about this pair is that the stitching is equally fine on both. We don't have the history of this muslin piece, but I like to imagine that perhaps it was sewn by someone who had been trained in a fine shop, and used her skills at home to create a beautiful garment for herself out of whatever she had at hand."

"If I had something that pretty I wouldn't hide it under a skirt!" Allie exclaimed.

Sarah smiled. "Neither did they," she said. "These were designed to be worn under a half skirt, so that all the beautiful stitching was prominently displayed."

"Huh," Allie said. "Maybe they weren't so different from us."

Sarah nodded. "That's exactly why I've set this exhibit up the way I have," she said, "to tell the stories of the women who made these pieces. I didn't just choose the quilts that were valuable or unusual. I chose the ones that tell us something about the way life was when the quilts were made. It's a different way to understand the history of Massachusetts, and the history of our whole country. We have lots of books telling us about the wars that were fought, and the laws that were made. But these quilts tell us a different part of the story, about what it was like for the women who lived during those times, and the things they did to keep their families safe and warm, and bring some beauty into their world."

"Did a Massachusetts settler make this one?" Harry Butler asked incredulously. Harry was another member of the fair board and a deacon at Sarah's church. He pointed up at a brightly colored bedcover of pieced silk, embroidered with lively scenes of strange animals fleeing from the figures of tiny men into jungles of thread.

"You have a good eye," Sarah laughed. "In fact, this wasn't made in Massachusetts. It was made in India, and imported to the colony by the British East India Company. I included it in the exhibit to remind us that global trade isn't new in our generation. In fact, the original colonies were full of people and goods from around the world. Many of the women who made Massachusetts what it is today were born on other continents before moving here to start a new life with their families. This quilt is an example of how interconnected the world was, even at the dawn of this country. And it was imported quilts like this that may have eventually inspired Massachusetts women to begin quilting themselves."

"Not to mention it's one of the most valuable in the exhibit," Allie added.

"That's right," Sarah said, smiling with an effort, despite the interruption. "As some of you may know, our very own Allie Turnquist is a substantial quilt collector, and this piece happens to be on loan from her collection."

"I paid an arm and a leg for it," Allie said. "My husband almost died. But now it's worth more than my car."

"We're very grateful," Sarah said.

She guided the group through the rest of the exhibit. The quilts she had selected for display really did tell the story of the state itself. The staid patterns of the early colonists mirrored the seriousness and simplicity of the settlers who had crossed the ocean to find the freedom to worship in their own way. The quilts created from scraps discarded by textile factories signaled the entrance of women into the industrialized workplace, and the creativity they brought to making the most of everything, including fabric their bosses threw away. The vibrant Victorian crazy quilts, gorgeous hodgepodges pieced according to no particular pattern, captured the hope and prosperity of that era. The pale pastels of the Depression-era quilts showed that even in those hard times, women had found a way to create beautiful patterns from worn-out clothes and inexpensive calico. In every era, the quilts told a different story, but one theme was always the same: women making something beautiful out of scraps that anyone else might have consigned to the trash.

At the end of the exhibit, the group came to a stop below a very large quilt. It wasn't as flashy as many of the others they had seen, but the more a person looked, the more there was to see. On a simple cream background, various figures in gray and chestnut felt had been stitched onto the quilt, then embellished with simple black-and-white thread. The first square showed a large boat, its deck crowded with embroidered animals. In the next, a man in an unmistakable pilgrim's hat accepted an armful of vegetables from a Native American.

"Now this one is out of order," Peter Wimber said.

Sarah nodded. "This one is much earlier than many we've just seen," she said. "But I saved it for last because it's the most important quilt in the collection."

"And perhaps in the state," Allie added.

"Perhaps," Sarah said with a little smile. This quilt was, in fact, the coup of the exhibit, and she was pleased that Peter had noticed it. "This is one of the earliest bed quilts in Massachusetts. It actually predates any of the quilts owned by the Boston Historical Society."

"Why isn't it in a museum?" Lily asked, her expression worried.

"Because this is one of Maple Hill's own treasures," Sarah told her. "It's been in Helen Baxter's family for over two centuries, and it's never been out of their hands."

"I've seen photographs of this," Peter said. "But it's never been on display before, has it?"

"No, it hasn't," Sarah replied, with a little flutter of pride—and anxiety.

"How did you manage it?" he asked.

"I've done some work for Helen, so she was willing to trust me with it," Sarah said. "And after all, it won't be leaving Maple Hill."

Peter nodded, his gaze fixed on the quilt, clearly impressed.

"I wish I could get her to trust me with it," Allie said. "I've offered her twice its weight in gold."

"She's not interested in selling?" Peter asked.

"That's putting it mildly," Allie said. "She's turned me down more times than I can count."

"The colors might not look like much," Sarah said, stepping back to address the whole group. "But they're hand-dyed, using nuts and berries. The embroidery is also unusual. It's another example of a person with natural talent who most likely didn't have the resources to afford a whole palette of threads. But look at what she was able to do with the simple black and white. In some ways, it looks very modern."

"It's gorgeous," Carolyn Johnson breathed.

"It's got a nice tie-in with our quilt competition this year, as well," Sarah said.

"You've heard about this, right?" Allie said, addressing the reporters. "We're offering a much bigger prize this year.

And we're introducing a new system of judging. Much more scientific than before."

Sarah struggled to keep a smile on her face. Allie had sprung the idea of a new judging system on her earlier that day, armed with a folder full of charts and what seemed like pages of scoring categories. When Sarah had objected, Allie had sailed out of the judging office, insisting they would work it all out later. Now she was pushing her opinion to the papers, without having worked it out with Sarah first. "I've always thought it was really more an art than a science," Sarah said.

Allie smiled her dazzling smile. "Not in front of the press!" she said. "We need to keep our methods secret!"

Lord, I know I'm supposed to love Allie, Sarah prayed. *But I am going to need your help.*

"Well," said Sarah, "we've got lots of wonderful entries this year, but one in particular I think you'll be interested in." Sarah had already selected it as the grand-prizewinner, but she kept that information to herself for the time being. "Janet Stevens, one of Maple Hill's most talented quilters, sewed an homage to this quilt this year. She even went so far as to hand-dye the fabrics using antique methods. It's an absolutely beautiful companion piece to this, and it ties together the quilt competition and this historical exhibit beautifully."

Peter Wimber still gazed intently at the quilt, which was separated from the crowd by a large table spread with historical information. This had been one of Sarah's innovations—it kept the crowds a good distance from the quilt, but also offered them the opportunity to learn more if their curiosity had been piqued. "Do you mind?" he asked, leaning in.

"Of course not," Sarah said, pulling the table away from the wall so he could slip closer. "Please." She watched as he moved in to stare up at the bold shapes and intricate stitching. But then a flash of silver in the corner of the quilt caught her own gaze.

Looking closer, she recognized it as one of the straight pins she used in her prize-judging system, to temporarily mark a top contender. What was it doing on this priceless antique?

Her stomach lurching, Sarah glanced quickly over the rest of the quilt. Janet Stevens's copy had been as faithful as possible, but having worked closely with both quilts, Sarah knew exactly how to distinguish them. In the antique, some of the embroidery threads had come loose, while Janet's new stitches were smooth and perfect.

Sarah scanned the face of the quilt, hoping against hope that she would find a loose thread. Her search was in vain. Each stitch was in place. Then she glanced down at the left corner of the quilt, which she knew should show a slight stain. The corner was freshly dyed and pristine.

The quilt hanging on the wall was not the priceless antique. It was Janet Stevens's flawless copy.

Sarah's eyes darted to Peter Wimber. If anyone else in the crowd might recognize the switch, it was him. But he simply gazed at the figures on the quilt in evident wonder. The rest of the little gathering started to drift toward the door.

"Congratulations, Sarah," Harry said. "You've put together a heck of a show."

"This is wonderful," Abby McCormick told her. "I'll look forward to writing this article. I think it may even rank as front page news."

"Thank you," Sarah said weakly.

Allie stayed planted near Sarah, soaking up the praise, Lily beside her. "Mom," Lily said as the crowd began to thin, "they put my jams out in the domestics barn. Do you want to go see them?"

"I've seen them at home, honey," Allie said. "They've been all over the kitchen all week."

Lily watched her mother for a moment. Then she slipped out the door.

Allie squeezed Sarah's arm tightly. "Great job," she said. "We'll talk soon about the new judging system. You're going to love it."

Sarah watched Allie go, her own head spinning. *What was Janet's quilt doing here? And if it was here, then—*

Peter broke into her thoughts, extending his hand. "Sarah," he said. She took his hand and shook it. "You ought to be proud," he told her. "This is a real accomplishment."

"Thank you so much for coming," Sarah said. "It must have been a long trip."

"It was my pleasure," he said. He glanced up at the gray and chestnut quilt again. "Amazing. The handiwork is still pristine. The family must have taken good care of it. You don't see something like that every day, even in my business."

"No," Sarah said, "you don't."

He smiled and went out the exit, leaving Sarah alone among the quilts. In the silence, she could no longer avoid the question that had been trying to invade her mind ever since she recognized Janet's copy: if this was Janet Stevens's quilt, where was the priceless antique?

 CHAPTER TWO

I t's just some kind of mistake, Sarah told herself as she slipped out the exit and around the corner to the textiles judging office she shared with Barbara Benson, who was overseeing the knits competition. The office took up one corner of the exhibition hall, but it could be entered only from the outside, through a door in the outer wall. *There must be a simple explanation.*

But as she stepped into the large private room where the many fair entries were received and judged, her chest grew tight. *Lord,* she prayed. *I'm not even sure what to say. Please make this come out right.*

The room where Sarah had judged the quilts and planned the quilt exhibition was nothing fancy—slab concrete with metal walls that reached up to the high pole barn ceiling, and a dented metal desk. In fact, Harry Butler had joked with her that a few years ago it had served as a makeshift infirmary for the vet to examine animals that fell sick during the fair.

Most of the other fair categories—jams and jellies, prize fruits and vegetables, children's art—were simply judged in the exhibition halls themselves. But because of the number of entries the quilt contest had drawn this year, and the high value of the pieces in Sarah's exhibition, the fair board had devoted an entire room to textiles this year. With Jason's help, Sarah had set up tall wire shelves to organize and protect the quilts and knits that had been entered in the fair, including crocheted afghans and blankets. For the past few days, as she had checked in the quilts and pored over them, she'd had the sense that she was working in a kind of library of fabric. She loved the flashes of beautiful color and stitching everywhere she looked, and the way the soft blankets absorbed the sound of her footsteps.

Now her sense of peace and accomplishment was shattered. Worry started to fill her rib cage as she unlocked the door, flicked on the light, and stepped in. Overhead the fluorescent light buzzed, then began to glow stronger.

Janet's quilt wasn't one that would have been easy to lose track of. In fact, Sarah knew exactly where she had left it: when she had finished the judging that afternoon, she had set it squarely on the center of the desk she had been working at, as a kind of present to herself. The work was so fine that she planned to look it over one more time before replacing it on the shelf with the other prizewinners she had selected. Now her desk was bare, as she had expected. But that didn't mean the original antique wasn't somewhere on the shelves, returned to the office for some unknown reason. Sarah went right to the shelves where she had stored the precious historical quilts as they had arrived, some hand delivered by museum interns or private owners, some sent through various courier services. The shelves were empty, just as they ought to be with the exhibit now hanging. And with a quick glance, she didn't see Helen Baxter's missing quilt anywhere.

Sarah frowned. If the original quilt had been returned to the office, it ought to be close at hand. Had it fallen behind something?

Sarah checked below and behind the shelves. Nothing seemed to be out of place. She stepped back and stared at the second group of shelves, still full of the entries for the quilt contest. Sarah had actually been quite careful not to mix the two categories: the quilt contest quilts were all stored in high-quality clear plastic bags, carefully labeled, and alphabetized by quilt maker's name, while the quilt exhibition entries had mostly arrived in archival boxes and quilt rolls, which were now stacked neatly to the side.

Sarah did a quick visual survey of the quilt contest entrants, finishing with the winners, which she had stacked together on the lowest shelf. Then she went back through each quilt by hand. She turned the bags over. She opened them on the chance that the missing quilt might somehow be hidden in the folds of another. She started from the beginning, and went through each bag again.

Flushed with worry, she stood up and surveyed the room. Her eye caught the jumble of empty boxes and tubes in the corner. Was there any chance that the missing quilt had been returned to its box?

Quickly, Sarah found the wide cardboard container that Helen had used to transport the precious quilt. It was empty. With fading hope, she rattled through the rest of the boxes and tubes. Nothing.

Crestfallen, Sarah sank down at the desk. Her hands closed on a stray piece of heavy card stock: Janet Stevens's entry card for the homage quilt. Could Janet know anything about the missing quilt? Was it possible that she had come to collect her quilt for some reason, gotten confused, and taken the wrong one? Or even that she had made the switch on purpose? Sarah didn't like to think about the possibility that she was dealing with a theft instead of a misunderstanding, but the antique quilt was very valuable, and Janet had certainly had enough time to acquaint herself with how much it was worth as she studied it to make the copy.

Sarah pulled her cell phone from her purse and dialed the number on the entry card.

On Janet's end, it rang several times. Then a message came on. When the beep sounded, Sarah hesitated. She wasn't even sure yet herself what had happened. How much should she share with Janet?

"Janet," she said after a moment, "this is Sarah Hart. I have an important question for you regarding the quilt contest. Would you please call me back as soon as you're able when you get this? Thanks so much."

In the silence after she hung up, the consequences of the fact that the quilt was missing began to spin through her mind. First of all, how would she tell Helen? She felt a strong responsibility to protect the treasure that had been handed down safely through so many generations of Helen's family. It had taken Sarah years to convince her to share that treasure with the rest of the world, and Helen had only allowed the quilt to go out of her home because of her trust in Sarah. Sarah couldn't even begin to think of what words she could use to tell Helen that the quilt was missing.

And besides Helen, there was the quilt contest itself. The winners would need to be hung in the prize hall in just a few days, for the big weekend celebration surrounding the close of the fair. Until then, Sarah would have a slight advantage over whoever had taken or switched the quilt. If she didn't share the news with anyone, the culprits might think they had gotten away with it, allowing her time to investigate while their guard was down. But if she didn't have the quilt back by Friday, Helen wouldn't be her only worry. Sarah would have to explain how she had lost track of a priceless antique to the fair board, *Patchwork Magazine*, and Allie Turnquist, who had put up the funding for all of this.

There was only one solution. She had to find the quilt and bring it back safely before the prize ceremony on Friday.

Lord, she prayed, *you know where Helen's quilt is. Please help me find it.*

When she finished, she felt steadier and more determined. She opened her bag and pulled out one of her familiar quilting notebooks. Usually she used these to record her progress on the restoration of a single quilt or the solution of a mystery, but she had filled this one with details about the quilt exhibition and contest. There were still some empty pages in the back. Sarah turned to a blank page, and began to write down the facts.

The last time she was sure of the whereabouts of both quilts was at about 4:30 that afternoon. At that time, she was certain that Janet Stevens's copy quilt had been on her desk because she had seen it as she carried Helen's quilt out of the office to the exhibit hall. Sarah had saved Helen's quilt for last as they had hung the exhibition, and had gone back to the textile office to get it herself, keeping her promise to Helen that she would be responsible for whatever happened.

As she supervised the volunteers who were hanging the quilt, making sure they took exquisite care of it, Allie had arrived, Lily in tow, to talk about her new judging scheme. That was about 4:40. Before Sarah had been able to think of a polite way to put Allie off, Carolyn Johnson had arrived. They had just discovered a glitch in the fair schedule, Carolyn had told Sarah, and they needed her help to work it out. Before they had left, Allie had extracted a promise from Sarah to look over the new judging system later that night, around nine o'clock.

Then Sarah had gone with Carolyn, grateful to have some time to think over the new judging rules before she had to confront Allie again. Sarah and Carolyn had spent the next forty minutes negotiating with Angie Bolen, who headed up the Junior Homemaker awards, over the fact that the quilt and Junior Homemaker awards ceremonies had accidentally been scheduled at the same time. Ultimately they had agreed to hold both ceremonies together, which might bring new audiences to both events. At that time, around 5:20, Sarah had returned to lock up the quilt office and the exhibition hall before going home to get ready for the tour. If anything had happened to the quilts, it must have been in that brief window of time.

I can't believe it, Sarah thought. *After all the work I did hiring security for this exhibition, something happened to the quilts before the public was even allowed in.*

She shook her head. Well, at least the fact that the public hadn't been allowed in yet narrowed her list of suspects. Who else could have possibly been in the hall while she was gone?

All Sarah's volunteers had left before she had that afternoon, but Allie and Lily had still been in the exhibition hall when Sarah left, and Allie made no secret of her desire to own the missing quilt. She made an obvious suspect, but Sarah had trouble believing that Allie would undermine both the exhibition and the contest she had funded by stealing the quilt. Then again, Allie had paid astronomical prices for quilts before. Maybe all her generosity surrounding these events had just been a ploy to get the quilt out of Helen's hands so it would be easier for her to "collect." But Sarah had been with Carolyn and Angie for almost forty minutes. Had anyone else visited the hall during that time? Could someone else have had the opportunity to switch the quilts?

In her purse, Sarah's phone let out a peal. Sarah fumbled for it, and glanced at the caller ID: a local number she didn't recognize. Probably Janet calling back, she thought, and answered.

"Mrs. Hart?" The voice was a man's.

"Yes," Sarah said. "That's me."

"This is Dr. Canaday, over at Bedford Manor," he said.

"Oh!" Sarah said. "Is everything all right?"

"I'm calling with an update on your father," the doctor said. "I know one of our nurses spoke to you earlier this week about an infection your father has been fighting."

"I know he hasn't been feeling very well," Sarah said. "He seemed worn out when I saw him a few days ago."

"Unfortunately, he hasn't been responding well to the antibiotics. We'd hoped he'd be out of the woods by now, but he seems to be declining."

"Is it serious?" Sarah asked.

"With patients your father's age, anything can be serious," Dr. Canaday said. "I'm still hopeful that we'll be able to knock this infection out with another round of medication. But I wanted to make sure that you understand that the situation does have risks."

"Is there anything I should be doing?" Sarah asked.

"Well, seeing you is always good medicine for him," Dr. Canaday said. "He brags to the nurses about his wonderful daughter for the whole day after you visit. Other than that, we're doing everything we can."

"Thank you so much," Sarah said.

"You're welcome," Dr. Canaday said. "Let me know if you have any other questions."

"I will," said Sarah. "Thank you."

She laid her phone down on the desk and closed her eyes. Worry over her father wiped all other thoughts from her mind. More and more these days, he seemed to have problems no one really understood, without easy solutions. In some ways, dealing with the mysteries of her father's failing mind and failing health was harder than dealing with her husband Gerry's death, even though Gerry had been younger, and went faster. At least then she had known what they were facing, and there were things she could do for him each day: take him to appointments, organize his medicines, hold his hand. She would do anything she could for her father too, but there never seemed to be anything concrete to do. And the memory losses her father had already suffered left both of them in a kind of twilight world. He still had the same voice, and face, and sweet spirit, but he couldn't consider her problems and give her the good advice she had depended on all her life. It was especially hard, since the good advice she wanted most these days was about how to help him.

With effort, she looked down at her notebook. She couldn't go to see him tonight, since visiting hours were over. She would go first thing tomorrow morning. But in the meantime, she still needed to find the quilt.

She glanced down the list of facts she had collected. Her volunteers had already gone by the time she had left Allie in the exhibition hall. They couldn't tell her whether anyone else might have come or gone. Was there anyone else who might have seen something?

She closed her eyes again. As she did, a memory floated into her mind. When she and Carolyn had left the hall together, a chorus of young voices had called after them from the walkway between the livestock barn and the exhibition hall. When they had turned back, they had seen Sarah's granddaughter Audrey and Martha's granddaughter Lexie, both waving at them like crazy. Beside them had stood a young man about their age, doggedly hosing down a reluctant Jersey calf.

Carolyn and Sarah had stopped briefly, while Audrey had excitedly explained everything she had learned in the last few minutes about cows, calving, and grooming cattle. It had done Sarah's heart good. She hadn't been sure how her sophisticated West Coast granddaughters would react to the pleasures of a country fair, and she had been touched by Audrey's enthusiasm. But now she realized the moment might have had more than sentimental value—if the girls had stayed for any length of time after Sarah left the hall, they might have witnessed something that could help Sarah find the quilt.

Sarah picked up her phone again and dialed Audrey's number.

Audrey answered on the second ring. "Hi Grandma," she said. "What's up?"

Sarah smiled despite herself. No matter what was happening, hearing her granddaughter's voice always lifted her spirits.

"We just met a piglet!" Audrey exclaimed, before Sarah had a chance to respond. "And a pair of lambs named Zeus and Thunder. Zeus is so cute. He's black, with a little white blaze on his face, and white feet, and a white tip on his tail, like he let it drag in a bucket of milk. Did you know sheep have long tails when they're born?"

"I'm not sure I did," Sarah said.

"They do," Audrey said, taking a professorial tone, "just like dogs. They bob them when they get older for health reasons. I wanted to take him home to keep for a pet, but Lexie says he'd only grow up to be a sheep, and she doesn't think mom would like that."

Sarah smiled again at the image of a full-grown sheep barging around her son's neat home, bumping into the furniture and begging at the table. "I'm not sure about that either," Sarah said.

"And then!" Audrey continued. "We met a colt named Hershey. He was just exactly the color of a Hershey bar. They didn't hose him down, though. They just brush his coat out with combs and a—" she hesitated momentarily, "—curry brush. I asked if it had anything to do with Indian food, and everyone acted like I was crazy. But half of them didn't even know curry was a kind of food."

"It sounds like you were there for quite a while," Sarah said.

"What time is it?" Audrey said. In the background, Sarah could hear Lexie give her the time. "Wow. I guess so. But I could have stayed there all night. We even met a pig that weighed even more than me and Lexie put together. He did *not* want his bath. Jesse says it's no use washing a pig down anyway. As soon as they get back to the pen, they'll roll in any dirt they can find."

"Are you girls still here at the fair?"

Audrey hesitated again. Then she offered a cautious "Yes…" Her voice turned up with uncertainty at the end.

"Does your mother know where you are?" Sarah demanded.

Another pause. "Kind of?" Audrey said.

"I've never heard of that particular variety of permission before," Sarah said.

"Okay!" Audrey said, confessing. "Mom thinks we're on our way home. But we're watching them build the Ferris wheel now! I've never seen anyone put a Ferris wheel together before!"

"Well, you need to get home soon if your mother's expecting you," Sarah said. "But I was hoping I might still have a chance to see you tonight."

"Is everything okay?" Audrey asked, worry creeping into her voice.

"Of course, dear," Sarah said. "You're over on the midway?"

"We're behind the lemonade stand near the Ferris wheel," Audrey said. "It's not open yet, but when we stand near the building, we just blend into the shadows, so nobody's tried to chase us away for a while."

Sarah smiled at her granddaughter's ingenuity. Maybe the sleuthing genes ran in the family.

"I'll be over there in just a minute," Sarah said. "I have a few questions I hope you can answer."

CHAPTER THREE

Grandma!" Audrey whispered.

Sarah looked around, startled. Audrey and Lexie had blended so thoroughly into the shadows of the lemonade stand that even Sarah hadn't caught sight of them at first glance. Overhead, a giant span of metal studded with yellow lights clanged into place, completing one of the triangular "pie pieces" that held the big circle of the Ferris wheel in place.

Audrey detached herself from the hulk of the lemonade stand, Lexie following just behind. Sarah kissed Audrey in greeting, and gave Lexie a quick hug. "Hello, girls."

"Nice to see you, Mrs. Hart," Lexie said politely.

"How's the quilt display?" Audrey asked. "Is everything ready?"

Audrey was just making conversation, but Sarah felt a quick tinge of anxiety. "We're getting there," she said. "In fact, that's what I was hoping you girls might be able to help me with."

She paused, wondering how to begin her questioning without alerting the girls to the fact the quilt had gone missing. "After we got the quilts all hung this afternoon," she finally said, "somebody went in and moved some things around."

"Uh-oh," Audrey said. "Aren't those quilts worth a lot of money? Did you get everything back where it belongs?"

"I'm working on it," Sarah said. "But I'm also wondering who would have moved them. I was hoping that you two girls might have seen something. Do you remember anybody coming or going from the quilt hall while you were watching the livestock being groomed?"

Audrey's face became serious with concentration. "I might not have seen everybody who came and went," she said. "I wasn't paying much attention."

"I'm not sure I'd say that," Lexie said with a smirk. Audrey gave her a warning glance, but Lexie's grin only got bigger. "You were paying quite a bit of attention...to Jesse."

"I was curious," Audrey insisted, her face darkening with a blush that was evident even in the low light. "About the cows."

Sarah nodded, trying to keep her expression neutral. She might have been over sixty, but she still remembered the days when she and her friends went to the fair to see and be seen. Even when she was married, she and Gerry would stroll through the fair together, keeping an eye on the kids and holding hands like they were teenagers. Although in those days, Gerry won stuffed animals for Jason and Jenna instead of for Sarah.

She tried to be patient while the girls focused on her question. They had been in a prime spot to watch comings and goings from the hall. When Sarah had left to sort out the Junior Homemaker and quilt awards, only one door was unlocked: the one that opened out onto the little alley that faced the livestock barns. She deliberately hadn't opened the exit door on the far side of the exhibition hall in order to keep curiosity seekers to a minimum while the exhibit was hung. "Do you remember seeing anybody?" she asked.

Audrey nodded, eager to change the subject. "Mrs. Turnquist," she said. "I think she came out just a little after you did."

Of course they would have seen Allie and Lily leave, Sarah thought. "She's done a lot to help us with the exhibit and the contest this year," Sarah said.

"They can afford to help," Lexie said. "They are *so rich*. Lily always had the best birthday parties. She had a clown when we were little. I always wanted a clown for my birthday, but Mom never let me have one."

"Clowns are creepy," Audrey said.

"*Lily* is creepy," Lexie said.

"That's not nice."

Lexie shrugged. "You haven't known her forever like I have," she said. "I'm just saying what everyone knows is true. She's not like the rest of us."

"What do you mean by that?" Sarah asked.

"She's so quiet," Lexie said.

"Well, some people are just quiet, honey," Sarah said.

"Yeah," Lexie said. "But then she gets way too into things. Like the Junior Homemaker competition. I mean, the fair can be fun, but she won't talk about anything else. And things that actually *are* fun, she doesn't care about at all. Like last year. Mrs. Turnquist rented out the whole skating rink one night. But Lily would barely skate, even though it was her own party."

Sarah felt a pang of sympathy for Lily. But so far, the girls hadn't really told her anything she didn't already know. "Were Lily and Allie the only people you saw in the hall?" she pressed.

"No," Audrey said, her brow still knitted, trying to re-member. "There were a few others."

The back of Sarah's neck pricked. Now they were getting somewhere. "Did you recognize any of them?" she asked.

"Mr. Connolly," Audrey said, mischief dancing in her eyes.

Sarah's heart gave a little tug, but her eyes narrowed at her granddaughter. Audrey was delighted with the fact that her grandmother and Liam had been on a few dates, but this was no time for teasing. "And what would Mr. Connolly be doing at the quilt exhibit?" Sarah asked.

Audrey gave an elaborate shrug. "I don't know," she said. "You'd have to ask him. All I know is he was awfully worried about getting the mud off his shoes before he went in the exhibit hall."

"Did he ask you where I was?" Sarah said. She had been certain that Audrey was just tweaking her about her friendship with Liam. But apparently Liam had been there. Why would he have come so early, and alone?

"I barely saw him go in," Audrey said. "He didn't really stop to talk. I wasn't even sure it was him until he came out."

"It was Mr. Connolly, all right," Lexie agreed. "I get a caramel latte from him every time I can get Grandma to buy me one."

Sarah smiled at Martha's softheartedness. But that didn't explain what Liam had been doing in her quilt exhibit.

"How long did he stay?" she asked.

"Not very long," Lexie said.

Audrey nodded. "Not even five minutes," she said. "It almost seemed like he walked in, and then walked right out."

Sarah's forehead furrowed as her mind worked to make sense of the facts. She couldn't think of any reason for Liam to handle the quilts, or a reason for Liam to be in the exhibition hall at all. Could he have had something to do with the missing quilt?

"Was he carrying anything when he left?"

Lexie looked at Audrey. Audrey looked at Lexie. Both of them shook their heads.

"But when he came out, he seemed kind of..." Audrey paused, searching for a word.

"Guilty?" Sarah suggested.

Audrey shook her head again. "No," she said, "more like embarrassed."

"He didn't even say hello to us," Lexie said, "and Mr. Connolly always says hello to everyone."

Sarah crossed her arms. The girls seemed to have told her everything they knew about Liam's visit. "Was he the only person you saw?" she asked. "Did anyone else go in while I was gone?"

"There was someone else," Audrey said, her eyes lighting up. "I think she worked for the fair. She was wearing one of those turquoise shirts."

She nodded up at the workers who were hammering the Ferris wheel in place. Most of them wore grubby work shirts, but a few sported the familiar turquoise polo shirts that all the carnival vendors would be wearing in the booths and games when the fair opened tomorrow.

Sarah's heart sank. A woman in a carnival shirt? That cut the list of suspects down, but not by much. Half the carnival staff seemed to be women. "Do you remember anything else about her?" she asked.

"She was blonde," Lexie offered.

"And she was small," Audrey added. "I think she wasn't even as tall as me. I noticed as she went by."

Now they were getting somewhere. Audrey was average height for her age, but a grown woman her size might stand out in a crowd.

"And she had a tattoo," Lexie said.

"I didn't see that," said Audrey.

"Probably because it wasn't on Jesse," Lexie teased.

Audrey opened her mouth in protest, but nothing came out.

"It was a butterfly," Lexie said, turning back to Sarah, "on the inside of her wrist. I remember because at first I thought she must have been hurt, and it was such a strange place for a bruise. But then I realized it was a tattoo. It was a pretty one. Just a black outline, with blue wings."

Sarah nodded. That gave her something to go on. "Thank you, Lexie," she said. "That helps."

Lexie smiled.

"She wasn't the only one," Audrey added, "from the carnival."

"What do you mean?" Sarah asked.

"There was another person with a turquoise shirt," Audrey said, "a man. Do you remember him?" she asked Lexie.

Lexie hesitated. Then her eyes lit up. "Yes!" she said. "But he didn't stay for very long. He went in, and then he came right out."

Two workers from the carnival, Sarah thought. If she was looking at a theft, that made sense. It would be hard for one person to switch the quilts on his own in that time frame, although it was possible. But how would the carnival workers have known about the other quilt, to switch it? They were strangers in town.

"What did he look like?" Sarah asked. "Do you remember?"

"Like a teddy bear," Lexie said.

"A teddy bear," Sarah repeated.

Audrey nodded. "She's right," she said. "He had big brown eyes, and a brown beard, and he was kind of round-looking. Not really heavy. Just kind of ... solid."

Sarah was quiet for a minute, turning over the clues they had just given her. Then another question occurred to her. "How did you girls get in here?" she asked. "The front gate isn't open yet."

"We came with Mom," Audrey said. "She was helping with some of the displays in the antiques exhibit." Sarah nodded. Every year for the fair, Maple Hill residents displayed favorite antiques that touched on the town's history. The relics might not mean much to anyone else, but they gave a wonderful glimpse into Maple Hill's history: playbills from the old movie house, old-fashioned baseball uniforms from a local team, photographs of the men and women the streets were now named after.

"Is your mom still here?" Sarah asked.

Audrey shook her head. "She finished up and went home," she told Sarah. "We wanted to stay, so she said it would be okay if we walked back later."

Sarah glanced around at the twilight on the half-finished midway. "Are you staying much longer?" she asked.

Lexie shook her head. "We need to go soon. I have to be home by eight-thirty."

Sarah looked at her watch. "Would you girls like me to drive you home?" she asked. "You've only got a little more than half an hour to walk home."

"No, that's okay. We'll leave in a minute," Audrey said.

Sarah gave her a hug. "You be careful," she said. She gave Lexie a little squeeze as well, her mind already racing through who she ought to approach next about the quilt. Could she find the mysterious carnival workers in the dark? Would it make sense to go over to The Spotted Dog to ask Liam what he had been doing at the exhibit? "Thanks for your help," she said. "You girls were very observant."

Audrey grinned. Then her grin faded. "Wait!" she said. "I almost forgot. There was someone else."

"Someone else in the quilt exhibit?" Sarah asked.

Lexie looked at her quizzically, but Audrey nodded. "Mrs. Andrews," she said.

"Oh!" Lexie said. Now she nodded too. "That's right!" she said. "I saw her too!"

"Mrs. Andrews?" Sarah repeated. "Shelly Andrews?" Shelly Andrews was a young wife and mother who Sarah knew in passing from Wild Goose Chase, the local fabric and yarn store. They usually greeted each other from opposite sides of the shop, since Shelly was a passionate knitter, and Sarah stayed mostly among the bolts and fat quarters of quilting fabric. But Sarah had always liked Shelly. She was open and friendly, and her knit creations were sought-after items at Maple Hill's charity raffles.

Audrey nodded. "I wasn't sure at first," she said. "When she went by, I said 'Hello, Mrs. Andrews' and she didn't answer. I thought maybe I was wrong about who she was, but then I saw the back of her jacket and it said 'Andrews.' It was one of those racing jackets. Black, with red silk sleeves. I guess she just didn't hear me."

Sarah nodded. Audrey's description did match Shelly. Her husband Mike raced stock cars on the weekends at a nearby track. Sarah's excitement began to build. Shelly had a real eye for detail in her knitted work, so there was a good chance she might have seen something useful during her visit to the exhibition. If Shelly had taken a good close look at the quilt while she was there, it was even possible that Shelly would be able to help her nail down exactly when the quilts had been switched.

She checked her watch: a few minutes before eight o'clock. It was a little late for a visit, but Shelly was almost sure to be at home now. And if Sarah went right away, she could still make it back in time for her nine o'clock meeting with Allie about her new judging scheme.

"Girls," she said, "how would you like a ride home, after all?"

A few minutes later, Audrey slammed the car door shut outside Lexie's house and turned to wave at Sarah. "Thanks Grandma!" she said. "You're the best."

Sarah waved back and watched to make sure Audrey and Lexie made it safely to the house. Then she pulled away from the curb and drove the few blocks to Shelly Andrews's home.

The Andrews lived in a snug bungalow on one of the last streets of town. The houses were a little smaller here than in some neighborhoods, but the yards were neat and the gardens were full of bright orange, yellow, and red flowers. A friendly light glowed on the Andrews's porch. The dark shadows of the forest that began where the neighborhood ended rose behind the house.

Sarah parked at the curb, got out, and went up to the door. When she knocked, it opened almost immediately.

A redheaded boy, about six or seven years old, looked up at her curiously. He was wearing a pirate hat, a pair of blue and white striped shorts, and swimming flippers.

"Hello," Sarah said. "Is your mother home?"

The boy drew himself up to his full height of about four feet tall. "Do you know the magic word?" he asked.

Sarah pursed her lips in pretend concentration. "The magic word...," she mused. "Could you give me a hint?"

"Adrian!" called a woman's voice from the back of the house. "What are you doing up there?"

Adrian's piratical courage quailed somewhat at the voice of his mother. "If you want a hint, I want a cookie!" he said.

Sarah smiled in spite of herself.

"Adrian!" the voice called again. It was close enough now that Sarah was sure she recognized it as Shelly's.

Adrian's eyes widened. He gave the door a heroic push. As it swung shut, Sarah caught one last glimpse of him dashing for the back of the house. A moment later, the door swung open again.

Shelly stood on the threshold, smiling ruefully. "Sarah," she said. "I see you've met my son."

"He's a very good negotiator," Sarah said.

"Yes," Shelly said, "if we can only teach him to use his powers for good and not evil. Come on in."

"I'm sorry to bother you so late," Sarah said.

"No problem at all," Shelly said. "I'm always up for a bit of grown-up conversation." She gestured around the entryway. Toys were strewn on the carpet. A few coats hung neatly on blue-painted pegs, including the black and red racing jacket the girls had seen earlier that night, but below it on the floor was a tangle of children's sweaters and shoes. "Believe it or not, those were all hung up this morning," Shelly added.

"I believe it," Sarah said. "Jason used to upend three rooms in the time it took me to put one back in order. But I could never get him to have that same enthusiasm for cleaning things up."

"Never, huh?" Shelly said. "I keep hoping if I keep at it, maybe…"

"Well, Jason's got children of his own, now," Sarah told her. "So now he cleans up behind them."

"I don't know if I can wait that long," Shelly said.

Sarah smiled. "It'll pass faster than you think," she told the young mother.

Shelly nodded. "That's what they say," she said gazing down at the pile of little clothes on the floor. Then she shook her head and looked back up. "Well, Sarah, what brings you here?"

"I'm hoping you can help me," Sarah said. "You know, I've spent a good amount of time this summer putting together the quilt exhibit and contest over at the fair."

When Sarah mentioned the fair, Shelly's smile faded. Sarah noticed, but she was struggling with a problem of her own: how to explain what had happened with the quilts without giving away too much information. The last thing she needed was for word of the problem to get around town while she was still trying to track down the missing quilt.

"I heard about that, yes," Shelly said. "It sounds like quite a project."

"It has been," Sarah said. "And I've loved every minute of it. But this afternoon, while we were hanging the quilts, we had a bit of confusion I'm trying to clear up. Just a few things that got switched around. It happened while I was out of the hall. My granddaughter Audrey happened to be standing outside, and she mentioned that she saw you go in while I was gone. I know you've got just a fantastic eye for detail, and I was hoping you might have seen something that would help me clear up our problem."

Shelly's polite smile had returned, but when she spoke, her voice was precise and cold, like someone speaking to a salesperson on the phone. "I'm sorry," she said, "I haven't been to the fair today. Your granddaughter must have made some kind of mistake."

"Actually, that's what she thought at first," Sarah said. "But after she thought about it, she was quite sure. She said you were wearing Mike's racing jacket, with 'Andrews' stitched across the back." She gestured to the jacket on the rack.

Shelly glanced back at the jacket with a startled expression, as if it had snuck up on her without her noticing. Then she looked back at Sarah and shook her head emphatically. "I'm sorry," she said, "I wasn't there."

"Are you sure?" Sarah pressed. "It would be so helpful if you'd seen anything at all."

Now even Shelly's forced smile vanished. "I didn't see anything," she said, talking slowly, as if she was explaining something to a stubborn child, "because I wasn't there."

Sarah took a deep breath, looking into Shelly's eyes. After a minute, Shelly looked down at the floor. "I'm sorry I can't help you," she said, her voice low.

"No," Sarah said. "I understand. I'm sorry to have bothered you."

Shelly looked up again. "I hope you do get your problem sorted out," she said, her voice sincere again.

Sarah nodded, but a new suspicion of Shelly had already started to take root in her mind. "I'm sure I will," she said.

"Well, good night," Shelly said.

"Good night," said Sarah.

She stayed on the porch as Shelly closed the door. Just before it swung shut, Sarah caught one last glimpse of the red silk sleeves of the racing jacket, and the bold white stitched letters that spelled out Shelly's last name on the back.

CHAPTER FOUR

"Now Sarah, I understand that you're not crazy about this idea," Allie said. "You can't hide it from me."

In fact, Sarah hadn't been trying to hide her lack of enthusiasm for Allie's new judging scheme at all. Sarah had actually begun the conversation by saying that she thought the old system worked just fine. She didn't see any reason to change it. Allie, of course, had ignored this. Sarah wondered if Allie's breathless, confidential tone worked on other people, because it certainly wasn't working on her.

In a chair at the far end of the long table, Barbara Benson, who was judging the knits category, kept her head down over a bright blue blanket worked with tiny white stars. She knew better than to get involved in the discussion, although Sarah had seen sympathy flickering in her eyes when she glanced up.

"Lily," Allie said, "where are those charts? Show her the charts."

"You have them, Mom," Lily said. "I gave them to you."

"You did?" Allie said. "I do? Where are they?"

"You put them in your bag," Lily said, and pointed.

Sarah watched Lily as Allie scrambled through her expensive black leather purse, which seemed big enough to pack for a long weekend. Lily observed her mother without a trace of the annoyance most kids sometimes betrayed for their parents, as the inevitable embarrassment of the teenage years set in. Instead, Lily's eyes followed her mother anxiously, almost as if she were the mother and Allie were the child.

"Aha!" Allie said, pulling out a sheaf of papers in a bright red folder. "Here it is." She laid the folder down on the table between them and flipped it open. Inside was a chart with a dizzying array of categories and boxes. Just looking at it made Sarah tired. "Isn't this beautiful?" Allie asked.

Beautiful wasn't exactly the word Sarah would have used to describe the charts.

"Lily made them," Allie said. "It was all my idea, of course, but I can barely use the computer. It crashes if it even hears me coming. But Lily can do anything on it."

"Well, yes," Sarah said weakly. "They seem to be very well done." Even though Allie had brought Lily into it, Sarah couldn't give up her ground. She simply didn't believe this was the best way to judge a quilting contest. Or *any* way to judge a quilting contest. So much of a successful quilt was about the response it elicited in the heart: the beauty, the thought, the small surprises carefully worked into the patterns. How could that possibly be reflected in a chart filled with numbers?

Sarah drew one of the sheets from the pile. "The thing is," she said, looking down at it, "I just don't know how a system like this can capture the essence of a quilt. There's so much about a good quilt that's hard to put into words. Even how each quilter chooses one pattern over another, for instance, or—"

"Well, that's all right here!" Allie interrupted. She pointed a well-manicured finger at one of the first items on the list that ran down the page. "Pattern choice, you see? And here's where you enter a number. Anything from one to ten. I thought at first it might be better to have one to a hundred, but Lily thought that was a little complicated."

Sarah looked at Lily gratefully. Lily gave her a little smile. At the end of the table, Barbara Benson seemed almost frozen over her stack of knits, as if afraid that any sudden movement might call attention to the fact that she was there, and give Allie the bright idea of trying the system out on her too. She didn't need to worry, Sarah thought. Quilts were Allie's passion, not knits.

"Just look," Allie said, stabbing her finger at the page. "I really think you'll find everything you could think of is on here. Pattern choice. Color choice. Difficulty. Originality. Quality of materials. Quality of stitching. Borders. And then points for each."

"But some quilts don't even have borders," Sarah said. "Points for originality will penalize quilters who are keeping heritage traditions alive. And giving points for quality materials only rewards people who are able to afford more costly fabrics."

"This isn't just my idea, you know, Sarah," Allie said. "I based this system on the ones they use at some of the very best competitions in the country. If it was good enough for them, I certainly thought it would be good enough for Maple Hill."

Sarah noted that a few minutes ago Allie had been trumpeting the fact that she had made the system up all by herself but decided to let that detail go. "I understand those kinds of systems can be useful in bigger events, when they're receiving thousands of entries, with multiple judges," she said. "But the quilt contest in Maple Hill has always been a small town event. We've just judged it by heart." Lily nodded politely, but under Allie's penetrating gaze, Sarah's explanation sounded weak even to her.

"This year's event isn't just a small town affair," Allie said. "Isn't that what you told me when we first talked about staging this quilt exhibition? That you wanted to do something that wasn't just about the town, but the whole region? All those quilts you have hanging in there aren't just from Maple Hill. They're from the whole state, and they're going to draw visitors from the whole state. And the quilt contest is different this year too. I don't need to remind you that there's quite a bit more money involved in it this year than usual."

My money hung in the air, unspoken.

Sarah sighed. What could she say? She knew she owed Allie for her generosity to the fair this year—she just wasn't sure how much she owed. Did making a big donation really give Allie the right to change the competition Sarah had overseen for years? She decided to try one more tactic.

"It does look like an interesting system," she allowed. "If we really felt we needed a system to handle the entries this year. But I've already finished judging the quilts. I'm afraid it's too late to try the system out. Maybe we could think about using it next year," she said.

As proof, Sarah pulled her list of winners from her bag and pushed it across the table to Allie. As she did, she saw Janet Stevens's entry at the top of the list with a little pang. What if Allie demanded to see the winning quilts here and now? Had Sarah foolishly overplayed her hand?

"Well, this is wonderful!" Allie exclaimed. "It'll give us a chance to see how the new system compares to the old one."

"I'm sorry," Sarah said, completely taken aback by Allie's enthusiasm over what Sarah had thought was an airtight excuse. "What do you mean?"

"Look, Sarah," Allie said, "I know you're a great judge of quilts. I've never had any question about the pieces you choose, and I've been following the contest for years. I even agree with your rankings. But the fact of the matter is we can't keep on depending on you like this. What would we do if you suddenly couldn't judge for some reason?"

Sarah crossed her arms, slightly bemused by how breezily Allie was predicting some kind of trouble for her. But then she thought of her father's declining health, and realized how real the possibility was.

"Or if you just decide one day that you're tired of judging," Allie said. "Where does that leave us? We need to put something into place now so that our judging will be fair, and scientific. This is the way of the future," she said. "It's how we'll protect this tradition for our children."

Sarah just stared. Taking Sarah's lack of objections for encouragement, Allie looked down at Sarah's list of winners. "Let's just start at the top," she said. "Janet Stevens, grand-prizewinner. Where do we have that quilt?"

Sarah froze. Without realizing it, Allie had stumbled on Sarah's one point of weakness.

"Isn't there a stack somewhere?" Allie said, looking around. "You didn't just leave them mixed in with the others, did you?"

"No...," Sarah said.

Lily began to hunt through the stack of winning quilts Sarah had piled neatly on the judging table. "Here's Molly Cunningham's, Mom," she said. "It's second place."

"Great!" Allie said, taking the quilt from her daughter and setting it down between her and Sarah.

Bless that child, Sarah thought briefly.

"Now," Allie said, "we just work our way through the sheet. Choice of pattern." She raised her pen over a blank chart and looked up at Sarah expectantly.

"Well, Molly actually designs her own patterns," Sarah said. "She created this one herself. It's not from any book."

"Wonderful," Allie said. "So where would you place that score?"

"High, I suppose," Sarah said. "She's a wonderful pattern designer. I'd say a nine or a ten."

"Nine point five," Allie said, calling the words out as she filled in the numbers. "And I guess she'd be high in originality, as well, then."

"I guess so," Sarah said.

"What score would you give it?"

Sarah could hardly believe that she had been dragged into a project as ridiculous as trying to put a score of one to ten on the product of Molly Cunningham's marvelous imagination. But it was better than explaining to Allie why Janet Stevens's prize quilt was hanging among the antiques in the exhibition hall, and that the actual antique was missing.

"A ten," Sarah said.

Following Allie's prompts, she worked through the whole list. When they had filled in every box, Allie tapped the numbers quickly into a small brass-plated pocket calculator that she pulled from a corner of her gigantic purse. "Ninety-six point five," she said, "out of a possible hundred. Not bad."

Sarah sighed. With this round lost, she didn't see how she could object to running the rest of the winning quilts through the same exercise. Luckily, there weren't that many of them, fewer than a dozen. She hoped she could have them finished and squared away tonight before she went home. She was tired, and she would rather be hunting down the missing quilt, but it was the only way to get Allie out of her hair. "All right," she said, "I'll go through the rest of these this evening before I go."

"All of them?" Allie said. She sounded shocked, even compared to the high drama she put into most of her statements.

"It's not a big deal," Sarah said, lifting another quilt from the winners' pile. "There are only a dozen of these."

"A dozen?" Allie repeated. "Sarah, we had almost two hundred entries this year."

Sarah laid down the pen she had just picked up and looked at Allie. "I wasn't planning to rejudge all the quilts," she said. "Just the winners."

"But that wouldn't be fair, would it?" Allie said. "I mean, what if we get different winners using the new system?"

Suddenly, Sarah realized the magnitude of what she had just gotten herself into. "I very much doubt that," she said.

"But we won't know!" Allie said. "Not until we judge them all. We owe it to our contestants. They spent a lot of time and energy on these quilts."

I know that, Sarah thought. *I already looked at every single one of them.* But now she was thoroughly stuck. If she had agreed to use Allie's system on the winners, how could she refuse to go through the rest of the quilts as well?

"I wouldn't try to finish it all tonight," Allie said, her voice concerned. "There's no call for that. And besides, we have until Thursday, when the winners list is due. You'll have plenty of time between now and then."

Except that I need to find the missing quilt by then too, Sarah thought to herself. "All right," she said, defeated. "I'll see what I can do."

Allie stood up and collected her purse. "You're going to do great," she said, giving Sarah's arm a pinch. "I just know it. I can't wait to hear how it all goes!"

"I'll let you know," Sarah said wryly.

"Thanks so much for your cooperation," Allie said. "I think you'll love it when you get used to it."

"We'll see," said Sarah.

Lily trailed her mother to the door. After Allie went out, Lily paused and looked back. "Have a good night, Mrs. Hart," she said. "It was nice to see you."

"Nice to see you too, Lily," Sarah said.

Lily gave her a little smile and went out, closing the door carefully behind her.

Sarah sighed.

"You've got your work cut out for you," Barbara said, finally lifting her eyes from her own judging now that the coast was clear.

"Yes," Sarah said, giving her a faint smile. "I'm afraid I do."

She picked her pen back up, spread the third-place quilt on the table, and began to fill in another one of Allie Turnquist's forms.

CHAPTER FIVE

A bright ray of sunlight fell across Sarah's pillow, teasing her back from sleep. When she opened her eyes, she was surprised to find the room full of morning sunshine. She curled deeper in the covers for a moment, relishing the soft blankets and the beautiful light. Then, one by one, the problems of the day began to crowd into her mind. She remembered the giant stack of quilts that still remained to be judged at the fair, the missing quilt, the call from the nursing home about her father.

She checked the time: just after nine. She had slept much later than usual, worn out by the late hours she had spent working through the quilts using Allie's system. Allie had been right—Sarah couldn't do it all in one night. But she had put a good dent in it.

Lord, she prayed as all the details swirled in her head, *you know exactly what I need, and where it is. Please lead me through this day, and help me not to forget that you're with me no matter what happens.*

As she sat up, all her swirling questions seemed to settle into perspective. People were more important than things, even if one of those things was a precious missing quilt. The first thing she needed to do was go to see her father. Then she would deal with everything else.

As she walked into Bradford Manor a while later, she heard a familiar voice call to her.

"Sarah!" Tiffany Henderson, one of Sarah's favorite nurses, greeted her from behind the visitor's sign-in desk at Bradford Manor. "Good to see you!"

"How is he doing?" Sarah asked, laying down the pen beside the visitor's log where she had just scrawled her signature.

Tiffany's gentle eyes were full of concern. She shook her head. "You can never tell with older people," she said. "A simple cold can knock them out, and the next day they'll be as good as new. But he didn't have a good day yesterday. I know he'll be glad to see you."

Sarah held up the plate of no-bake peanut butter balls she had whipped up before she came over, one of her father's favorites. "Well, I've got peanut butter cookies," she said, and offered one to Tiffany. "They seem to cure a lot of ills."

"They've cured a lot of mine!" Tiffany agreed, laughing.

Sarah went down the hall with a smile still on her lips.

When she reached her father's room, she was surprised to find him still lying in bed, the blinds drawn against the summer light. His breathing was labored, and he didn't turn his head when she came in.

She set the plate of cookies on the bedside table and sat down in the padded chair beside him. When he still didn't wake, she shook his shoulder gently. He opened his eyes slowly, as if his eyelids were almost too heavy to move, but when he caught sight of her, his expression brightened.

"Hello, sweetheart," he said. "Is it good to see you!"

Sarah leaned over to kiss his cheek. "Hello, Dad," she said. "I hear you aren't feeling too well."

"This isn't one of my best days," he said, softly.

"Well," Sarah said with a cheerfulness she didn't really feel, "I've got a brand-new plate of peanut butter cookies here for you. How would you like one for breakfast?"

A mischievous grin played across her father's lips. "We can't tell your mother," he said.

Sarah's mother had passed away years before, but when Sarah was a child she and her father had shared all kinds of harmless secrets. She smiled at the memory and took a cookie from the tray. "Of course not, Dad," she said.

But when she turned back, his eyes were closed again.

"Dad," she said, "did you want your cookie?"

"Oh, thank you, honey," he said, without opening his eyes. "Maybe another time. I'm a little tired."

Sarah sat frozen for a minute with the cookie in her hand. She had seen him sick before, but she had never known him to refuse a sweet, especially not one she had made.

After a long moment, she replaced the cookie on the plate and covered the plate back up with the little film of cellophane. "Well, I'm going to leave them right here," she said. "You can have one whenever you want."

Her father didn't answer. His breathing was deep and labored again, as if he had already fallen back to sleep. Sarah watched the well-loved lines of his face as his chest rose and fell with each breath. *Lord,* she prayed. *Please be with him.* Then she stood up, kissed him, and went out.

In the parking lot, she checked her phone for the first time that morning. There were no messages.

That was strange, Sarah thought. She would have thought Janet would have returned the call by now. Maybe she hadn't picked up her messages yet for some reason. Or maybe she just didn't understand how important it was. In either case, a second call couldn't hurt. She scrolled through her contact list to Janet's number, and dialed.

Janet's line rang several times, and then her message played, followed by the familiar beep.

"Janet," Sarah began, "I'm still hoping to talk with you as soon as possible. I've got a question about the quilt exhibition that's very urgent. If you're able to call me back as soon as you get this, I'd be grateful." She added her number, then hung up, feeling uneasy. She had never known Janet to be so difficult to get in touch with before, especially not when Sarah made it clear she needed to talk about something important.

The fact that Janet was so closely acquainted with the quilt meant that she knew as much about its value as anyone else in town. Sarah couldn't quite imagine Janet hatching a plan to copy the quilt and switch it out, but large amounts of money could entice people to do strange things, things you would never suspect of them. And who else would know about the homage quilt, in order to form a similar plan?

The thief was obviously using Janet's quilt in order to hide the theft and buy some time. And who else besides Janet would have known enough about both quilts to make the switch? There were a handful of other possibilities: friends of Janet's or Helen's who knew about the project, Allie Turnquist, a few quilting publications that had been notified in advance. But that still left Janet as a primary suspect.

Mulling this over, Sarah got in her car and headed downtown, toward the fair. But as she passed The Spotted Dog, she slowed, then slipped into a nearby parking space. Liam was another person the girls had seen at the exhibition hall that evening, and she hadn't talked with him yet. It would be good to see a friendly face, and hear Liam's levelheaded take on everything that was going on. And maybe a good cup of chai would help clear her head.

Murphy, Liam's gregarious corgi, was lolling on his dog bed like a self-satisfied Roman emperor when Sarah came in. But as soon as the bell by the door chimed over Sarah's head, he leapt to attention, surveying the newcomer to his domain with a glint in his eye. When he recognized Sarah, though, he dissolved into an eager puppy, galloping between the chairs and tables of the coffee shop to meet her by the door, where he immediately thrust his black-and-white rump in the air for a little scratch. When Sarah knelt down to oblige him, he fell over on his side, all four paws in the air, begging for her to rub his belly too.

"You know you're one of the only people who gets that reaction from him," Liam called from behind the counter. "With other customers, he really is a bit more of a guard dog."

"I don't believe it," Sarah said, then addressed the wriggling Corgi. "That's not true, is it, Murphy? You're just this sweet with everybody."

Murphy licked her hand and gave a satisfied little whimper as she rubbed behind his ears.

Sarah gave him one more pat and stood up. Murphy remained splayed on the ground at her feet, gazing up at her with an air of disbelief, as if he couldn't fathom that she could be finished celebrating their reunion already.

The sweet, spicy scent of chai was already emanating from behind the counter, where Liam was frothing hot milk in a small silver pitcher. As she walked up, he poured the milk neatly into a paper cup, then finished it with a cloud of whipped cream.

"Chai latte," he said, pushing it toward her. "Two percent, with whip."

Sarah pulled out her wallet and laid several dollar bills on the counter.

"Oh, this is your free latte of the month," Liam said. "Part of our frequent-customer program."

"I didn't know you'd started a frequent-customer program," Sarah said.

"We did," Liam said. "Although right now it's invitation-only."

Sarah smiled, picked up the latte, and left her dollars on the counter. "Well," she said, "then consider that a deposit against my next one."

Murphy trotted up behind her, his tags jangling, but when she looked down he walked right by, his nose high in the air, and settled back onto his dog bed.

Liam shook his head and smiled back at Sarah. "He's got a big heart, but he's a little sensitive," he said.

"I suspect he'll forgive me eventually," Sarah said.

Liam nodded. "So how's it going over there at the fair?" he asked. "I read a bit in the paper about it this morning. The article was glowing. It sounds like the reporter loved the exhibit."

"Actually, that's part of why I came in," Sarah said. "I've run into a bit of a problem with the exhibit. A few quilts got switched around while I was gone from the hall yesterday."

"Anything serious?" Liam asked, his normally merry eyes full of concern.

"I hope not," Sarah said. "But Audrey and Lexie were standing out beside the barn when it happened, and they said they saw a few people go in and out, including you. I wondered if you saw anything that might help me understand what went on while I was gone."

Liam glanced away from her, smiling with what seemed to be slight embarrassment.

"The girls say they saw me, do they?" he asked.

Sarah's brows drew together in confusion. She could hardly believe it. Was Liam going to deny he had even been there, just like Shelly Andrews?

"They did," she said. She took her first sip of the latte. At least it was the same as always: warm and sweet. A feeling of well-being rolled through her body as the tea slipped down her throat.

"Well," Liam said, his eyes dancing as his familiar smile returned, "maybe I was."

Sarah took another sip of the chai. "Well," she said, "if you had been there, what might you have seen?"

"Oh, I wasn't there for long at all. Not long enough to see anything."

"Nobody else was there when you were?" Sarah asked.

He shook his head.

"And did anything seem …," she hesitated, still not wanting to share too much of the secret, even with Liam, "out of place?"

"It all looked great to me," Liam said sincerely. "The little I did see. But I don't know much about quilts, Sarah, except what I've picked up from you. I'm not sure I know enough to have been able to tell if anything was out of place, or not."

He held her gaze steadily. It really seemed to be everything he knew. This time, Sarah was the first one to look down.

"If I saw anything that might help, you know I'd tell you," Liam said.

Sarah nodded. "I do," she said. "And can you remember why you were there?" she asked.

The trace of embarrassment crossed Liam's face again. "It just wasn't important," he said. "Perhaps I was just looking for you."

"All right," Sarah said, collecting her purse and drink.

"Will I see you over there this week, then?" Liam asked as she turned to leave.

"Are you planning on coming out to the fair?"

"I wouldn't miss it."

"Well, I guess I'll see you then," she said.

"I'll look forward to it," Liam told her.

The bell chimed over her head again as she went out.

Because its sound was still echoing in her ears, it took Sarah a moment to realize that the ringing she now heard wasn't from the bell in the store, but the phone in her bag. *Janet,* she thought immediately, and sent up a quick prayer of thanks as she scrabbled, one-handed, to find the phone amid the jumble of her personal items.

She answered it on the third or fourth ring, her purse sliding down her arm, her chai splashing from side to side in the paper cup.

"This is Sarah," she said. "Hello."

"Sarah?" a woman's voice said. It was familiar, but too old to be Janet's. Before Sarah could place it, the voice went on. "This is Helen."

"Oh, Helen!" Sarah said, trying her best to sound calm and friendly, despite the sudden knot in her stomach. "How are you doing? What can I do for you?"

"I'm doing just fine, dear," Helen said with a little laugh. "Thank you for asking. About as well as can be expected, I guess."

"Well, that's good to hear," Sarah told her.

"The only thing is that I'm a little nervous," Helen said. "I know it's silly, but I've never let that quilt out of my sight for this long. I'm sure you're taking even better care of it than I could, since you're such an expert with quilts. But I just thought I'd call and see if you could ease my mind. How are things going over there? Is everything all right?"

For a moment, Sarah longed to simply confess the whole mess to Helen and get it off her chest. But even as the words rose to her lips, she knew she couldn't say them. Helen was an old woman, barely able to leave the house. If Sarah shared the problem with her, Helen wouldn't be able to do anything but sit alone and worry about it. There was still a good chance that the quilt was missing due to some kind of simple mix-up. And even if that wasn't the case, Sarah was in a better position than anyone to find it: she knew the quilt, she knew the quilting community both in Maple Hill and beyond, and she knew Maple Hill itself. Sharing the burden with Helen at this point would only be selfish. It would upset Helen, and it wouldn't accomplish anything.

Sarah took a deep breath. "Things are going just fine," she said. "We hung the exhibit yesterday, and it looks beautiful. The reporters who were there said wonderful things about your quilt."

"And what about the quilt that Janet Stevens made?" Helen asked. "Have you had a chance to see it yet?"

"I have," Sarah said. "It's just beautiful. You can barely tell the difference between the two of them."

Helen giggled. "She worked so hard on that!" she said. "I didn't really want her to take the quilt away, and she didn't want to take a chance on staining anything in my kitchen when she made the dyes, so she set up a fire and a pot in my backyard, to try to make some of those old dyes and match the fabric. You should have seen the kinds of things she put in it! Oak bark, and berries, and chestnuts! She had a line out there with all the swatches hung up, just like a rainbow of grays and browns. I loved to look out my window and see them all fluttering in the breeze. But she matched them, exactly like the original dyes. She'd do it over and over, till she got it just right."

"She did excellent work on the shapes and stitching too," Sarah said. "I think you'll be really delighted when you see it."

"I can't wait!" Helen exclaimed. "You know, if I could get around better, I'd be over there today. But my son promised me he'd come and take me over for the closing ceremonies later this week, after you hang the winning quilts up on Friday. So I'll just have to wait. But it does give me something to look forward to."

"I'm glad," Sarah said. "We're so grateful to you for trusting us with your quilt. The exhibit wouldn't be the same without it."

"Oh, listen to what a silly old woman I am," Helen said. "I can't believe I was worried about anything. I'm sorry I bothered you with my little attack of nerves. It's just that the quilt's been in our family for so long, and I'm a little set in my ways. It's not always easy for me when things change. But this is a change for the better, I just know it. I'm so proud to have the chance to share my quilt with everybody in Maple Hill. After all, it's part of their history too."

"Well, we owe you a big debt for caring for it so well for all of these years," Sarah said.

"Oh no," Helen said. "That was easy. You've got the hard job, putting on a show for all these people. But I'm sure everything will go beautifully."

"I'm doing the best I can," Sarah promised, feeling a little sick.

"I'm sure you are, dear," Helen said. "Well, I should let you go. I'm sure you have more important things to do than soothe my nerves."

"I'm glad you called," Sarah told her.

"You're sweet," Helen said. "I'll see you Friday! It'll be so exciting to see it up there on display."

"I hope it'll be a special day for you," Sarah said.

Helen broke the connection, and Sarah slipped the phone back into her purse.

Dear Lord, she said, *you heard all my promises to Helen, and you know I meant them. Please help me keep my promises.*

CHAPTER SIX

Seven, eight, four, six, nine...," Sarah murmured to herself, tallying up the scores on one of Allie Turnquist's forms. The project still seemed ridiculous to her, especially with the pressing question of finding Helen's missing quilt. But Sarah had never been able to do a halfhearted job of anything once she began it, so she had been poring over the quilts for several hours, making careful judgments in each category, even when one quilt was clearly superior to another.

"Seventy-seven," she said, marking the total carefully at the bottom. She leafed through the stack of finished score sheets, slipping the newly completed one in between a quilt that had scored seventy-four and another that had scored seventy-eight. This was Sarah's own addition to the system: it would make it easier to pick out the winners at the end. Then she stood up to replace the quilt carefully in its clear plastic bag on the wire shelf.

When she reached for the one below it, her hand came back with only an empty bag and entry form.

"Hmm," Sarah said, surprised. "What's this?" She shook the bag open and pulled the crumpled entry form out. In careful printing, Janet Stevens had listed her name, address, and the title of the quilt that now hung where the priceless antique should have been: "Maple Hill Homage." Sarah felt a pang of worry. Until now, she had done a good job of focusing on the judging, hoping that she might come up with a new tack for finding the quilt if she just let the problem rest for a few hours. Not to mention that no matter what she did to find the quilt, she had to finish the judging by Thursday—and the sooner she could get it done, the better.

But now, when she scooped up the quilt that had rested under the empty bag and sat down again to work through the score sheet, she found it impossible to concentrate. *Choice of Materials,* the score sheet insisted, but Sarah had seen so many quilts already that morning that they had all started to blend together. Did the fabric in this quilt deserve a six, or more like an eight? She had worked scrupulously all morning to be fair in her comparisons, but now all kinds of fabrics swirled through her head, mixed up with the emotion surrounding the antique quilt's disappearance: Liam's evasion, Shelly's rudeness.

She had never known Liam to try to hide anything from her. And she had never seen Shelly Andrews act so frightened and cold. What could possibly have gotten into them? Was there one answer that could explain both behaviors?

Sarah worked through several scenarios, but one leapt out at her. What if the girls had been mistaken? She didn't think Audrey and Lexie would mislead her on purpose, but they had been distracted by the sights and sounds of the fair, not to mention the handsome young farmer Audrey seemed to have a crush on. Anything they saw would have been out of the corners of their eyes. Maybe they thought they recognized Shelly and Liam, but they had mistaken them for someone else.

And maybe the judging would go better if she took a little break from it.

She pulled her phone from her purse and dialed Audrey's number. Audrey answered on the first ring. "Grandma?" she said, her voice high with excitement.

She sounded as if she had answered the phone from the middle of a fireworks display or a war zone. A steady rat-a-tat-tat fired in the background.

"Audrey?" Sarah said. "Where are you, dear?"

"We're at the fair," Audrey said. "It just opened."

Sarah took a deep breath. Maybe this was one of God's ways of helping her find out the truth. "That's wonderful," she said. "So am I, and I was hoping to see you."

"Okay," Audrey said as a volley of noise went off in the background.

"Could you come over to the quilt barn in a few minutes?" Sarah asked.

"Um ...," Audrey said. "No?"

Sarah adjusted the phone by her ear. It wasn't like Audrey to refuse Sarah a favor.

"Is everything all right?" Sarah asked.

Audrey hesitated, then let out a little squeal. "It's *fine!*" she exclaimed.

"Where are you?" Sarah demanded, even more non-plussed.

"We're right on the midway," Audrey said, "at a game near the lemonade stand. From last night. You remember?"

"I'll be right over," said Sarah.

She found the girls just where Audrey had said, at a gun range under the shadow of the Ferris wheel that was now turning lazy circles in the sky. Lexie stood at the rail of the game, wearing a pair of large but obviously fake sound reducers on her ears. Her eyes narrowed, she shot steadily at a moving row of dented aluminum soda cans. Audrey stood beside her, clutching a gigantic purple dog with a lolling red plush tongue and large, hopeful eyes.

"Grandma!" she stage whispered when Sarah walked up. "I'm sorry we couldn't come over. Lexie's on a roll."

A cola can tumbled from the conveyor belt with a clatter. The carnival worker, a clean-shaven, middle-aged man with a shock of peroxide blond hair and a weather-beaten face, flipped a switch that stopped the belt.

"That wins one of these," he said, gesturing to a line of brightly painted mirrors depicting dragons, fairies, woodland scenes, and a suite of current pop stars. "Or you can go on."

Her expression fierce, Lexie pulled three crumpled dollar bills out of her pocket and mashed them down on the counter. The carnival worker flicked the switch once more, and the parade of pop cans began to slide by again.

Audrey held up the giant purple dog to show her grandmother, using both arms to support his bulk. "Lexie won this!" she said. "Now she's winning me one!"

Sarah gave the overgrown stuffed animal a pat on the head. "Impressive," she said. "I didn't know Lexie was such a good shot."

"Neither did we!" Audrey exclaimed. "We just thought it'd be fun to play the game, but then she kept hitting things. We're the first customers of the day, so at first the guy thought it was a fluke. But now it looks like she can really shoot."

Another soda can, this time for orange drink, toppled from the line in the back of the booth.

"One more round," the carnival worker said. He already seemed weary, despite the early hour. "For the big prize." He pointed at the row of prestige prizes that hung from the awning overhead: a whole pack of huge blue, red, and purple dogs.

"I don't know if I want blue or red," Audrey confided to her grandmother.

"Well, dear, these games are hard to win," Sarah said. "I wouldn't get your hopes—" Her words of wisdom were interrupted by the rattle of another can. Lexie pulled her headgear off with an expression of triumph.

"Another big win!" the man in the booth said with an attempt at heartiness. He lifted a red and white striped hook toward the line of dangling dogs. "Which one of these fellas are you going to take home?"

"Hello, Mrs. Hart," Lexie said politely when she noticed Sarah. Then she turned to Audrey. "Audrey, which one do you want?"

Audrey threw her head back to examine the curious faces of the stuffed dogs. After a long moment, she pointed up at a blue one. "That one," she said.

Obligingly, the man reached up with the stick to unhook the loop of string the dog hung from. He lifted the gigantic stuffed animal down. Audrey pushed the purple dog at Lexie, and embraced her new pet.

"I'm going to call him Bear," she said, her voice somewhat muffled beyond the dog's giant head. "Thanks, Lexie, I love him!"

"Thank you," Lexie called to the man.

He nodded and sat back down on his wooden stool. "You're quite a shot."

"What are you going to name yours?" Audrey asked Lexie.

Reluctantly, Lexie followed the two of them away from the scene of her victories. "I don't know," she said.

"Girls," Sarah interrupted again, "do you have time to answer a few more questions for me?"

"Sure, Grandma," Audrey said. "What are they?"

"Well," Sarah said, "I just had a few questions about the other night."

The girls nodded in unison, Lexie from over the shoulder of the purple dog, Audrey cheek to cheek with the blue one.

"I was just wondering," Sarah continued. "I know you were excited to be at the fair, and you were busy watching—" Audrey's expression turned anxious at the incredibly embarrassing prospect of discussing her crush with her grandmother. "—the animals get groomed," Sarah finished, to save her granddaughter's dignity. "When you saw Mrs. Andrews and Mr. Connolly." She paused, wondering how best to phrase the question, then just decided to plunge in. "Well," she said, "are you sure it was them?"

The girls looked at her as if she might be just a little bit slow. Sarah knew the expression. She had gotten familiar with it when Jason and Jenna were teenagers, and baffled by the fact that God had given them a mother who so clearly couldn't understand *anything*.

"I read Mrs. Andrews's name right off her jacket," Lexie said. "I don't know how I could make a mistake about something like that."

"I saw it too," Audrey said. "And I recognized the coat, from when she comes to pick up her daughter at school."

"But did you see her face?" Sarah asked, remembering Shelly's insistence that she hadn't been at the fair. "Are you sure?"

Audrey nodded. "I did," she said. "But how many racing jackets that say 'Andrews' on them are there in Maple Hill?"

Audrey had a point, Sarah realized. Despite Shelly's insistence that she hadn't been at the exhibition barn—or anywhere near the fair—the girls had no reason to lie about whether or not she had been there. And they seemed absolutely certain about the jacket in particular, which Sarah had seen hanging in the front hall when she went to visit Shelly.

The only other explanation for the girls seeing that jacket was that somebody had stolen it from Shelly's house, worn it to the fair, and then returned it later that evening, all without Shelly or anyone else in the Andrews house noticing. That was theoretically possible, but it didn't really make any sense. No, the simplest explanation was probably the best. The girls had seen Shelly Andrews in the exhibition hall, and for some reason, Shelly Andrews didn't want to admit she had been there.

"And you're sure you saw ...," Sarah hesitated again. "Mr. Connolly?"

Now the girls' expressions changed from slight pity to outright disbelief.

"Mr. Connolly?" Lexie repeated. "I've known him all my life."

"I'm sure it was Mr. Connolly," Audrey agreed. "Nobody in town really looks like him." A bit of mischief lit up her eyes. "I think you'd know that better than anybody, Grandma."

Now it was Sarah's turn to blush, but she quickly turned her thoughts back to the problem at hand. The girls were certain that they had seen both Shelly and Liam in the quilt exhibition hall. So whatever Liam's strange evasions had been, they really were evasions—not just a way of humoring her.

"Well, thank you, girls," Sarah said, turning to go.

"Is everything all right, Grandma?" Audrey asked. "You look worried."

Sarah reached out to give Audrey a little squeeze. "I'm just looking for something, honey," she said.

"Something important?" Lexie guessed.

Sarah nodded.

"Well, did you talk to the lady with the butterfly tattoo?" Audrey asked. "I bet she's around here somewhere. Or that other man too. All the carnival workers are working the rides and games now."

Sarah shook her head. Between her father's health and the quilt judging, she hadn't gotten that far down the list. But Audrey was right. Now was probably as good a time as any to try to locate the quilt exhibit's other uninvited visitors—while all the fair offerings were in full swing, but before the evening crowds arrived and it got dark.

She gave Audrey a quick kiss. "That's a good idea," she said. "You girls have fun."

"Do you want to go for a ride next?" she heard Audrey ask Lexie as she set off into the midway.

"I don't know," Lexie said. "Do you think the dogs will fit in the seats with us?"

The lights of the midway blinked bravely at the games and under the awnings, but day wasn't really their element, and they couldn't do much yet to compete with the strong morning light. On one end of the midway was a giant slide ride, complete with turquoise, magenta, and yellow flags dancing at the top of the stairs where the children waited to take their turns sliding down. At the other end was the Ferris wheel. Between them was a long double row of games, concessions, and smaller rides.

It was the perfect time to scan the booths for workers who fit Audrey's and Lexie's descriptions of the woman with the butterfly tattoo and the bearded man. Crowds were thin, and the workers watched the passing strangers carefully, sizing up which ones might stop at the game they captained, or take a detour to the window of the caramel apple vendor.

But as she studied them, Sarah couldn't avoid their attention. "Five darts, three dollars!" shouted a red-faced, heavyset worker with a broad smile.

Sarah smiled back, but shook her head. "Not today," she said.

"Come on!" he called back. "I bet you've got some real power in that arm!"

Farther down the line, a wiry college student with a trim goatee lifted a rubber duck from a miniature river to show her the number printed on its belly in permanent marker. "Everyone's a winner!" he promised.

Sarah shook her head again, and moved on.

A number of the fair workers were women, and several of them were blonde, but most didn't fit some other part of the description. Sarah was drawn to the corn dog stand by a flash of blonde curls, but when she got closer, she saw that the woman whose head they graced towered over the other workers in the booth, and Audrey and Lexie had said the woman they saw was petite.

Hope rose in Sarah's heart at the sight of a blonde woman resting in a lawn chair beside the gate to the Swing Ride, but when the woman stood up to safely fasten the next group of children into their seats, she saw that she was of average height, and a quick glance at both wrists showed no tell-tale tattoo. The men were even easier to sort through—again and again she glanced into their faces, but all the men she glimpsed working the games and rides were clean-shaven.

Sarah made a second loop around the midway, then came to a stop at the elephant ear stand. Every year, she promised herself she would have only one, and every year somehow that number climbed higher as the fair went on. She really should wait at least until tonight to buy one of the doughy, fried, cinnamon-sugar covered treats.

But if she bought one now, she told herself, she might also be able to collect some valuable information from the worker at the counter.

"One, please," she said, handing over a few small bills.

A moment later the carnival worker, a middle-aged woman with tinted glasses and tight brown curls, pushed the confection onto the aluminum counter at the window.

"Excuse me," Sarah said. "I just had a quick question."

The woman looked at her with slight surprise, checked behind her to see that there was no line, then looked back at Sarah.

"Yeah?" she said.

"I'm looking for a woman who works with the carnival," Sarah said. "She's small, with blonde hair."

"What do you need her for?" the woman asked, somewhat protectively. "There's no trouble, is there?"

"Oh no," Sarah said. "I helped set up the quilt exhibit this year, and I heard she came to visit it. I just wanted to ask her a few questions. She has a butterfly tattoo," Sarah went on, and pointed at her wrist. "Here."

The woman studied Sarah for a second longer, then seemed to decide she might be all right. "Sounds like Cherie," she said.

"Cherie?" Sarah repeated. "Do you know where I might find her?"

"Down to the end of the midway," the woman told her. "Under the Slip-Slide."

Sarah pulled the warm, greasy plate out of the window. "Thank you so much," she said.

The woman nodded as Sarah turned away with her pastry.

But when Sarah returned to the foot of the slide, she didn't see anyone who matched the girl's description. One of the slide operators was resting in the big swath of shade the ride threw across the fair, and a few games stood around it, all operated by men, all without beards. After a quick survey of the area, Sarah saw only one other possibility: a small crowd gathered around what seemed like a large easel.

When she got closer, she realized how she had missed it on her first loop of the midway. Hidden by the crowd, seated on a little stool, was a petite blonde woman, drawing a quick-sketch caricature of a little girl with red braids and a complete constellation of freckles.

As the woman's hand flashed over the paper, capturing the shape of the girl's eyes, button nose, and wide smile, Sarah could clearly see a butterfly tattoo on her wrist.

CHAPTER SEVEN

There you go, sweetie," the blonde woman said, handing over the drawing she had just unclipped from her easel.

The little girl gazed at the drawing, her eyes wide with wonder. "Do I really look like that?" she asked, looking up at her mother. "She's so pretty!"

"You're even prettier than that," the mother said, rumpling the girl's red hair.

"And what about a little bit of—" the artist opened a small vial of glitter and pigment and used her thumb to trace a shimmering glow around the girl's figure on the page.

"Fairy dust!" the girl exclaimed.

"That's right," the blonde woman said, nodding.

The girl's mother pulled out her wallet and paid for the drawing. "Thank you," she said.

"Oh, she's so cute," the blonde woman said. "It was my pleasure." She slid the payment into a small pouch at her waist as the family wandered off. When she looked up again,

Sarah was the only person standing there. Now she could see the woman's name tag clearly. Just as the lady who sold her the elephant ear had said: Cherie.

"You here for a quick sketch?" Cherie asked Sarah cheerfully. "It only takes a minute, but the image lasts forever."

Sarah smiled and shook her head. "Not today," she said. "I'm just interested in watching."

"Well, there's no charge to watch!" Cherie said. "Although there hasn't been a whole lot of traffic yet this morning."

"I bet it will pick up this evening," Sarah observed. She didn't want to dive into direct questions right away. Cherie was a complete stranger, and Sarah couldn't guess how she would react. And Sarah had found, over time, that she could learn a lot about a person simply through small talk. "You must have to work so fast, with children for subjects."

Cherie laughed. "Oh, it has its challenges," she said. "But I like doing it better than anything else in the world. My sketches may not hang in galleries, but I get to make a living doing what I love."

Sarah nodded. "We had a portrait done of my daughter at the fair years ago. Now her kids love it. It's a little glimpse of their mommy when she was a young girl."

"That's wonderful!" Cherie exclaimed. "I love to hear stories like that."

Cherie was so friendly and open that for a moment Sarah was tempted just to ask her straight out what she had been doing in the exhibition hall. But it would be better to keep her motives to herself for the time being.

"Do you sketch the whole day?" Sarah asked.

"Just until eight," Cherie said. "Then I'm off for the evening. A few years ago, we kept the booth open till the midway closed, but it was nothing but trouble. I can barely see to sketch in the dark, and when the crowd gets big, people get frustrated because they can't see what's happening either. So now I just close up shop when the sun starts to go down."

"Still," Sarah said, "that's a long day."

As they were speaking, a young mother led a reluctant towheaded boy up to the bench where Cherie's subjects sat to be sketched. He looked at it doubtfully, but his mother scooped him up and settled him down on it.

"But how could I mind that?" Cherie asked, smiling at him. "With all these beautiful faces to draw?"

Immediately, the little boy began to explore his surroundings: specifically, the various means of escape from the bench. He scooted his rump forward and dangled his legs toward the ground. Then he straightened up, only to lean dangerously far back.

"I hope you really are quick," the mother said. "I'm not sure how long I'm going to be able to keep him there."

"Well, I see you're busy," Sarah said quickly, backing away.

"Nice to meet you!" Cherie called over her shoulder. "Now," she said, turning to the little boy, "what's your name?"

"Batman," Sarah heard the boy announce as she walked off.

Then Sarah paused, with the uncanny feeling that someone had just called her own name.

"Sarah!" the voice cried again. The second time, Sarah placed it immediately. She turned around to see Allie Turnquist tottering around the unevenly packed earth of the fairgrounds in a pair of impractical black suede heels. Sarah couldn't see the brand, but she knew without a doubt the main message the unusual shoes were trying to get across: they were expensive.

"Hello, Allie," Sarah said.

"I'm surprised to see you here!" Allie said.

"At the fair?" Sarah asked, puzzled. Where else would Allie expect her to be?

Allie shook her head. "Out on the midway like this," she said. "Just enjoying yourself. I mean … you're not finished judging the quilts yet, are you?"

In fact, I was, Sarah thought. *I was done judging them yesterday morning. Before you insisted that I judge them all again.* "I was just taking a quick break," she said instead.

Allie raised her eyebrows like a disappointed parent. It seemed like a role she was well practiced in. "I can see you're not enthusiastic about this new system," she said. "But it means a lot to me. I know it might take a lot of work, but I think it's worth it to do it right."

If Allie only knew how much trouble Sarah was having cutting any corners, despite her frustration with the new system. Thinking of it, a smile sprang to Sarah's lips.

Allie took this for agreement. "Thanks for understanding," she said. "I know you're going to do a great job."

"I was just heading back to the hall, in fact," Sarah said.

"Well, enjoy yourself," Allie said.

"I'll do my best," Sarah called over her shoulder.

Dispirited, Sarah made her way back to the textiles office. *Lord,* she prayed, *I don't seem to be getting very far on my own. Please show me the way forward.*

When she stepped inside, the room wasn't empty. Lily Turnquist sat on the table, tracing her finger idly along the ditch of a line of stitching that ran down the quilt Sarah had left behind when she went out to meet Audrey and Lexie.

"Hello, Lily," Sarah said. "What brings you here?"

"Mom and I stopped by to see if you were here yet," Lily said. "Then Mom had to go do something, but she said I could stay and look through the quilts. They're one of my favorite parts of the fair. My hands are clean," she added when she saw Sarah glance at them. "I know about taking care of quilts. Don't worry."

Sarah set her purse on the desk and sat down. She located her eyeglasses and put them on. Lily pushed the quilt toward her. "Thank you, dear," Sarah said.

"Do you mind if I stay here?" Lily asked. Something in her voice made it sound as if she was sure Sarah would mind.

"Not at all," Sarah reassured her. "But I'm afraid I might not be great company. I have stacks of these to get through before Thursday."

"I know," Lily said, her voice small.

Sarah had already bowed her head over the blank face of a new score sheet, but something about the resignation in Lily's voice made her look up.

"You said the quilt competition is one of your favorite parts of the fair," Sarah said, more gently. "But I didn't notice that you'd entered anything. Isn't it one of the events for Junior Homemaking?"

Lily seemed to sit up a little straighter under Sarah's attention. "Well, yeah, it is," she said. "There's sewing, knitting, quilting, needlework, baking, canning, agriculture, hobbies, antiques, and floriculture. But you don't have to do them all. You just have to make enough entries in different categories overall. It helps to have a lot of diversity," she added, obviously parroting the advice of one of the contest organizers.

"I see," Sarah said. "Well, I imagine you have plenty to enter in antiques, with all your mother's quilts."

"Oh no," Lily said. "She always tries to make me, but I won't do it. The antiques category is for things you've found or collected yourself. And it's better if they're from right here in Maple Hill. Mom's quilts are mostly from other parts of the country, and I didn't really help her collect them. She'll say I did, because she likes to show them off. But I didn't."

"Well, she could enter them herself if she really wanted to," Sarah suggested.

Lily shook her head. "She said she doesn't think it's really worth it unless I win something," she explained. "But I don't want to win that way. Someone did that last year—her mom collects antique clothes, and she entered a bunch of them in the fair as if they were hers. I guess she said she goes along with her mom on buying trips and helps her choose. I don't think that's really the same as something you collect yourself. She didn't win, though," she finished with an air of satisfaction.

"That's right," Sarah said. "I think it was Kaylee Jones last year, wasn't it?"

"Kaylee had to win," Lily said philosophically. "She was a senior, and she'd been entering the contest ever since she was thirteen."

"I can understand your not wanting to enter your mother's quilts," Sarah said. "But you could always make your own. Especially if they're something you're interested in too."

"I tried once," Lily said.

"What did you make?" Sarah asked, encouragingly.

"Just a double Irish chain," Lily kept her voice self-deprecating, but Sarah could see the enthusiasm lighting in her eyes. "But instead of using only three colors, I made the center stripes out of all kinds of fabric. So it was white, and green, and then one little line made from all kinds of calicos."

"That's an ambitious project for a new quilter," Sarah said.

Lily dropped her gaze to the bold navy and white squares on the quilt in front of Sarah. "Mom said it was nice," she said. "But she'd seen a lot just like it."

Sarah's frustration with Allie rose up again. "Yes, but this was one you made, not some stranger," Sarah said. "And I bet it was beautiful."

"Well, she's just seen so many quilts," Lily said. "I guess it's hard for her to get excited about them, unless they're really special."

"So what did you enter in the fair this year?" Sarah asked, trying to turn the conversation away from the awkward subject. The Junior Homemaker award was given to the local girl who won the most awards in the fair competitions each year, with preference given to girls who showed achievements across multiple categories the fair celebrated—not just baking and preserving, but gardening, animal husbandry, and collections. Midweek, the leading girls were interviewed in a pageant-style panel, but it didn't count nearly as much as the achievements themselves.

"All kinds of things," Lily said. Sarah was happy to see the excitement in her eyes. "I made sweet pickles, dill pickles, *and* hot pickles. The hot ones are gherkins. I love those. I entered a double chocolate cake and some cheese bread, and a dress I made with an inset at the hem pieced from old handkerchiefs. It's so pretty when the light shines through, because the handkerchiefs are more delicate than the rest of the fabric."

"That sounds almost like a quilt," Sarah observed. "I think you might be a natural."

"Maybe," Lily said without smiling, and then went on. "Last year I got second place, after Melissa, and they said it was because I had concentrated so much on domestic, and not enough on agricultural and hobbies. So this year I raised a peacock and some rabbits and entered them."

Sarah raised her eyebrows, trying to imagine a peacock strutting across Allie Turnquist's carefully manicured lawn, followed by a line of docile rabbits. "How did your mom feel about that?"

"Well, I didn't raise them at home," she said. "Our new house is out in the country, and Mr. Parker's farm is right behind us. He let me do some chores around the farm in exchange for boarding Rosie and the kids."

"Rosie? Kids?" Sarah asked.

"My peacock," Lily told her. "And I call the rabbits 'kids.' John, Paul, and Ringo. They're dwarves, so they still fit in my hand, even though they're almost a year old now. They're so cute."

"That's an impressive set of entries," Sarah said.

"And a butterfly collection," Lily added, "for the hobby category. I caught them all myself. At first it was hard to chloroform them, but most of them live for only a few days anyway, and this way someone can enjoy how beautiful they are for years. They're all from here in Maple Hill. You wouldn't believe how many different ones I found."

"Really? How many?" Sarah asked, genuinely curious.

"I have twenty specimens in the display box," Lily said. "But two of them are swallowtails. They're my favorite, so I couldn't resist. I put them at the top and bottom in the middle row, to make kind of a column."

"See, you *are* a natural," Sarah teased. "That's exactly the kind of decision a quilter makes, arranging different pieces."

"Maybe," Lily said. As if to deflect attention from herself, she flipped a nearby quilt over, revealing a familiar pattern of simple blocks.

"Log Cabin," she said instantly.

"Very good!" Sarah said. She shouldn't be surprised that Allie's daughter would know so much about quilts. After all, she would have seen a lot of them as her mother hunted for new finds and brought them home. But it was an impressive feat for a girl her age to know a quilt pattern by sight.

"Quilts are so different," Lily said, turning over the next one to reveal a Victorian-style crazy quilt made from scraps of jewel tone velvets.

"They're just as different as the people who created them," Sarah said.

"I guess so," Lily said. She looked up with a curious expression. "I know this is a new quilt, and somebody probably bought all these pieces new to make it," she said. "But I noticed in the exhibit of antiques that even some of the old quilts had lots of fabric that all seemed to match. And it didn't seem to be worn out like it would have if someone had really used it for a dress first. Were all those old quilts really made of scraps of old clothes and blankets?"

"That's a good question," Sarah said, impressed again. "You're right. Many of the old quilts were made from recycled garments. But in the 1840s fabric production became industrial. Women didn't have to spin thread and weave it themselves. And many more people could afford relatively cheap manufactured material. So people were buying fabric, brand-new, for the express purpose of making quilts with it."

"You know what else I liked?" Lily asked. "That quilt with the lovebirds and the roses. It wasn't exactly appliqué. Or it was appliqué, and something else. Like someone had cut a piece they liked out of a printed pattern, and then sewn it onto a plain background."

"That's broderie perse," Sarah said. "It became popular when very vivid chintz started arriving from India. People would cut out highlights of the designs, and create new designs with them."

"It's nice to see just one thing on a plain background," Lily said. "You can see it better, somehow."

"It's a very creative thing to do with a print," Sarah agreed. "But in some ways, that's the heart of quilting: taking something that already exists, and re-creating it so that it can be seen in a new light."

She reached out to unfold the crazy quilt Lily had uncovered the moment before. "Crazy quilts have always been one of my favorites," she said. "I just think they're a perfect blend of creativity and order. The piecing," she said, tracing the outline of a block with her finger, "can be totally abstract." She ran her hand over the joyful jumble of colors, patched together at weird angles. "But the squares themselves add up to a whole quilt with four perfect corners."

"I love the embroidery," Lily said, pointing to a lady-bug stitched from shiny red and black thread, and a zinnia picked out in bright magenta.

"You'll love this," Sarah said, opening the quilt panel by panel until she found what she was looking for: a delicate spiderweb, in silver thread, spread over the face of several squares.

"That's beautiful," Lily breathed.

Sarah patted the soft nap of the velvet. "This certainly placed high in the competition this year," she said. "But Janet Stevens's homage quilt was just remarkable. Nothing could compete with everything she did—duplicating the handwork, dying the fabric. Especially since she did it all so well."

Lily hopped down from her perch on the table. "I'm afraid I'm in your way," she said. "I should let you go."

"Oh, you're not in my way," Sarah objected. "But I do have a lot of work to do here. And I'm sure you can find something more fun to do than sit in this little room with me."

"This *was* fun, Mrs. Hart," Lily said. "But I know you've got lots to do. I'll see you around."

"Have a good time today," Sarah called after her.

A blade of bright morning sun cut the room as Lily stepped out into the light. It winked out again as the door swung shut behind her.

Lord, Sarah prayed, *it doesn't matter how you do it, but please hear Lily's hopes. Help Allie Turnquist see what a treasure she's got in that girl.*

CHAPTER EIGHT

A fternoon faded into evening as Sarah painstakingly worked through over a hundred quilts, with only a few short forays into the fairgrounds in search of something slightly more healthy than an elephant ear for lunch and dinner. When she returned from her evening meal—a Styrofoam cup of macaroni and cheese and a caramel apple, which counted as something fresh, she told herself—she settled back down at the desk.

By now, she had judged all but a few dozen quilts. But despite her deep concentration on the task, something nagged at her. A moment later, she remembered what it was.

She flipped open her phone, and dialed the nursing home. "Yes, hello," she said. "It's Sarah Hart. I'm just calling to check on my father William Drayton. He wasn't feeling well when I visited him earlier today. I was hoping you could tell me how he's doing now."

"He's been running a slight fever all day," the nurse answered. "But he seems to be resting well now. He spent most of the day sleeping."

"Has his temperature changed at all?"

"Not significantly," the nurse said. "It's gone down from just over a hundred to just below."

"That's not too high," Sarah said.

"No," the nurse agreed. "We just don't like to see any kind of fever over an extended time. We're hoping it breaks during the night."

"And you'll let me know," Sarah asked. "If anything changes?"

"Of course," the nurse said. "I hope we'll have some good news for you tomorrow."

"I hope so," Sarah said. "Thank you so much for taking such good care of him."

"Oh, he makes it easy," the nurse said. "He's such a sweetheart."

Sarah smiled. "He is," she agreed. "Have a good night."

"Thank you," the nurse said, and ended the connection.

Sarah sat with the warm phone in her hands for a moment, thinking of her father. The conversation about fevers and temperatures reminded her of all the times he had cared for her when she was sick as a child. He was never as expert as her mother, who could take a temperature, dispense a pill, and flip a steak all in the same breath, but something about the careful, somewhat halting way that he slipped a thermometer into her mouth and then furrowed his brow as he read the results always made her feel loved and safe.

It was strange to think that now he was the one who needed that kind of care. And it was strange to think that he might not remember all the days he had spent sitting by her side through the various colds and flus of her childhood, even if she did bring them up. Since they had happened long in the past, he might still have some faint memories of them, but there was also a good chance he would respond to her attempts to prompt his failing memory with his familiar, "Is that right?"

Sarah had come to terms with her father's disappearing memory, but sometimes, like now, it still caused her sadness. That was part of the process of caring for a loved one with Alzheimer's too, and she let herself feel it. Her sadness was a way of honoring her father and all the memories she still had of their good times together. But she also comforted herself with a thought that had helped her many times as her father grew weaker: no matter what memories or details he lost track of, he was still the same man she had always known. Generous, mischievous, openhearted, quick to think about the needs of others. In some ways, she wondered if the way the details of her father's life had been erased, leaving only the man himself, was a little glimpse of heaven, where the worries of this world would fade, and where each person could take only who they were, and not any of the achievements or possessions they had collected.

Of course, there was nothing heavenly about Alzheimer's itself. It was a harsh disease, and Sarah was lucky that it hadn't changed her father's personality, as it did with many other patients. But she also knew that God embedded hope even in the deepest suffering, and this was a nugget she had found although her father slipped further and further away from her.

Lord, she prayed, *I know you can still speak to him in his heart, even if his mind doesn't work as well. Please let him know you are with him tonight. Please comfort him, and be his Father.*

As she slipped her phone back into her purse, a knock sounded on the door. *Allie,* Sarah thought. *Here to make sure I haven't escaped.*

"Come in," she called, her voice resigned.

But when the door opened, it revealed another familiar figure: Sarah's best friend Martha.

Sarah's face broke into a smile. "Martha!" she said. "What are you doing here?!"

Martha slipped into the room, her shoulders dramatically hunched like some international spy on a television thriller. "Shh!" she said. "We don't have much time! But I think I can get you out of here if you'll just follow my instructions."

Sarah laughed and stood up to give her friend a hug.

"You're *still here?*" Martha said, her voice incredulous. "Didn't you tell me you were coming in to do the judging yesterday morning?"

Sarah shook her head. "It's a long story," she said. "Allie Turnquist—"

Martha groaned. "Say no more," she said. She sank down in the chair beside Sarah's and picked up one of the judging sheets Sarah had been working through all day. She inspected it for a moment, then dropped it back on the table. "On second thought," she said, "tell me everything."

Sarah took her seat again and explained the whole snarl with the judging to her friend, from her completed winners list to Allie's insistence that she judge the whole set of them again.

"I wish I'd been there," Martha said. "It would have been harder for her to railroad the two of us."

Sarah took a long breath. "I don't know," she said. "Allie's a force of nature." She picked up a judging sheet and gazed at the long row of numbers. "And maybe she's right," she said. "Who knows how fair I am when I operate on gut instinct? Maybe it's time to get more scientific. And it *is* Allie's money we're giving away for the prizes this year. I guess she has a right to her opinions about how we choose the winners."

"The prizes *are* big this year," Martha said. "Almost enough to get me to enter something. I thought, even if I won third place, that's still enough to buy a new stove."

"Or go on a cruise with your best friend," Sarah said.

"I don't know," Martha said. "Does the cabin on the ship clean itself at the press of a button, like a new oven?" She twirled around in her chair to regard the stacks of knit blankets and quilts, neatly stacked on their wire racks.

"Those are the ones you've done?" she asked, nodding at the vast bulk of quilts that Sarah had already judged and reshelved.

"Yes, thank goodness."

"You're getting there," Martha observed.

"I am," Sarah said. "The list is due tomorrow, but I think I can finish it up with a few more hours in the morning."

Martha scooted forward in her seat to peer closer at the knit blankets on the other set of shelves. "And these are the knits entries?" she asked.

"Yep," Sarah said. "Barbara Benson judged those on Tuesday, when I was here working through the quilts."

"And Allie's not making her use the new system?"

"Nope," Sarah said, grimly. "I'm the only guinea pig."

"She just doesn't think the knits are as interesting, since she doesn't collect them," Martha said.

"I think that might be the actual truth," Sarah agreed.

"Well, that's her loss," Martha said, reaching out to feel the texture of a bright red wool throw. Unlike most of the other blankets, it was woven of a single color of yarn, but with a rich pattern of vines and flowers worked into the stitches. "This has to be Annie Fitzgerald's," she said. "She loves to make these single-color pieces. And she always works in wool. She won't touch acrylic with a ten-foot pole, even though it's easier to care for. Am I right?"

"That it's Annie's?" Sarah asked. "I don't know."

"Don't you have a book of the secret identities around here somewhere? There must be some list of which names correspond to the entry numbers."

"I don't know," Sarah said, glancing over the desk. The fair volunteer who had checked in the quilts as they were entered had given her a folder full of forms with the quilter's names matched to their entry numbers. Maybe Barbara had been given a similar one for the knits. But if she had, it was probably well buried under the piles of quilts and judging forms, finished and unfinished. Sarah scrabbled halfheartedly through the mess.

"There!" Martha said.

"Where?"

Martha pulled a slim red plastic folder from under the corner of a recently rebagged quilt. "I could see the 'K' on it," she explained, turning the cover to face Sarah. "Knits," a handwritten label proclaimed, just like the "Quilts" on Sarah's corresponding folder.

Martha flipped it open and thumbed through. "Aha!" she said triumphantly. "Annie Fitzgerald. Number twenty-three. Do I know my Maple Hill knitters, or what?"

"Impressive," Sarah agreed.

Martha handed the folder over to Sarah and stood up to get a better view of the knits on their racks. "Let me see if I can do it again."

Sarah set the folder obligingly in her lap while Martha perused the racks. "Jennifer Quinto," she said, pointing to a crocheted cotton throw, cream colored, with botanical specimens embroidered onto the finished design. "Nobody else does crochet lace like this. Even I would barely dare." She looked at Sarah expectantly. "Well?" she said.

Sarah fumbled with the plastic folder. "What's the number?"

"Forty-one."

Sarah flipped through the pages. Forty-one was, indeed, the work of Jennifer Quinto. "You got it," she said. "It's Jennifer's."

Martha grinned and turned back to the racks. She thumbed through a few more blankets, then drew another one out. This one was a traditional chevron-patterned afghan, but with a unique color pattern: pink blended to rose, then changed to dusky evergreen before lighting up into gold that changed to sky blue. Unlike other afghans, the colors never repeated. It was a gorgeous symphony of hues. "Shelly Andrews," Martha said. "Nobody else works with color like this. She's not actually using variegated yarn— she's got a whole palette of individual colors she's collected, and she works them together by hand. They're just amazing." She pulled at a red ribbon sticker attached to the thin plastic bag. "This looks like one of the prizewinners," she said. "I'm not surprised. She deserves it."

"What number?" Sarah asked.

"Fifty-three," Martha said.

Sarah flipped through the book. "Nope," she said. "Not Shelly."

Martha turned back. "Check again," she said. "I'm positive about this one. It's not just that nobody else works like her in Maple Hill. It's that no one else works like her *anywhere*."

Sarah looked down at the page, looked back up, and shook her head.

"Let me see that," Martha said.

Sarah handed her the notebook. "Mary Matthews," Martha read. She frowned. "I've never heard of her."

"The contests drew a wider group of entrants this year because of the big prizes," Sarah told her. "Maybe she's from out of town."

"Hmm," Martha said, and swiveled to face the racks. She pawed through a few more pieces, then pulled another out. "This one must be hers, then," she said, showing Sarah a thick afghan with a scattered popcorn stitch and similar intricate shading, again in a chevron pattern.

"Number?" Sarah asked.

"Fifty-one."

Sarah flipped back a page. "Here's Shelly's," she said, looking down at entry number 52.

"Fifty-one?" Martha asked. "Am I right?"

Sarah flipped back one more page, to 51. She shook her head. "This one's a Candace Drew," she said. "It's a prizewinner too. Third place in the full-size category."

"Really?" Martha said, the disbelief evident in her voice. "I've never heard of her, either."

"Did you really think you knew all the knitters in Maple Hill?" Sarah teased.

"I know, I know," Martha said. "But isn't it a little hard to believe there would be two knitters this accomplished in Maple Hill whom I haven't met?"

"I'll give you that," Sarah said.

"And I can't believe anyone else would have the palette of colors necessary to make something like this," Martha went on. "There must be a hundred yarns in this piece. I know it's taken Shelly years to build up her collection. Mike doesn't make a lot of money, and a lot of what he does make goes to the racetrack."

"It *is* strange," Sarah agreed.

Martha sighed. "Well, which one *is* hers?" she asked.

"It's just a throw," Sarah said. "It may be small enough you've been missing it. Number fifty-two. But she did take first prize with it."

"Fifty-two," Martha said, rooting through the plastic bags. "Fifty…here it is. Oh, this is beautiful. She's outdone herself."

She turned back, pulling a delicate lacework throw from a plastic bag. It was a floral pattern, but not with any kind of formal symmetry: instead, lilies and daisies, roses and violets, were scattered across the surface like volunteers popping up of their own accord in an actual garden. Martha let the bag fall to the ground and held the piece up by its corners.

"Well, you see what I mean," she said, "about the palette of yarns."

Sarah nodded. The original pattern had probably called for simple splashes of individual colors, but Shelly had worked delicate hue changes and rich contrasts in all over the blanket, using dozens of shades. The effect was almost like a watercolor painting. "It's really beautiful," she said.

They took in all the details of Shelly's intricate work for a long moment. Then Martha folded it up and replaced it carefully in the bag.

"Well," she said. "I guess I have some new friends to make. Mary Matthews and Candace Drew." She checked her watch. "Speaking of which," she said, "the demolition derby starts in ten minutes. Lexie and Audrey are saving seats with some of their friends. Do you want to join them with me?"

"What time is it?" Sarah asked.

"Seven fifty," Martha told her.

The quick-sketch artist, Cherie, got off work at her booth at eight o'clock. Sarah hesitated.

"I can't," Sarah said.

"You have a better offer?" Martha asked, surprised.

"I have something I have to do," Sarah said.

Martha's eyes twinkled. "You're tracking down some mystery," she said. "Aren't you?"

Sarah smiled back. Her friend knew her too well. A few minutes later, she had shared all the details of the story with Martha.

When she was done, Martha deposited Shelly's entry neatly on the wire shelves and gave Sarah a quick hug.

"I think the girls can handle the derby on their own," she said. "I'm coming with you."

Sarah smiled. After keeping the secret to herself, it was a relief to share it with someone. And maybe Martha would be able to see something she hadn't seen yet. At this point, she was willing to try anything. She shuffled her papers into some semblance of order, picked up her purse, and made sure the room was locked.

Then she and Martha stepped out into the riotous lights of the midway.

It took them only a few minutes to reach the quick-sketch stand at the foot of the giant slide, which was now glittering with orange, pink, and yellow lights. On Sarah's cue, the two of them faded into the shadows of the stories-high slide, slipping through the darkness as children squealed with delight overhead. The two friends were close enough to see Cherie clearly, but too deep in the shadows to be easily seen themselves.

Cherie was just finishing a drawing of a pair of sisters, about nine and seven, wearing matching blue western shirts with red gingham lining at the collars and cuffs.

"They're so sweet," Martha whispered. "You could make a pair of those for Amy and Audrey."

"Shh," Sarah said.

"Here you go," said Cherie, unclipping the thick paper from the board and handing it to them.

Both girls reached for it at the same time.

"It's mine!" the younger one said. "It's a picture of me!"

"But I'm in it too," her older sister said reasonably.

Still, neither of them released their grip on the drawing until their mother pulled it firmly from their hands.

"I should have had you make two," she told Cherie ruefully.

Cherie smiled, dropping her pens into a box and snapping the lid shut. "I know a lot of people put them up in the living room," she said. "Then there's no question about which kid gets to keep it."

"That's a good idea," the mother said.

"*Now* can we go on the Ferris wheel?" the older girl asked.

"Have a good night!" the mother told Cherie.

Cherie touched one of the joints on her easel and the whole top folded down. "You too," she said.

The family drifted off into the thick of the fair, and Cherie unzipped a large black portfolio to put away her unused paper. A moment later, she was off down the midway, carrying the portfolio in one hand and the folded frame of the easel in the other. Sarah couldn't believe how quickly the sketch station had disappeared.

"If sketching doesn't work out, she could always do a vanishing act," Martha observed as they followed her out into the crowd. Cherie worked her way down the midway, staying to the middle, where she avoided the fairgoers who tended to clump and cluster in groups near the concessions or around the games. Sarah and Martha followed her, taking pains to keep out of sight, but their efforts were unnecessary—wherever Cherie was going, she was focused on getting there, and she didn't give one backward glance.

She led the way to the far side of the park, where the demolition derby announcer was calling out the names of the drivers as they took the field, to hoots and applause from the crowd. Behind the stands was a darkened area, full of equipment trucks and staff trailers where the carnival workers lived and slept. Cherie walked past the final exhibition barn, and slipped into the gloom.

Sarah hesitated for a moment under the lights of a kiddie ride composed of wide-eyed green flying dragons. Then she dove into the dark, Martha close on her heels.

They picked up Cherie's shadow quickly, moving faster now without the obstacles of the midway. Sarah and Martha hurried to catch up, trailing Cherie between the shadows of farm equipment and empty truck beds to a row of mobile homes. The dwellings were lit by a string of exposed light bulbs that had been hung down the center of the aisle that separated them.

Sarah and Martha hung back in the darkness, watching as Cherie walked down the row to a mobile home about a third of the way down. She climbed the rickety aluminum steps, fiddled with the door, then slipped inside.

"What do we do now?" Martha whispered.

Sarah folded her arms, wondering the same thing. "We could knock," she said. "Maybe the surprise would startle her into telling us something."

"Or we could come back when she's gone and search the place ourselves," Martha suggested.

But before they reached a conclusion, Cherie emerged again. Her turquoise fair uniform was gone, replaced by a pretty red peasant top and a loose olive green skirt. She went lightly down the stairs and started off down the row of houses. About halfway to the end, she took a quick turn and seemed to disappear between two of them.

"We're in luck!" Martha whispered.

Sarah and Martha broke out of the shadows they had been standing in, and went quickly to the trailer they had just seen Cherie leave. Light glowed inside, but blinds in the front windows hid most of the contents. Sarah slipped up the low steps and tried the doorknob. It gave a quarter-turn under her hand, but then it wouldn't budge.

"Locked?" Martha asked.

Sarah nodded. "But there's no blind on the door," she said. Martha joined her on the top step.

Through a pane of scratched plastic, Sarah could see a tiny kitchen and living area, obviously being used by several people. The pillows of the couch were in disarray, and half a dozen unmatched and unwashed plastic cups stood around the room on various shelves and tables. Other than the clutter, the room seemed clean. Sarah glanced around, looking for any clue to the missing quilt. Most of the items in the room were nondescript: an overstuffed love seat, some recent magazines, a gray sweatshirt, which hung over a kitchen chair, turned inside out.

"See anything?" Martha asked.

Sarah shook her head. But as she did, her eye caught something. Under the kitchen counter, where a dishwasher might have been installed if the trailer were stationary, was an empty space. A few large pots rested there, but so did the familiar shape of a sewing machine, along with the unmistakable folds of about a dozen fat quarters in a wicker basket. Someone in the trailer was a quilter. And behind the sewing machine was a tantalizing shadow: a large blanket of some kind, not resting in even folds but wadded hurriedly, as if it had been stashed there to keep it out of sight of prying eyes.

"Do you see that?" Sarah asked, pointing.

"Looks like someone was trying to get it out of sight, quick," Martha said.

Around the corner of the trailer, something shuffled in the grass. The two women darted down the stairs and concealed themselves around the opposite corner just as the shadow of a man emerged from one of the gaps between the trailers. In the dim light, Sarah couldn't make out much of his features. But she could be sure of one thing: he was the first carnival worker she had seen that week who wore a beard. She crept as close as she could, trying to make out any other identifying characteristics.

The man hesitated when he stepped out into the light, but then he climbed Cherie's steps, where he peered into the window for a moment.

"What is he doing?" Martha hissed.

Sarah shook her head and held her finger to her lips. When Audrey and Lexie told her there had been two carnival workers, she had assumed that they must have been working together, but this man didn't look as though he belonged on Cherie's doorstep. In fact, when he finally did knock, he barely made any sound at all, almost as if he didn't really want to be heard.

He and Sarah and Martha all waited silently in the dark to see if anyone would answer. No one did. Apparently, Cherie had left the trailer empty. The man descended the stairs, and then disappeared into the darkness.

Sarah followed him, Martha on her heels. But there was no sign of him. They walked the entire length of the row, in hopes of picking up his trail. Laughter burst from a few of the trailers as the workers celebrated the end of a long day. A lullaby drifted out of another. But neither Sarah nor Martha caught another glimpse of Cherie or the bearded man.

Both of them seemed to have vanished without a trace.

CHAPTER NINE

I n the crisp morning air, Sarah pulled her fair badge out of her purse and showed it to the athletic booster at the gate. "You're here early, Mrs. Hart," the football mom said, reading her name from the badge.

"Oh, you know how it is," Sarah said with a smile, "always so much to do."

The football mom smiled back and waved her through.

But when Sarah stepped inside the fence that ringed the fairgrounds, her smile faded. There was so much to do, she didn't know how she could possibly do it all. The list of quilt winners was due that day at noon and she still had several hours of judging to do, not to mention the final calculations that would establish the winners of the contest. But tomorrow was Friday, when the winners would be announced and their quilts hung as part of the evening's awards ceremonies.

If she didn't find the missing quilt by then, she would have a whole host of problems she couldn't bring herself to think about: Allie's reproaches, insurance issues, police involvement, legal tangles. And more important, she would lose Helen's trust.

It had been easy to bury herself in the work of judging the quilts. At least she knew she could do that and do it well, and she could see the progress she was making. In contrast, all the sleuthing she had done to find the missing quilt seemed to leave her right back where she had started. Right now, the quilt judging seemed urgent, and it would be easy to hurry over and pick it up again. But if she didn't start making progress in finding the missing antique, she was going to have much bigger problems than Allie Turnquist's new judging system.

She thought back to the exhibition barn where she had first discovered the switch. She had questioned the girls closely about who had been in and out, but she had never really investigated the area itself. Maybe whoever had switched the quilts had left some clue behind.

A moment later, Sarah was striding toward the quilt barn. *Lord,* she prayed. *Please give me clear eyes to see anything you want me to see.*

To her relief, the quilt barn was deserted except for the young man from the security company who had been hired to keep the quilts safe from curious fingers. Sarah nodded at him, then made a beeline for the other end of the hall, where Janet Stevens's homage quilt still hung in the place of honor.

She looked over the surface of the large table that sat under the quilt, preventing the crowd from getting close enough to touch it. It was covered now with informational materials, but when Sarah had left the exhibit hall that Tuesday afternoon, all the cards with facts about the quilt had been neatly stacked in one corner.

Sarah pushed the cards aside and peered at the table. Was it her imagination, or could she see blurred footprints on the false-wood plastic veneer?

I wish I'd thought of this sooner, Sarah thought, her heart sinking. *These have been smeared around by the crowds for two days now.*

Still, despite the indistinct outlines of the footprints, she thought she could make out two separate sizes. One seemed to be some kind of sneaker. The other seemed more like a pointed boot.

I wonder if the girls would remember anybody's shoes, she thought. She doubted it. They might have noticed who was going in and out, but not their footwear.

With a sigh, Sarah knelt on the dusty cement, and poked her head under the table. It was hard to make out anything in the shadows, but something sparkled against the wall.

Sarah reached into the gloom and scrabbled in the dust that had collected against the wall, but her fingers didn't connect with anything. When she straightened back up, she saw why. The glimmer in the shadows hadn't come from an object. It was glitter, now sparkling on her fingertips in the morning sun that streamed through the back entrance.

"Ma'am?" the young guard stood behind her, his voice concerned. "Is everything all right? Do you need some help?"

Sarah looked up into his worried face and smiled to re-assure him. "Oh, thank you, no," she said. "I'm sorry. I was just looking for something I lost."

The guard's face relaxed. "Oh, all right," he said agree-ably. "Did you find it?"

Sarah shook her head. "Not yet," she said.

The guard offered his hand. She took it and rose to her feet.

"Can you tell me what it was?" the guard asked. "I can keep an eye out, and let you know if I see anything."

His eyes were earnest, and he was eager to help. At the sincerity in his voice, Sarah's stomach dropped. This was a little taste of what it would be like to have to tell all the people who had trusted her that the quilt was missing if she didn't find it by tomorrow.

"Oh, thank you," Sarah said. "But if I didn't find it here, it must be someplace else."

"Well, good luck," the guard said.

"Thank you so much," Sarah said, and went out into the midway. The booths and rides that seemed so magical at night seemed slightly worn now, their garish colors faded by the morning sun. Inside the booths, workers cleaned coun-ters, filled napkin holders, and ran potatoes through slicers, turning them into fresh French fry wedges. But the front gates hadn't opened yet, so the midway itself was deserted.

Sarah walked back to the judging hall, turning over the new clues in her mind. Two different sets of footprints. Or was that really what she had seen? How was it possible that two separate people had climbed up onto the table in the brief window of time when she was gone, without attracting any notice? She thought again of Liam and Shelly. Both of them were hiding something from her, but they might hold some valuable information—like whether or not they had seen somebody lurking around that table at the end of the hall.

Suddenly a new thought struck Sarah. She had assumed the footprints must have been left at different times, but if the muddled prints really belonged to two people, maybe they had been working together. Her mind spun, trying out combinations of her current suspects. But even Cherie and the bearded man, who she had been sure must have been in cahoots, hadn't seemed at all together when she had seen them last night. And she couldn't imagine Allie Turnquist working with Cherie, Liam working with Shelly, Cherie working with Liam. At the end of all the possible permutations, none of them seemed to fit.

And then there was the glitter. It wasn't such a surprise to see glitter on the floor of an exhibition hall. In the floral category, entrants sometimes dipped roses or lilies in florist's glitter to add shimmer to an arrangement. But the floral displays were two barns over. It was unlikely that so much glitter could have been tracked from one barn to another, and even less likely that it would have ended up under a table that hadn't been moved since the exhibit opened. But Sarah had seen glitter recently: it was part of Cherie's artistic tool kit. She thought again about the mysterious shadow wadded under the kitchen counter in Cherie's trailer. More and more, Cherie seemed like a strong suspect.

Sarah glanced at her watch. It was 10:30, half an hour before the fair would open and she could find Cherie again at the quick-sketch stand. Before Sarah could do any more sleuthing, she needed to turn in her winners list. She slipped around the corner of the exhibit hall into the textiles office and settled down at the desk where she had already spent so many precious hours that week.

An hour and a half later, she folded the last quilt, wrapped it in its plastic bag, and replaced it on the racks. Then she sat back down to add up and compare the totals. When she was finished, she pulled the highest scores in each category, then slotted them into their places: first, second, and third in the various divisions, and the grand-prize-winner.

She shuffled through her papers to find her original list, and laid the new one and the original side by side.

They were exactly the same.

Sarah gave a little laugh of disbelief. All that work, just to arrive at the very same conclusions she had arrived at by instinct three days ago. Just wait until she told Allie. She tried to imagine Allie abashed at having made Sarah waste so much time, but even as a warm sense of vindication rose in Sarah, she glanced down at the quilt in the grand-prize slot: *Janet Stevens. "Maple Hill Homage."*

Maybe I should involve the police now, she thought. After all, the quilt was worth a fortune, and the longer she waited, the farther away it might be taken. But right now, for all the thieves knew, they had gotten away with it. That meant they were feeling safe, and might get sloppy and give away some crucial clue. Once the thieves knew the theft was discovered, there was a much higher chance that they would work quickly to dispose of the evidence, one way or another.

For the time being at least, it was still her responsibility. She had a better chance than anyone of bringing the quilt home safely. Still, she was already worn out from all the work of preparing for the fair. She had thought this week would be one long celebration, but it seemed more overwhelming by the hour.

Lord, Sarah prayed, *I thought this quilt exhibit was a blessing from you, but it's turning into a nightmare. Please show me what your plan is in all of this. And please help me keep all my promises. Please help me find Helen's quilt.*

A sense of peace stole over Sarah, even though she didn't know any more than she had a moment before. *Thank you,* she prayed.

A knock sounded on the door.

"Who is it?" Sarah called.

Without answering, Allie Turnquist swept in. "There you are!" she said. "I was here last night and noticed there were still some quilts to be judged, so I thought I'd come over and make sure everything was all right."

"Actually, I just finished!" Sarah said brightly. She pointed to the two winners lists, side by side. "This one has my original selections," she said. "And these are the results, with the new system."

Allie looked from one list to the other, then back again. "Well, well..." She drew out the word as the truth dawned on her. Then she looked up in surprise. "But these are both the same!" she exclaimed.

"I know," Sarah said, trying to keep from sounding a bit superior. After all, she ought to feel some sympathy for Allie. She had worked hard on her system, and Sarah had just proved that it was no better than the old one. Maybe all the work she had done had been worth it after all, if it set them free from the complicated judging system in future years.

A wide smile broke out on Allie's face. "Well, this is wonderful!" she said.

"It is?" Sarah asked, bewildered again by Allie's reaction.

Allie squeezed her shoulder. "Yes!" she said. "Don't you see? It proves my system works! There's no clearer proof than getting identical results! I couldn't have asked for anything better!"

The only difference is that the new system takes four times as long, Sarah thought.

"You know what?" she said, picking up one of the winners lists and rising from her chair. "I need to get these over to the fair office. They're due."

"Oh, don't let me keep you," Allie said. "I can't wait to announce this! It's going to be wonderful. We'll talk soon."

Sarah managed a smile and went out, heading up the slight hill to the fair's main office.

Gloria Hampshire, one of the fair board members, was manning the desk. "You're just under the deadline!" she said when Sarah walked in. "I don't remember you working down to the wire like this last year."

"It's a long story," she said, handing over the list.

Gloria looked down at it. "Janet Stevens," she read. "Good for her."

Normally, Sarah would have shared Gloria's excitement for Janet, but this morning it was hard. Janet's name was a reminder of the lost quilt hers had replaced. And Janet still hadn't responded to either of Sarah's urgent calls.

Gloria's eyes traveled down the list. "Some of these names I don't recognize," she said.

"We drew from a wider area this year, I think," Sarah said, "because of the exhibit and the extra prize money."

"That's great. Anything we can do to strengthen the fair." Gloria flipped open the three-ring binder that held the entrants' handwritten personal details. "Yep," she said. "This one's from Dexter." Dexter was a town about half an hour north of Maple Hill.

Something stirred in Sarah's mind: the memory of Martha's insistence that the colorful knits they had looked at last night must be Shelly Andrews's handiwork. It might not have anything to do with the missing quilt, but maybe it was worth asking about. "You know what," Sarah said, "do you have the entry forms for the knits?"

"I sure do," Gloria said. "You need something from them?"

"I'm just curious about a few of the winners," Sarah said. "There was a Mary Matthews..." Gloria began to flip through the forms while Sarah struggled to remember the other name.

"Well, she's right here in Maple Hill, it looks like," Gloria said, looking up.

"She is?" Sarah asked. "Where?"

"It's a post office box," Gloria told her. "But it's in Maple Hill."

"What about..." Sarah began. Then the name flashed into her mind. "Candace Drew," she finished.

Gloria looked down and shuffled some papers again. "Oh, she's right here in town too," she said. "Over on Olivet. Number three five nine."

"Do you know her?" Sarah asked.

Gloria shook her head. "But I don't know *everyone* in Maple Hill," she said, and laughed. She shut the book, picked up the winners list, and slipped it into a large manila envelope labeled "Prizewinners." Sarah scrawled the address Gloria had given her on an envelope and smiled. "Thanks for this," she said.

"Anytime," Gloria called after Sarah as she went out.

Address in hand, Sarah stopped at the fair entrance to get her reentry stamp, then walked through the meadow the fair used for parking to her car. Olivet was right in town, just a few short minutes away, and it wouldn't hurt to pay Candace Drew a visit, to see if somebody else in town really had adopted Shelly Andrews's distinctive style of knitting.

And if she didn't turn up any more clues to the missing quilt, maybe a drive would give her a chance to clear her head, and think about where to begin looking again.

Just before she reached her car, she ran into Martha.

"You're here early," Sarah said. "What brings you here?"

"My best friend has been traipsing through the shadow lands of the fair at all hours of the day and night," Martha told her. "I'm here to make sure she stays out of trouble."

"Well, this time I'm looking for trouble outside the fair," Sarah said. "I've got an address for one of the pieces you thought might be Shelly's. Do you want to go meet the artist?"

"What are we waiting for?" Martha asked. "Let's go."

Three five nine Olivet was a modest ranch house with an assortment of kids' toys scattered in the yard. When Sarah knocked, the door was answered promptly by a young man with a brush cut wearing a gray T-shirt. He held a baby in one hand, and a stuffed knit giraffe in the other.

"Can I help you?" he asked, friendly but slightly surprised.

"I hope so," Sarah said. "I'm looking for Candace Drew. I just wanted to speak with her about one of her entries in the knits section at the fair. It's a remarkable piece."

The young man's surprise turned to confusion. He shook his head. "Well, she doesn't live here," he said. "Are you sure you have the right address?"

Sarah looked down at her scrap of paper. "Three five nine Olivet," she said.

"That's it." Then he shrugged. "But there's no Candace here," he said.

The baby had begun to pull at the young man's ear. He shifted it on his hip.

"Cute giraffe," Martha said. "Someone make it for you?"

The young man grinned. "My aunt," he said. "She's a great knitter."

"You're right about that," Martha said. "There aren't many women in town who could pull that off."

"She knit Joel here a whole ark full of animals when he was first born," he said. "And you should have seen the colors on them. I've never seen anything like it. They weren't like just a regular sweater," he said, addressing the baby. "Were they, buddy?"

"And do you mind if I ask who your aunt—?" Martha began.

"Nope, not at all," the young man said. "It's Shelly. Shelly Andrews."

For a moment, as the pieces came together in Sarah's mind, she couldn't think of anything to say. Work that looked just like Shelly Andrews's, registered to the address of one of her family members. Had Shelly entered her own work in the competition under several names so she could win more of the cash awards?

"Is everything all right?" the young man asked.

Sarah collected herself and gave him a smile. "Oh yes," she said. "You've been so helpful."

"Thank you," Martha added.

"Glad there was something I could do," the young man said. "I hope you find this Candace Drew!"

The door swung shut.

"Well," Martha said. "I think we have a good idea of where to look now."

Shelly Andrews didn't live far from her nephew. Sarah pulled up at the simple bungalow just a few minutes later. But when she rang the bell, no one answered. Sarah waited a few minutes, then rang again, and knocked. Still nothing.

While Sarah had been knocking, Martha had been investigating the yard.

"Look at this," she called. "Did you know she was neighbors with Janet Stevens?"

Sarah stepped down off the porch. Through the Andrews's backyard, she could see the leafy vines of Janet Stevens's famous Concord grapes, planted along the line that separated the Andrews's yard from hers.

"Have you talked to Janet yet?" Martha asked.

"She hasn't returned any of my calls," said Sarah. "But I haven't tried knocking."

The two of them cut through the backyard, and circled around the house to the front walk. Sarah had just rung Janet's bell when a lanky workman in a battered painter's cap came around the far side of the house.

Sarah jumped.

"I'm sorry, ladies," he said. "Didn't mean to startle you. You looking for Ms. Stevens?"

Sarah nodded.

He pushed his hat back. "Well, she ain't home," he said. "Ain't been here for days, I guess."

"When was the last time you saw her?" Sarah asked.

The workman folded his arms. "Earlier this week," he said. "I guess it was Monday. I remember it because there was a gentleman here too, and they were having an argument. Both of them seemed pretty heated about it. I came over to make sure everything was all right, and she said it was." He spread his hands out to indicate he had been unconvinced. "So what can you do?" he asked.

"Did you hear what they were arguing about?" Sarah asked.

"This may sound crazy," he said. "And I don't know if I'm right or not. But to me, it sounded like they were arguing about—a quilt?" His voice turned up at the end, as if he couldn't quite believe anyone could work up so much emotion over something as unimportant as a quilt.

"People get worked up about all kinds of things," Martha said encouragingly.

"Ain't that the truth," he said, spreading his hands again. "They were talking about a quilt, and I heard some numbers too, like they were talking about money. A lot of money," he added.

"And you haven't seen her since?" Sarah asked.

The workman shook his head. "I'm only here every few days," he said. "Doing odd jobs, and helping with the garden. So that don't necessarily mean anything. But usually I'd see her sometime during the week."

He caught the worry on Sarah's face. "You don't think anything's really wrong, do you?" he asked.

Before Sarah could answer him, her phone rang. "I'm sorry," she said. She pulled it from her purse, and glanced at the caller ID. It was the nursing home. "I'm sorry," she said again. "My father is sick. I ought to take this."

The workman nodded and backed away.

"Hello?" Sarah said into the phone.

"Mrs. Hart?" a woman's voice asked. "This is Tiffany."

"Tiffany," Sarah said. "How are you doing?"

"Just fine," Tiffany said hurriedly. "I'm calling about your father."

"How is he doing?" Sarah asked. "Is everything all right?"

"I'm sorry, I can't say that it is," Tiffany said. "The fever hasn't broken, and he seems to be struggling. We think it'd be best if you come over."

CHAPTER TEN

S arah, wait." Tiffany stopped her just as Sarah rounded the corner of the nurse's desk, rushing down to her father's room. Martha had offered to come with her, but Sarah had told her she would call if she needed her.

"Isn't he down there?" Sarah demanded. "Did you have to take him to the hospital?"

"No, no," Tiffany said soothingly, coming around from behind the desk. She put her arm around Sarah and gave her a comforting squeeze. "He's there. It's just that he's finally resting comfortably. The doctor ordered some sedatives for him right before I called you, and they seem to be working now."

"I'd just like to look in on him," Sarah said. "Would that be all right, if I'm quiet?"

"I'll come with you," Tiffany said, walking beside her down the hall.

When they reached William's room, Sarah stopped in the doorway and looked in. Her father was sleeping on his back. He did seem peaceful, as Tiffany had said, but his breathing was as labored as it had been the day before, and his face was pale, with two bright flushed spots high on his cheeks.

Lord, watch over him, Sarah prayed. Then she stepped out of the room and turned to Tiffany, who had waited in the hall. "What happened?" she asked.

"Well, he's been struggling with this infection, as you know," she said. "This morning he woke up with congestion and continued fever. He didn't want to eat or drink, which makes both of those symptoms more severe. About an hour ago he was very uncomfortable, and his fever spiked to a hundred and one point five. I finally got him to sip something, which seemed to help, but he became very uncomfortable from the heat, and he was having trouble breathing. Sometimes when patients are agitated, they're able to recover more quickly if we sedate them, so Dr. Canaday ordered a prescription to help him get some rest this afternoon."

"You sounded so upset when you called me," Sarah said. "I was worried."

"I'm sorry," Tiffany said. "I was too. We hate to alarm anyone, but we also want to be in contact with family if anything serious is going on."

Sarah sank into one of the hallway visitor chairs. "Can you help me understand what's happening? How bad is this infection? What should I expect?"

"I wish I could tell you," Tiffany said. "With older people, it's a delicate balance. A virus that you or I might fight off in a day or two can keep them down for weeks. But on the other hand, once they fight something off, their recovery can seem almost miraculous. The bottom line is we just don't know."

Sarah took a deep breath and let it out, working to calm herself.

"I'm sorry I upset you," Tiffany said, laying a hand on her arm.

Sarah clasped her hand. "No," she said firmly. "I'm glad you called me."

Down the hall, a phone rang at the nursing station. "I'm sorry," Tiffany said. "I have to—"

"Go ahead," Sarah said.

She stepped into her father's room again and stood for a moment, watching him sleep, as she knew he must have watched her a hundred times when she was a child. *Lord, I know he's in your hands,* she thought. *Please do what's best for him.* She leaned down and kissed his cheek, very gently. Then she went out.

In her car, she dialed Jason's number. He picked up on the first ring.

"Hi, Mom," he said. "Everything okay?"

"Hi, honey," she said. "I'm just over at the nursing home. I just came to see Grandpa William and he's not doing very well. He's—" she paused. If the doctors and nurses didn't really understand what was happening to her father, how could she explain it to Jason? "He's fighting an infection," she said. "And he's pretty weak. It might be nothing to worry about, but I wanted to let you know."

Jason was quiet for a moment. "Okay," he said. "Thanks for telling me. How are you doing?"

Her son was trying to take care of her, Sarah realized, just as she was trying to take care of her own father. Tears rose up in her throat, but she pushed them back down. "All right," she managed.

"You sure?" Jason asked. "I can be there in a few minutes."

"Oh, there's nothing you can do," Sarah said.

"I can take you out for lunch," Jason said. "And try to cheer you up."

Sarah smiled. "No, honey," she said. "That's all right. I just wish there was more I could do for him."

"You do everything anyone could ask," Jason said.

"That's what he always did for me," said Sarah.

"I know he did," Jason said.

"It's funny," Sarah said. "I know he gets wonderful care at Bradford Manor, but it still means so much to me to be able to take care of him."

"That's been a big part of your life," Jason said. "For a long time."

"It has," Sarah said. She sighed. "I guess I just need to be able to give him into God's hands, whatever happens."

"That sounds right to me," Jason said. "Almost like something Grandpa would say."

Sarah smiled and blinked back tears.

"I'll try to check in on him later today or tomorrow. But are you sure you don't want me to come down there?" Jason asked. "Or have lunch at The Spotted Dog, on me?"

"No, thank you, honey," she said. "It was good just talking with you."

"Love you." Jason said.

"Love you too," Sarah said.

She sat for a minute with her phone in her hands. Then she pulled out of her parking spot and headed for the fair.

No more score sheets to fill out, she thought as she walked through the fair gates. *This time I have only one job to do: find the missing quilt. I just wish I had a better idea of how to do it.* The clues she had accumulated swirled together in her mind: Janet Stevens's disappearance, the mysterious stranger in her yard, evidence that Shelly Andrews may have entered a piece under a different name, the mysterious shadow in Cherie's trailer, and the bearded man on her doorstep. But try as she would, the pieces never seemed to fit together into any pattern.

She found herself standing outside the quilt exhibition barn through sheer force of habit. *Back at the beginning. Again,* she thought.

But when she stepped inside, she realized she hadn't been to visit the exhibition during normal hours since the fair had opened.

The place was filled. Dozens of people stood below the quilts she had so lovingly collected from around the state.

Some of them craned their necks to see the intricate decorative hand-stitching. Some ducked their heads to read the historical blurbs Sarah had prepared. Children chattered to their mothers about the details they observed. Teenagers squinted up at the vivid fabric canvases.

For the first time since the exhibit went up, Sarah stopped inside the door and simply looked at the quilts themselves. *It was a good exhibit, after all,* she thought. One that she would be excited to visit herself. Through a year of polite requests and traded favors, she had managed to assemble a collection that touched on the highlights of every important moment in quilting throughout the state's history.

The exhibit opened with a gorgeous example of a handmade bed blanket, quilted at a bee in the early 1800s. It was a significant piece because along with it, history had also preserved the diary of one of the makers, so that the hands of the women who made it were not anonymous, as the creators of so many other quilts were. That diary added enormously to the value of the quilt by proving that the women who made it had been the wives and mothers of some of the most important men in Massachusetts, including a judge, a doctor, and one of the state's most prominent ministers.

The petticoats Sarah had highlighted on her own tour and the chintz appliqué that Lily had mentioned to Sarah as her favorite hung next to each other, along with several examples of the quilts that average housewives were able to make after the explosion of cheap fabrics that American textile mills produced in the second half of the nineteenth century. The dawn of the industrial age was also represented by a piece made of found scraps, this time the ones collected by a textile worker who sewed gorgeous creations at night. A very early machine-sewn quilt came next, accompanied by an early sewing machine. A girl with a pair of corn yellow braids stood by it, tracing her finger along the machine's beautiful enameled design of vines and birds. Sarah smiled. Even though she loved all the advantages of her own modern machine, she still wished contemporary manufacturers would pay as much attention to the beauty of their models as the original sewing machine makers had. The older machines were so exquisite that even antique collectors who couldn't sew a stitch prized them for their elegant design. The machine-sewn quilt was followed by a friendship block quilt, a variation on the quilting bee. Instead of being sewn at a bee, friendship block quilts were created by various quilters first working on their own individual squares at home, all from the same pattern.

Several later quilts represented the importance of the quilt in the Civil War era. One had been sewn especially for auction to raise funds for the war effort. After the war quilts came Sarah's beloved Victorian crazy quilts, one in rich flannel, one pieced by a seamstress from the scraps of satin dresses she sewed for wealthier women. Sarah had represented the resurgence in interest in quilting during the Depression with a piece that featured giant gray dahlias, each petal cut from a piece of worn-out men's suiting.

A few modern examples of the recent resurgence in quilting followed, and then the exhibit culminated in Maple Hill's own treasure, the oldest quilt in the state. But as Sarah looked up at Janet Stevens's homage, all the warmth and satisfaction that had built in her vanished. A father pointed out one of the hand-dyed images to his daughter: he was pointing up at a fake. A mother leaned in to get a better view of the almost invisible stitches: she was studying a replacement, not the real thing. People had come from hundreds of miles to see these quilts, a once in a lifetime gathering—but they weren't seeing the quilt she had promised them.

Sarah shook her head, trying to dispel the feeling. She glanced under the table and at the ghosts of the footprints on the tabletop, now smudged by another day's worth of visitors' hands. She didn't see anything she hadn't seen before, so she looked back up at the quilt.

Again, she was struck by how much work Janet had done to replicate the old antique. Sarah was adept at repairs, and she had sewn a few homage quilts in her time, but never anything as involved as this. For one thing, it was just so large: a queen-size quilt, almost unheard of in its time because of its extravagant size in an age when many beds were just barely wide enough for their occupants.

Wait, Sarah thought. *The size. Of course!* When she had looked for clues around the exhibit hall, she hadn't thought about the clue held by the quilt itself. It was gigantic. Even folded to its smallest dimensions, it would still be quite a bit larger than an overstuffed grocery bag. Sarah had wondered about what kind of shoes had been worn by the people the girls had seen coming and going. But she had ignored a much more obvious question: *what had each of them been carrying?* Even if the girls were busy watching the animals being groomed, it would have been hard for them to miss someone wrangling a package that size.

Sarah pulled her phone out and dialed Audrey. Audrey's cell phone went to voice mail, so Sarah tried Jason and Maggie's house line. Maggie picked up on the third ring.

"Sarah!" she said. "To what do I owe this pleasant surprise?"

"Actually, I'm trying to reach one of your beautiful daughters," Sarah said. "Is Audrey at home?"

"She sure is," Maggie said. "Is everything all right?"

Sarah hesitated. She didn't want word of the missing quilt to get out, but she knew she could trust Maggie—and Maggie had a tendency to think the worst if she didn't know what was going on. Besides, it would be a relief to share the secret with Maggie.

"I'm having some trouble finding a quilt that was lent to us for the exhibit," she said.

"Oh, Sarah!" Maggie said. "That's terrible!"

"It really is," Sarah said. "And I'll trust you and Jason to keep it quiet for now. But Audrey was at the fair the night it went missing, and I just had a few questions to ask her about it."

"Of course," Maggie said. "Audrey!" she called. In the distance, Sarah could hear footsteps clattering down the stairs, and Audrey's voice: "What? Mom, what?"

Maggie came back on the line. "And if we can do anything else to help, please let us know."

"Thanks so much," Sarah said. "I appreciate it. I just wish I had a better idea of what kind of help to ask for."

"Here she is," Maggie said. "Audrey, it's Grandma."

After a brief shuffle, Audrey's voice came across the line. "Grandma?" she said.

"Hi, honey," Sarah said. "How are you?"

"I'm fine," Audrey told her. "I'm going back to the fair tonight. My science teacher is in the dunk tank. I might not be a sharpshooter, but I can throw a softball." Various well-known citizens from around town were scheduled for shifts in the dunk tank all week. For a small donation to the local Kiwanis Club, Maple Hill's residents had three chances to knock them from their perch into the water by striking a target with a softball.

"You think he deserves a dunking?" Sarah asked.

"*Yes*," Audrey answered emphatically.

"Well, I'll be curious to hear how that goes," Sarah told her. "Audrey, I have another question for you."

"Sure," Audrey said.

"Tuesday night, when you and Lexie were standing outside the exhibition hall, do you remember any of the people you saw carrying a big package?"

"How big?" Audrey asked.

"The size of a paper grocery bag," Sarah said, "or bigger."

Audrey pondered for a minute. "I don't," she said. "I'm sorry."

"There's nothing to apologize about," Sarah said. "I'm just looking for something, and this might help me."

"Mrs. Turnquist had an awfully big purse," Audrey offered, "with all kinds of crystals around the handle."

"Was it big enough to hold a blanket?" Sarah asked. "Like a blanket from your bed?"

The line went silent for another moment. "No," Audrey said. "I don't think it was that big. And it didn't really seem like she was carrying that much in it. It seemed more like she was showing off the purse itself."

That sounded like Allie. "And nobody else was carrying anything?" she pressed, just to be sure. "Not Mrs. Andrews, or Mr. Connolly, or the lady from the fair?"

"Nope," Audrey said, her voice assured now.

"Well, thank you," Sarah said, her mind already turning. If *none* of the people Audrey and Lexie had seen leaving the building were carrying the quilt, how had it gotten out? The other exit had been securely locked. Sarah was sure about that. She had locked it herself, after letting the last volunteer out when they finished hanging the pieces.

Was there any chance it could still be in the building, hidden away somewhere? Hope rose in Sarah's heart for a minute, then faded again as she thought about the dimensions of the hall. She had gotten to know it quite well as she planned the exhibit, and there simply wasn't anyplace to hide an object the size of a quilt. The building had been designed for summer use, so it was made of simple single-thickness metal walls, with no insulation or hidden places where a quilt could be stuffed in the walls themselves. The floor was unfinished concrete, devoid of crawl spaces. And in preparation for the exhibit, Sarah had personally supervised the removal of the trash cans, trunks, crates, and various other junk that had collected there during the winter. There was nothing left in that exhibition hall besides the quilts hanging on the walls and the tables for the displays. And the tables didn't even have skirts on them, despite Sarah's best attempts. The fair board had liked the idea, but dismissed it as impractical.

"It sounds real pretty," Harry Butler had told her. "But they'll make it the devil to sweep in there each night. And if it rains, you won't have tablecloths anymore. You'll have mud flaps."

There was simply no place to hide a quilt in the hall. But if nobody had taken it out by the only exit, where Audrey and Lexie had been standing, where had it gone? And who had taken it?

"You're welcome," Audrey said. When Sarah didn't respond, she asked, "Grandma?"

At the other end of the exhibit hall, Sarah caught sight of a familiar figure. Liam had just come into the hall. He stopped at the first quilt and gazed up at it, taking in every detail. Then he picked up one of the information sheets and began to read.

"Thank you, honey," Sarah said again, somewhat nonsensically. "That helps a lot."

"Okay," Audrey said.

"I'll talk with you later," Sarah said, glancing at Liam to make sure he hadn't seen her yet. "Love you."

"Love you too," Audrey said.

Sarah shadowed Liam through the exhibit, making sure to keep out of his line of sight. She watched him closely for any clues he might give away: quilts he avoided or lingered by, interactions with strangers. But he passed among the quilts just like anybody else in the exhibit, except perhaps paying a bit more attention than most. He stopped for several minutes under Janet Stevens's copy, leaning forward once to get a better view of the unusual natural dyes, and then went out.

Maybe now he'll lead me to whatever he's been hiding, Sarah thought, following him into the midway. A few paces behind him, she waited as he stopped to watch a group of children spin around on the carousel, cheered on a young man who tried unsuccessfully to win a prize for his girlfriend at the basketball hoop game, and stopped to look longingly at a candy apple through the glass of a concession booth.

Sarah hung back in the crowd when he stopped at the candy apple booth, congratulating herself on her skill in tailing him. But when Liam reached the elephant ear booth a few yards down, he stopped suddenly. There wasn't anywhere for Sarah to go, unless she wanted to dive into the duck pond on her right. And she would hardly blend in with the crowd of toddlers gathered there. Reluctantly, she slowed her steps but continued toward him, scanning the surrounding midway for a convenient place to hide.

Before she found one, Liam spun around. He looked straight at her. "Sarah Hart," he said, delight dancing in his eyes. "I believe you're following me."

"I am not!" Sarah returned heatedly. "I'm just...," she began, but trailed off. If he wanted to insist on defining everything, she was, in fact, following him. "You're the one who...," she began, and stopped again. Who did *what*, exactly? That was what she had been trying to answer when he had recognized her.

"What did I do now?" Liam asked, laughing.

"I know you were in the exhibition hall," Sarah accused him.

"Well, yes," Liam agreed. "Did you really think you could put up a quilt exhibit that causes this much fuss, and I would miss it? Of course I came over. It's a wonderful display, even for someone like me who doesn't know much about the subject. You should be very proud of yourself, love."

Sarah's heart softened at the compliment, but then she remembered his evasiveness at the coffee shop, and steeled herself. "But this isn't the first time you've seen it, is it?" she said. "You were here before the fair even opened. I have witnesses."

Liam's smile didn't falter. "Witnesses?" he said. "Is it really that serious?"

"It is to me," Sarah said. "I don't understand why you won't stop joking about it."

"Aye, Sarah," Liam said, chastened. "I was there, but not for long. And I can't say that I saw much. I'm sorry. I didn't realize how important this was to you."

"Was anybody else there when you went in?" Sarah demanded.

Liam thought for a minute. "Just Allie Turnquist and her daughter Lily," he said. "But she's working with you this year, isn't she?"

Sarah nodded. He seemed to think this meant she could trust Allie. She wished she felt the same way. "What was Allie doing?" she asked.

"Just talking," Liam said. "They didn't seem to be getting along very well, if that makes a difference."

Sarah wasn't surprised. Allie seemed impatient and frustrated with Lily in most of the conversations Sarah had overheard between them.

Then she realized that Liam hadn't actually answered the question she had asked him, back at the coffee shop. "And what were you doing there?" she asked again.

Liam dropped his eyes to the straw and gravel that lined the midway. "As I said before, love," he said, and raised his eyes again, "it's nothing to worry about."

Sarah could see that he was doing his best to make peace with her, but he still hadn't answered the question. She crossed her arms.

"I'll tell you what," Liam said, "let me make it up to you. Take a walk with me and I'll buy you any of the fair delicacies you want. Chips with vinegar? A fried Twinkie?"

Sarah thought for a moment, then shook her head. As she did, she caught sight of a familiar flash of blonde hair under the giant slide. Cherie was on duty again at the quick-sketch booth.

"I'm afraid I've got work to do," Sarah said.

Liam's smile faded slightly. He shrugged. "Well, if you need a break, I'll be around."

"All right, then," Sarah said, trying to keep the hurt out of her voice. Then she set off back down the midway to Cherie's booth.

CHAPTER ELEVEN

N ot so fast," Martha said, catching up to Sarah as Sarah turned toward the giant slide that sheltered the quick-sketch booth. "I was hoping I'd find you around here. How did things go with your father?"

"He was resting when I got there," Sarah said. She hesitated to say more, not sure whether she could handle talking about the topic without tearing up.

"Resting?" Martha asked. "Then why did they call you over?"

"They were just trying to do the right thing," Sarah said. "He'd been struggling all day."

"But he's better now?"

Sarah shrugged. "They don't really know," she said. Then she shared the fear that had been haunting her all week: "What if he doesn't get better?"

"Oh, honey," Martha said.

She wrapped Sarah in a hug. Sarah held on tight to her best friend. Tears rose up in her throat, but at the same time, some of the worry and weight that she had been carrying on her shoulders seemed to slide off under her friend's touch.

"I know how hard this is," Martha whispered.

"I know you do," Sarah said, and let her go.

"Is there anything we can do for him?" Martha asked. "Or you?"

"We're doing everything for him that we can," Sarah said. Again, Sarah forced her thoughts back to the problem at hand. "But you could help me find this quilt."

"I'm on it," Martha said. "Where are you going?"

"The quick-sketch stand," Sarah said. "I want to try to talk with Cherie again."

"Need a sidekick?" Martha asked.

"Would you take no for an answer?" Sarah asked.

Martha laughed.

To Sarah's surprise, Cherie wasn't the only person wearing the turquoise carnival work shirt at the quick-sketch stand. A young teenage girl, also with blonde curls, stood over her shoulder as she sketched, watching Cherie's confident strokes, and drawing her own on a large pad of paper that she balanced against her stomach. The wait to be drawn wasn't long—only one young couple with a pair of dark-haired boys in matching blue and white striped T-shirts. Sarah and Martha got in line behind them and waited as Cherie sketched them and the family exclaimed over the finished drawing. Then Sarah sat down on the subject's stool herself.

"Welcome to the quick-sketch booth," Cherie said with a big smile. "I'm Cherie, and this is my daughter Tansy. She's learning the ropes."

"Nice to meet you," Sarah said.

"You look familiar," Cherie told her. "I know I see a lot of people, but have I met you before?"

Martha shuffled behind Sarah. "I watched you work for a little while yesterday," Sarah said. "I've always enjoyed seeing people draw."

Cherie clipped a clean sheet of rag paper to her easel and studied Sarah's face. "So you must spend a lot of time at the fair," she said, making small talk.

"More than I like to admit!" said Sarah.

"She's practically running the whole thing this year," Martha broke in.

Cherie looked up at her and smiled, beginning to trace the lines of Sarah's face onto the paper.

"What are you organizing?" she asked.

"Have you heard about the quilt exhibit? And the big contest?" Martha asked.

Sarah watched Cherie closely for signs of nervousness, but Cherie's eyes lit up instead. She nodded vigorously. "I have!" she said. "In fact, I've been looking forward to it all summer."

"Really?" Sarah asked. "Why's that?"

"Can you turn your head for me, honey?" Cherie asked, pointing to the left. Sarah obliged. "Just like that. Perfect. Yes. I'm a little bit of a quilter myself," she said, picking up the thread from earlier in the conversation. "Not like the people who win the contests, I'm sure. But I read about this exhibit in one of my quilting magazines all the way back in the spring. And I do love to look at quilts."

"That's interesting," Sarah said. "Because I heard that a blonde carnival worker visited the exhibit before it even opened."

Cherie's pen, which had been darting steadily over the paper during this whole conversation, came to a dead stop. Over her shoulder, a warning showed on her daughter's face. She didn't have to say anything for Sarah to understand exactly what it meant: you leave my mom alone.

"Oh?" Cherie said.

Sarah kept her expression friendly, but she didn't break Cherie's gaze. It was Cherie who finally looked away. "Well, there are a lot of girls with blonde hair in the crew," she said. "I'm sure it would be easy to get confused."

"Well, yes," Sarah went on agreeably. "But they mentioned a butterfly tattoo too. I don't imagine there are too many of those around here, are there?"

Cherie dropped her hand, still holding the pen, to her knee. "You're not really here for a portrait, are you?" she asked.

Sarah shook her head.

Cherie glanced behind her. A father and his two- or three-year-old daughter had gotten into line while she and Sarah talked. Cherie stood up, pulled Sarah's half-finished drawing from the easel, and motioned for Tansy to sit down.

"I need a little break," she said. "Honey, can you take over for me?"

Tansy nodded as Sarah rose to her feet. "She's the best in the business," Cherie assured the father as his daughter toddled forward. "She knows everything I do, and then some."

"Hello, sweetheart. You look beautiful!" Tansy said to the little girl, who broke into a broad smile.

Cherie led Sarah and Martha a few steps away, into the shadow of the giant slide, so Tansy and the customers couldn't hear. "Look," she said, speaking low, "I don't want any trouble. You're right, I snuck into the exhibit. I couldn't wait to see it, and I never know what kind of time I'm going to have once the fair begins. Lots of places we're allowed to go look at the exhibits before they open. I didn't know it would be any problem here. I'm real sorry. Just please…I don't want any trouble. I didn't mean anything by it. I was just so excited to see everything."

The worry was evident in Cherie's face, but her story didn't explain the mysterious shadow hidden in the cubby with her sewing machine or the man who had followed her into the exhibit. "Well, all that would be fine," Sarah said, "except that a very important quilt was taken from the exhibit during the time that you were visiting."

"Taken?" Cherie asked, her eyes widening in surprise. "That's terrible. Which one? It looked like they were all there to me."

Sarah hadn't planned to tell Cherie the whole story, but Cherie wasn't likely to tell anyone else in town about the problem, and Sarah was running out of time. "The final quilt. The one by the door," she said. "They traded it with a facsimile. That's what's hanging in there now." Her eyes narrowed. "Are you sure you don't know anything about it?"

Strangely, a smile broke out on Cherie's face. "I don't," she said. "And I couldn't have traded the quilts."

"Why not?" Sarah said. "You don't deny you were in the exhibit hall alone, do you?"

"Come on," Cherie said, a slight smile still on her lips. "I'll show you."

With a quick glance at Tansy to make sure her sketch was still going smoothly, Cherie set off for the quilt exhibit hall. There was nothing for Sarah to do but follow. She glanced at Martha as she walked alongside her. Martha gave a broad shrug. Inside the hall, Cherie didn't break her stride. She marched up to the table below Janet Stevens's quilt, climbed up on it, and raised her arms over her head. They came almost a foot short of the rod that suspended the quilt. She turned around, her arms still raised.

"See?" she told Sarah. "There's no way. I could have pulled it down, but I never could have gotten it back up there again."

The other visitors to the exhibit began to turn and stare. From the other side of the room, the security guard came barreling over.

"Why don't you come down and we'll talk about it," Sarah told her.

Cherie dropped her arms to her sides and hopped down.

"Is everything all right here?" the security guard demanded.

"It's fine," Sarah told him. "She just wanted to get a closer look."

"That's exactly why the tables are there!" the guard insisted. "To keep people from touching the quilts!"

"I'm sorry," Cherie said.

The guard was unmoved. He folded his arms, unwilling to kick them out, but not sure what else to do. Sarah saved him from the decision. "We were just leaving," she said.

"Well," the guard said, his feathers still ruffled. "I think that's for the best."

"See, *this* is why I snuck in when nobody was there!" Cherie said to Sarah as they went out the exit. She checked Sarah's unsmiling face. "Not funny yet?" she said. "Okay."

The three of them stopped just outside the hall.

"How did you know you couldn't reach the top of the quilt?" Martha asked Cherie.

"I climbed up," Cherie said simply. "I wanted a closer look. And when I got up there, I realized how much bigger the quilt still was than me. So I tried to reach the top, but I couldn't."

"That's not the only way you could have switched the quilts," Martha said. "You could have found a ladder easily enough. Or a stool," she said.

Sarah remembered the other carnival worker the girls had seen go in after Cherie. Could she learn something about him from Cherie by surprising her with that fact? It was worth a try. "Or the man you were with could have done it," she added.

Cherie's brow wrinkled in confusion. "A man?" she said. "I wasn't with a man."

"That's not what my witnesses said," Sarah told her. It felt a little ridiculous, describing Lexie and Audrey as "witnesses," but maybe it would scare the truth out of Cherie.

Cherie smiled gamely and shrugged. "Well, I don't know who saw what," she said. "But I haven't traveled with any kind of man since Tansy's dad took off. And that was six years ago." She searched Sarah's face. "Look," she said, "I can tell you're worried about this, but I didn't take your quilt. What can I do to prove it to you?"

Cherie might have missed the man who followed her into the hall, Sarah thought. But how would she explain the hidden quilt Sarah had seen the night before, in Cherie's own house?

"I saw something that looked like it might be the missing quilt," Sarah said. "In your kitchen."

"My *kitchen?*" Cherie repeated. "When did you..." It took her a minute to process what Sarah had said. But when the answer came to her, she grinned. "Did you follow me home?" she asked, her voice full of amusement. She shook her head. "I've got to hand it to you," she said. "I wouldn't have guessed you had it in you. You must be pretty determined to find this thing."

Sarah nodded, wary.

"Well, I don't have it," Cherie said. "You're welcome to search my place if you want proof. In fact..." she glanced over at Tansy, now calmly sketching her second customer of the day. "Come on," Cherie said, and set off through the fair toward the workers' trailers. Sarah and Martha hurried to catch up.

A few minutes later, Cherie climbed the steps of her trailer, unlocked the door, and went in. Then she poked her head back out and beckoned to Sarah and Martha, who stood in the grass outside. "You two coming?" she asked.

"She sure doesn't act guilty," Martha said. She gripped the aluminum handrail and the two of them ascended the steps.

Cherie stood in the small trailer with her arms open. "It's four to a trailer in summertime," she said, "me, Tansy, and two other girls. So I'm sorry about the mess. But you take a look around at whatever you want. I've got nothing to hide."

Sarah didn't waste any time. She went straight for the kitchen cubbyhole where she had seen the sewing machine and the mysterious shadow.

"You *did* look in my windows, didn't you?" Cherie said, laughing.

"Is this yours?" Sarah asked, kneeling down to get a better look.

"Guilty," said Cherie. "I know it's crazy, but I take that little machine out on the road with me every year."

"I can understand that," Martha said. "I take my knitting anywhere I go. I always feel sorry for Sarah since her machine is so much bigger than my pair of needles."

Just beyond the machine was the wad of fabric Sarah had seen from outside. She reached back for it, being careful not to knock over the sewing machine as she did.

As soon as her hand connected with the fabric, she knew it couldn't be the missing quilt. Unlike the fabric of the antique quilt, which had a lot of irregularities, this blanket was smooth and cool: simple calico, and modern calico, at that.

"That's what I'm working on this year," Cherie said. "Do you want to see? Go ahead."

Gently, Sarah retrieved the half-finished quilt top from behind the sewing machine. When she straightened up, Cherie took the quilt from her and spread it out as well as she could in the small space. Cherie had used muted colors, like the missing quilt's, but that was where the resemblance stopped. Instead of the missing quilt's separate shapes on separate squares, this quilt's pattern spanned its whole surface: a gigantic bouquet of calla lilies, appliquéd in bold strokes across a background of pieced greens and gold. About half the appliqué was carefully pinned, not yet sewn, but from the quality of the work that was finished Sarah could tell that despite Cherie's modesty, she was an accomplished quilter.

"It's beautiful," Martha said.

"I do one every summer," Cherie said. "It keeps me out of trouble. I've made so many now, I'm actually running out of people to give them to."

"You do excellent work," said Sarah.

"Ah," Cherie said, "I just do what I can, here and there."

Sarah nodded, deflated by the adrenaline of confronting Cherie, and the disappointment at finding another dead end.

"I'm real sorry about your missing quilt," Cherie said. "But I promise you I didn't take it."

"I believe you," Sarah said. She stared down at the shapes of the beautiful white petals, but they couldn't tell her anything more than what she had already learned: this was not the missing quilt.

"I hate to rush you out," Cherie said, "but I really better get back."

As the three of them walked back through the trailers and farm equipment to the midway, Sarah was struck with another idea. She had been so busy making sure Cherie hadn't taken the quilt that she hadn't asked her what she had seen. Cherie was well acquainted with quilts and she had made herself especially well acquainted with whatever quilt had been hanging on the wall during her little unauthorized inspection. The question was had she seen the original, or the fake?

"Cherie," Sarah said, "did you see anybody else? While you were looking at the quilt?"

Cherie shook her head. "I wouldn't have been climbing around on that table if anyone else had been around," she said.

"What about the quilt?" Sarah said. "Do you think you'd remember which one you saw, if you saw it again?"

"I can't say," Cherie said.

Sarah wasn't sure of that herself. But it was worth Cherie taking a look.

"Listen," she said. "Would you have a minute just to look at the quilt again and tell me anything you notice? I'd be grateful."

"That's a great idea," said Martha.

"Tansy's probably convinced the manager to give her my job by now anyway," Cherie said. "Why not?"

A few minutes later, in the exhibit hall, Martha pushed aside the historical materials so Cherie could hop back up on the table again. At the other end of the hall, the guard looked at them with disbelief, then started over.

"I don't think he's going to be happy," Martha said.

Up on the table, Cherie looked back, worried.

"You take your time," Sarah said. "I'll deal with him."

"Let me see," Cherie said, leaning in to get a better look at the quilt.

"What's going on here?" the guard shouted, charging up.

"It's all right," Martha said. "Official fair business."

"Fair business?" the guard asked incredulously. "What is that supposed to mean?"

"I'm the organizer of this exhibit," Sarah said, dodging the question. "She's here with me."

"The organizer?" the guard said, and Sarah could almost see him ticking down a mental list of all the times he had seen her today, crawling around under the table, following Liam around like some kind of spy, and now defending Cherie's leaps onto the security barriers. "*You?*"

"You're welcome to radio the fair office and ask for confirmation," Sarah answered politely.

But apparently her demeanor, or the sheer ridiculousness of the whole day, was enough for the guard. He gave an "I've seen everything now" shrug and slunk back to his post.

Up on the table, Cherie turned around. "I'm pretty sure this is the same one," she said.

"How come?" asked Martha.

Now it was Cherie's turn to shrug. "I don't know. Spidey-sense," she said. "Nothing feels different."

A little twinge of excitement ran through Sarah. If Cherie was right, it could help her pinpoint the time the quilt was taken, and perhaps eliminate some of her suspects. But was Cherie's eye trained enough to detect the minor differences in the two quilts?

"What about this stitching, here?" Sarah asked, pointing to the cap of an acorn where she knew the stitching was visibly frayed in the original. In Janet's copy, however, the stitching was perfectly hidden.

Cherie shook her head. "Looks exactly the same to me," she said. "And I actually did spend a little time looking at that one, because it's got the two colors, the cap and the nut, but they look like they were just Velcroed on. I looked and looked for a stitch, but I couldn't find one."

It sounded like Cherie did have the attention to detail Sarah needed. And it also sounded like she had arrived *after* the quilts had been switched. Now all Sarah needed to do was tie down the time of Cherie's visit.

"Do you remember when you were here?" Sarah asked.

Cherie came to the edge of the table and Sarah held her hand to help her down. Cherie hopped onto the cement slab. "I do," she said, once she was on solid ground. "I got here a little before five, and I left a few minutes after. I know because I made it to the five o'clock staff meeting at 5:10. The boss made a big deal about checking the clock and making sure I knew how to read it."

"Sounds like a charming guy," Martha said.

That cut the window of time the thief had been in the building by almost half. It also meant that anybody who had come out of the building after Cherie must be innocent.

But what about the bearded carnival worker who had gone into the building just after Cherie? Had she really not seen him, or was she trying to protect somebody?

"My witnesses," Sarah began again, thinking about how Lexie and Audrey would laugh if they could hear themselves being described this way, "also say they saw another carnival worker come in, after you. Would you be able to help me identify someone based on a description?"

For the second time that day, Cherie became guarded. "I don't want to get anybody else in trouble," she said.

"This person came in after you," Sarah told her. "So I don't believe he could have taken the quilt." She hoped this was true. "I'd just like to talk to anybody who was there, and see if he saw anything that might help," she continued. "They said he was a man, brown hair, brown eyes, bearded?"

"A beard?" Cherie said, and frowned in concentration.

Sarah added the last detail she had. "One of them said he looked like a teddy bear," she finished.

Suddenly Cherie's eyes lit up. She laughed. "Earl!" she exclaimed. "That's got to be Earl McCoy. He doesn't just look like a teddy bear, he *is* one. He's one of the sweetest guys in the show. He works the bell and hammer game, for the little kids. But good luck getting him to tell you anything. I can never get him to say two words to me at a time."

"But we saw him at your trailer," Martha challenged, "the night we followed you."

"At my trailer?" Cherie said, obviously surprised. "I didn't see him there."

"After you left," Sarah said, "he went up the stairs and knocked."

Cherie shook her head as if there were all kinds of things that happened every day that she couldn't understand. "I don't know what to tell you," she said. "Are you sure it was him?"

Sarah wasn't. After all, she had never seen him before that night. She had no one to compare the man she had seen to. "I don't know," she said. "But he works at the bell and hammer game?"

Cherie nodded and pointed to the other end of the midway. "It's at the far end," she said, "under the Ferris wheel. He's on days and Jarvis Cheever's on nights. Or the other way around. It changes every week. But you should be able to find him there if you keep going back." She looked at her watch. "Speaking of which ...," she said.

"Oh, of course," Sarah said, jolted from her tunnel vision on finding the quilt. "Listen, I really appreciate all your help. I'm sorry for any misunderstanding."

"Oh, I understand," Cherie said. "That quilt must be worth a fortune. If it had been me, I wouldn't have just peeped in the windows. I would have broken in."

Sarah smiled.

"Well," Cherie said, "maybe I'll see you around."

"That would be nice," Martha said.

"I'll be here all week," said Sarah.

"See ya!" Cherie said, and turned to go. But instead of slipping out the exit door or crossing the hall to the entrance, she walked straight toward the nearest wall. When she reached it, a broad swath of sky and midway was visible for a moment. Then she walked right through.

Sarah and Martha looked at each other in shock. Then they bolted across the hall after her. When they reached the spot where Cherie had been, they found a section of the metal, complete with a thick handle, still swinging slightly in Cherie's wake. Sarah yanked the handle, and the section of the wall swung open.

Cherie was several yards away, climbing the low hill back to her booth.

"Cherie!" Sarah called.

Cherie stopped and turned. Sarah and Martha ran to catch up. When she reached Cherie, Sarah was puffing to catch her breath.

"Is everything all right?" Cherie asked.

"That door," Sarah said. "How did you know about it?"

"Oh, that," Cherie said. "Somebody showed it to me the other day. All the exhibition halls have them, so you don't have to walk all the way down the barn to get out. And for loading in bigger things. Just a little short cut."

"How many people know about them?" Sarah asked.

"I guess most of us do, by now," Cherie said. "Anyone who works with the fair figures it out, sooner or later."

All the careful clues Sarah had collected so far seemed to tumble down like a house of cards. "So anybody can go in or out?" she said. "Anybody who knows about it?"

Cherie shook her head. "Not in," she said, "just out. Look at the wall on the outside."

Sarah and Martha turned and looked back down the hill. The door she had come through just a moment before was gone, replaced by the smooth face of the outer wall.

"There's no handle on the outside," Cherie said.

So the suspects were still the same, Sarah thought with a wave of relief. This just offered a possible solution for another puzzle she hadn't yet been able to explain: how the thief got the original quilt out of the building without Lexie and Audrey noticing any bulky packages.

CHAPTER TWELVE

W
ell, it sounds like we need to talk to Audrey and Lexie again," Martha said. "If you can pinpoint the time the girls saw everyone come and go, you could eliminate some suspects."

Sarah nodded. "That's exactly what I was thinking," she said.

"And you're in luck!" Martha went on. "Mandy told me this morning that she's dropping the whole crew off here for lunch. I bet we'll find them by the food vendors."

"Let's go!" Sarah said, anxious to hear who had been in the hall before Cherie.

The two friends threaded their way through the midway crowd, mostly families with younger kids at this time of day. The fair hadn't slid into the intensity of the evening, when darkness hid everything but the frenzy of lights. During the day, everything seemed to be a little quieter, and things happened a little bit more slowly. Sarah liked the lazy feeling of the daytime fair, still with the familiar creaking of the rides and the sweet greasy smell from the food booths, but with the blue sky stretching overhead to remind them there was life beyond the fair.

They didn't find the girls amid the food booths, but a quick search discovered them in one of the nearby exhibition barns, where the prize horses were bunked for the week.

Martha was right about "the whole crew." Not only did they find Audrey and Lexie, but Amy, Pru, and Tina too. The lot of them were standing in front of a large chestnut stallion, who gazed down at them patiently as they munched on their fair treats.

Sarah and Martha greeted the girls with a flurry of hugs. "I'm glad to see you here," Sarah told Amy as she squeezed her and stepped back. "I thought maybe you'd started up your field hockey practices already."

"Not for a few weeks," Amy told her. "I was helping out with the five- and six-year-old soccer camp."

"That's so young!" Martha exclaimed. "Do they understand the game?"

Amy smiled. "We spend a lot of time telling them which way to run. And we've got one little girl who is always excited to kick it in the goal, no matter whose goal it is. But they've got a lot of energy, and they have a lot of fun."

"I'm sure they're glad to have you," Sarah said. "So how are you enjoying the fair?"

Amy's smile faded. "I don't know," she said. "Audrey made it out to be this big awesome thing, but I don't think I get it."

"What's not awesome about the fair?" Audrey insisted. "Look at this horse! You've never seen a horse like this before!"

"I've seen plenty of horses," Amy said.

"Where?" Audrey demanded.

"On TV," Amy answered.

"TV is not *real*," said Audrey.

"They don't *smell* on TV, either," Amy said.

Before Audrey could retort, Martha broke in.

"Girls, we need your help," she said.

All five girls looked at her. Martha looked at Sarah.

"I'm still trying to understand a few things about what happened while I was gone from the hall on Tuesday," Sarah began. "I know you told me everyone you saw there, but do you remember when they came and went?"

Lexie and Audrey looked at her doubtfully. The other girls, losing interest, wandered off.

"Who did you see first?" Sarah tried. "Do you remember that?"

"I'm not sure, Grandma," Audrey said, doubtfully. "I wasn't really paying all that much attention."

"Not to *those* people," Lexie said.

Audrey elbowed Lexie.

"Did Mrs. Andrews come out *after* the lady in the turquoise shirt?" Sarah asked.

"I don't really know," Audrey said. "No?" The upturn in her voice at the end of her response made it clear it was a guess.

"What about Mrs. Turnquist?" Sarah asked.

"Oh, she left early," Audrey said. Now her voice was confident.

"Are you sure?" Sarah pressed.

"Yep," Audrey said. "I remember thinking maybe she was trying to catch up with you."

Beside Audrey, Lexie was shaking her head. "I thought she left sometime in the middle."

Audrey shrugged. "I don't know," she said. "Maybe."

This was getting them nowhere. "What about Mr. Connolly?" Sarah said.

"Mrs. Hart," Lexie broke in. "This was a long time ago."

Sarah smiled at the teenage definition of "a long time." Lexie must think that Sarah had been alive pretty much forever.

"Well, do you remember if he was one of the first people to go in, or one of the last?" Sarah pressed.

"The first?" Audrey said.

"Really?" Lexie said. "I would have said one of the last."

Nothing about the girls' time lines agreed. The only thing Sarah had managed to confirm was what both girls had told her from the beginning: that neither of them had really been paying much attention to the comings and goings at the quilt exhibit.

Martha patted her on the back. "Well, we won't keep you girls any longer," she said. "You run along and have a good time."

Audrey and Lexie tore off to catch up with the other girls.

Sarah shook her head. "We don't know anything more than we did before," she said.

"Yes we do," Martha said. "We found out if we want to know the answers to our questions, we'll have to find them out from someone else." They both laughed.

Together, they walked arm and arm through the exhibition halls to the quilt barn. When they stepped inside, Martha gave Sarah an encouraging squeeze.

"Look at all these people," she said. "They're enjoying the fruits of all your hard work."

Sarah nodded and leaned back against the wall, watching the crowd that snaked slowly through the hall. For a moment, all the shuffling feet and upturned faces seemed to blur together: just a lot of visitors from Maple Hill and the surrounding towns, enjoying the peak of summer activities. But then one figure emerged from the crowd.

He didn't fit with the flip-flops and sundresses, the work boots and T-shirts that most of the crowd was dressed in. Instead, he wore a pair of crisp linen trousers and a carefully pressed dress shirt. From their cut and drape, Sarah could see that they were expensive, and if she'd had any question about that, her guess was confirmed by a pair of designer sunglasses that dangled at his collar. And he didn't gaze up at the quilts with a tourist's innocent wonder. Instead, he scanned the various patterns with a practiced eye, as if looking for some kind of secret embedded in them.

"Do you see that guy?" Sarah whispered.

"What guy?" Martha asked. Without answering, Sarah slipped into the crowd and began to trail him through the exhibit, Martha close behind. When he got to the final quilt, he stopped cold, peering up at the beautifully composed fabrics with keen interest. Sarah hung back, jostled by passersby as she inched her way along, trying to stay out of the man's line of vision without losing sight of him herself.

Suddenly, faint strains of "The Love Boat" soundtrack drifted through the hum of the crowd. The man looked down from the quilt, patted his pockets, then pulled a phone out of one.

Martha stifled a giggle as she and Sarah crept closer.

". . . impressive," the man was saying. The noise of the crowd swept his words away, and then Sarah caught a few more. ". . . value is debatable in this market."

"Is he talking about the quilt?" Martha hissed.

"I agree, it's unique," the man said. "But, Janet . . . ," and his voice dropped below audible range again.

Janet? Sarah thought. *Is he talking to Janet Stevens? What are they saying?* Now the crowd had pushed Sarah and Martha within a few yards of the man.

Suddenly, Martha took a few steps forward, placing herself squarely beside him, right in front of the quilt. The man glanced at her, clearly annoyed. Martha yanked on Sarah's arm, dragging her alongside.

"Just a minute," he said to the person on the other line, and moved back in the crowd.

Sarah and Martha held their place for a moment. Then Sarah dragged them to the side, where she could catch a glimpse of the man out of the corner of her eye. He finished his conversation, then strode through the crowd and took his place at the foot of the quilt again.

Again, Martha sidled up next to him. "You seem very interested in this quilt," she said.

For a moment, the man tried to pretend he hadn't heard her. When Martha didn't retreat, he raised his eyebrows. "It's an interesting quilt," he said.

Martha gestured for Sarah to join them. When Sarah hung back, she gestured again. Reluctantly, Sarah joined them.

"This gentleman is interested in this quilt," Martha told Sarah. "I thought you might like to share some facts about it with him. Sarah curated this whole exhibit, you know."

Martha was always a little more direct than Sarah, but Sarah had to admit this was a brilliant opening. What was the harm in the curator of the exhibit striking up a conversation with a visitor?

"It's the oldest in the state," Sarah began. "And it hasn't been on display since it was made. It's out of chronological order, but I just had to end the show with it. It's really the highlight, and something told me that this was where it belonged, from the time I started thinking about how to curate this group of quilts."

But instead of being drawn into conversation, the man pulled his sunglasses from his collar. "Excuse me," he said. "I'm late for an appointment."

"Friendly, isn't he?" Martha commented as the two of them hurried after him.

He exited the building, putting the sunglasses on as he stepped into the light.

He didn't get far before Sarah and Martha set out after him, following at a discreet distance as he headed for the fair exit. Just outside the fair gates, the two women stepped behind the giant fiberglass cow that would glide down Main Street during Saturday's parade, and watched as the man made his way up the hill between the rows of cars in the parking meadow. A few minutes later, the man reappeared, driving down the row in a cream-colored Mercedes convertible with the top down. He gunned the engine as he turned onto the drive that led away from the fair, and then he was gone.

Sarah stood in the shadow of the fiberglass cow's giant haunch, her mind racing.

"Have you ever seen him before?" Martha asked.

"No, I don't think so."

"Me, either," Martha said.

"It's funny," said Sarah. "I knew Allie Turnquist wanted this quilt, but I never thought about all the other collectors who might want it too."

"Do you think someone from out of town might be behind all this?" Martha asked.

"I don't know," Sarah said. "The thing is, nobody from out of town, that we know of, was in the hall, except the carnival workers."

"But they could have been working for someone else," said Martha.

Sarah nodded. "I want to go back to the hall," she said. "I need to look it over again, now that I know about the other exit."

Together, they circled the building, looking for clues. Cherie's exit had given Sarah an answer as to how the thief might have gotten the antique quilt out without the girls noticing, but it hadn't answered the question of where the quilt had gone. When they came to the secret door in the middle of the building, Sarah stopped and surveyed the surrounding area.

The exhibition hall lay parallel to the midway, at the top of a small rise. The secret door faced the midway, across the mud and gravel walkway from the carousel and giant slide. On the opposite side, the hill ran down to a second set of exhibition halls, where the horses, rabbits, and poultry were kept. At the far end of the exhibition hall lay another hall just like it, but it was configured to house sheep, goats, and cattle in low wooden pens filled with straw. That was where the calves and sheep lived that Audrey and Lexie had been so engrossed in.

"The thief didn't go out through the main door," Sarah said, "at least, not with the quilt."

"Lexie and Audrey would have seen it," Martha said.

Sarah nodded. "And if he came out this door, he'd have to carry it quite a ways before he reached cover again," she said. "Unless…"

She turned toward the quilt office, just around the corner of the building. It took her only a dozen steps to reach it.

"So he could have taken it to the office easily enough," she said.

"But then how did he get in with the other quilt?" Martha asked.

"He might have brought the other quilt with him when he came the first time." Sarah said. "It wouldn't have been hard. I only lock the quilt office at night."

Sarah inspected the muddy concrete around the door to the quilt office and the door itself, finding nothing out of the ordinary. But when she retraced her steps, following what must at some point have been the thief's path from the quilt office to the hidden metal door, she found a large rock nearby—large enough to hold the door open if somebody wedged it in before it closed.

"Look at this," Sarah said. She knelt down to get a closer look. The rock was half-covered in dry mud, and the imprint of a harsh right angle was pressed into the crumbling substance, as if it had, in fact, been used to prop open a door.

"So the thief went out and came back," Martha said.

"But how did he know about the homage quilt?" Sarah asked.

"Janet has been talking about it for months," Martha said. "Anybody in town could have gotten wind of it."

"But who knew where to find it?" Sarah said. "And who had the most opportunity to think about switching the two quilts?"

Martha's eyes widened.

"Allie Turnquist," Sarah told her. "And she has the best motive too."

Just then, her phone began to ring. She fumbled in her purse, found it, and turned it over to read the caller ID. Allie Turnquist.

"Hello?" Sarah said.

"Sarah," Allie said. "Thank goodness you answered. I'm here with Gloria Hampshire. We're just trying to pull the winning quilts for display tomorrow, and we need your help."

They were pulling the winning quilts already? Sarah thought. *But they wouldn't go up on display until after the awards ceremony tomorrow.* She had thought she would have more time—at least a whole day. "I'm a little busy," Sarah said. "Is it something we could do later tonight? Or tomorrow? I don't usually pull them until the afternoon they're announced."

"You're busy?" Allie asked. "Doing what? Are you at the fair?"

"Actually, I am," Sarah admitted.

"I know!" Allie crowed. For some reason, her voice had a stereo effect, almost like an echo.

Sarah glanced up. Allie peeked around the corner of the exhibit barn, waving her cell phone and grinning. "I saw you!" she said. "We were just getting stuck with these quilts, and I looked up, and there you were, out the office window. Isn't that lucky?"

It didn't seem to bother her that Sarah didn't respond.

"Okay," Martha said, stepping back. "It was great seeing you, Sarah. I'll see you soon!"

Sarah gave Martha a pained look, but Martha scooted away, leaving her in Allie's clutches.

"I love the way things are working out for us this year," Allie said. "Getting the identical results with the old system and the new system. And now you showing up, just when we need you!"

Sarah thought frantically, desperate for a reason to put off pulling the winning quilts. As she did, she studied Allie's face. In more ways than one, Allie was a mystery to her. But if she had stolen the quilt for her own collection, would she really insist on pulling the quilts this early? Wouldn't she want the theft to go undetected for as long as possible? Then again, Allie Turnquist was never a woman to shy away from attention.

Plus, as soon as it became obvious that one of the quilts was missing, Allie wouldn't be the one trying to answer everyone's questions. Sarah would.

"I was really just on my way—" she began.

Allie shook her head emphatically. "I won't take no for an answer," she said. Sarah believed her. "I can't imagine you've got anything to do that's more important than making sure this whole thing goes off without a hitch. Come on," Allie said, starting back to the quilt office with maddening confidence. Sarah had no choice but to follow. "It won't take more than a few minutes."

She was right about that, Sarah thought as she went after Allie. Working alone, Sarah could have pulled the quilts herself in under five minutes. That was all the time it would take to destroy Helen's trust in her, and taint the memory of the dream exhibition Sarah had spent a year creating.

Sarah stood outside the quilt office and took a deep breath. As soon as they pulled the stack of winning quilts, it would be obvious that Janet Stevens's was missing. And there would no longer be any way of hiding the fact that somehow, Sarah had lost an irreplaceable quilt.

CHAPTER THIRTEEN

L ook who I found just wandering the midway!" Allie called as Sarah walked into the office.

Lily sat on the judging table, her legs swinging. "Hello, Mrs. Hart," she said.

By the wire racks, Gloria Hampshire from the fair office stood frowning down at Sarah's list of quilt winners. Barbara Benson was combing through the knit entries, checking the numbers on the bags against her list, and pulling winners into a pile at her feet. She kept her head down, probably remembering the last run-in between Sarah and Allie.

"Sarah," Gloria said, looking up, "I'm so glad you're here. Maybe I just don't understand the system, but I can't even find the first quilt."

Suddenly, a new idea flashed through Sarah's mind. As Gloria had discovered, pulling the winning quilts would reveal that a quilt was missing.

But it didn't have to reveal *which* quilt.

Sarah's mind spun through the consequences. If she didn't let on that she had discovered the quilt switch, everyone would assume the homage quilt was the one missing. She would have additional time to search for the antique before she had to upset Helen or involve other authorities. Janet Stevens might be upset that her quilt was missing, but then again Janet wouldn't even answer her phone right now. And as far as bad news affecting the event went, the misplacement of a local quilter's piece was a far less interesting story than the theft of a priceless antique.

The plan had another advantage. It would give her a chance to watch Allie's reaction to the discovery that Janet's quilt was "missing." If Allie was the thief, the stress of pretending not to know about the switch might trip her into revealing something incriminating—and help Sarah get the antique back.

"Well, just go on," Allie said.

Gloria and Sarah looked at her. Allie waved her hand like she was commanding a limo driver to keep driving. "Go on!" she said. "We've been looking for it for ten minutes already. Let's make some progress. Go to the next one. I bet we'll find the one we're looking for while we're looking for something else."

Sarah studied Allie's face carefully. Was she nervous, or just impatient?

"Well, maybe Sarah will have an easier time finding it," Gloria suggested. "After all, she knows what it actually looks like. All I've got to go on is a name and a number."

"Sure," Sarah said. "This is Janet Stevens's quilt. It's an homage to the antique in the exhibition hall. So it's not going to be one of these more vibrant modern patterns. It's more grays and browns."

"She dyed it all herself," Lily offered.

"Well, I doubt it looks *exactly* the same," Allie said. "Nothing really compares to a true antique. It may not be obvious to the untrained eye, but it's obvious to those of us who know. That's what makes them so special."

Lily lapsed into silence.

Gloria was already sorting through the nearest stack of quilts. When she didn't find it there, she dropped to the next shelf down. Sarah made a show of looking through a few quilts herself.

"I just don't see it," Gloria said.

"I hate to say it," Sarah said, "but I don't either."

She turned back to catch Allie's expression. Lily glanced at her mom. Allie shrugged impatiently. "I already told you," she said. "Just go on. We'll find it while we're looking for the rest of them."

Working together, Sarah and Gloria pulled the other remaining quilts in about five minutes. Lily arranged them all in stacks, in descending order, with the first-place winners on top.

"But where is Janet's?" Gloria asked, starting to sound worried.

Sarah hesitated, trying to think of something to say that wouldn't be an outright lie. "Maybe it slipped behind something," she said.

"Or got out of order," Lily suggested.

"Should we just go through all of them?" Gloria asked, turning to Sarah.

That would be the sensible thing to do, if Sarah didn't already know the missing quilt was hanging in plain sight on the wall next door. "I guess so," said Sarah.

Together, Sarah and Gloria went painstakingly through each quilt, checking the numbers and patterns. When they reached the last one, Gloria straightened up, her face distraught. "It's really not here," she said, as if the idea were only just sinking in.

"I'm afraid not," said Sarah.

"This is awful," Gloria went on. "I feel terrible. She's been working on that quilt for months."

"Well, I know she put a lot of work into it," Allie said. "But it's not like it's really *worth* anything."

Sarah couldn't believe how casual Allie seemed, almost as if she had known from the beginning that the quilt would be missing.

"You have all the others?" Allie asked Gloria.

"Well, yes, but—"

"Then my work here is done," Allie said, standing up and slinging her giant purse over her shoulder. "I'll leave you ladies to it."

For once, the expression of disbelief on Sarah's and Gloria's faces seemed to register with Allie—although not very deeply. "Don't worry," she said breezily. "I'm sure it'll turn up somewhere."

Her heels clicked to the door, which thunked shut behind her.

"I'm so sorry, Mrs. Hart," Lily said, real emotion in her voice.

"Oh, thank you, Lily," Sarah said, laying one last quilt back down on top of the others. "We'll figure this out."

"I saw a quilt in the fair office," Lily offered. "It looked like an old one."

"Do you think it could have been Janet's?" Sarah asked.

"I didn't get a close look," Lily said. "But I think it was an antique."

And Lily really would know, Sarah thought. A bit of hope leapt up in her heart. Was it possible this had really just been some terrible mix-up after all? Had the missing quilt simply been carried over to the fair office at some point, lost in the shuffle?

"Do you remember anything like that, Gloria?" Sarah asked.

Gloria shook her head. "Not specifically," she said. "But we always find all kinds of things in the fair office when we open. Things seem to accumulate during the year. Entries that nobody picked up at the end of the last fair, and books and coats that board members leave during planning meetings. You wouldn't believe it."

Suddenly, Sarah was eager to get to the fair office. "Well, let's get these up there, then," she said. "Barbara, how are you doing there? Do you want to go with us?"

"I'm all set," Barbara said, finishing up her check of the winning knits. Shelly Andrews's winning garden blanket sat on top, but Sarah could also see the other two examples of her unmistakable watercolor palette style. Sarah's heart sank again. She had been so busy trying to find the missing quilt that it hadn't even occurred to her to wonder if she ought to report Shelly's deception to the fair board. Sarah didn't like the idea of taking that news to the board before she had a chance to confront Shelly directly about it. But she didn't like the idea of the fair board being duped and the large prizes going to the wrong hands, either. And what if Shelly had something to do with the quilt's disappearance? After all, if Shelly was capable of lying to the fair board when she entered the competition, she might be capable of taking the quilt as well.

Gloria had already gathered up half the quilts in her arms, and Barbara was carefully stacking the knits into the crook of her elbow.

"Do you need some help?" Lily asked.

Sarah scooped up the remaining quilts. "Thanks so much, Lily," she said. "I think we've got this."

The three women marched out of the quilt office in a haphazard parade, up the hill to the low ranch-style building that housed the fair office. Lily followed them out, but stopped at the bottom of the hill, watching them go.

"Quilts!" Carolyn Johnson exclaimed as Gloria came through the door, followed closely by Sarah.

"And knits!" she added when she caught sight of Barbara. "My goodness, you girls are early with these this year. It's an embarrassment of riches."

The three women set their plastic-wrapped piles down on the counters in a row. "But," Gloria said, "there's a problem."

"A problem?" Carolyn said.

"We're missing the winning quilt," Gloria said. "We just tore the whole quilt office apart, looking for it."

"Well, how could that happen?" Carolyn asked. "A quilt doesn't just get up and walk off."

"I'm sure it's just some kind of mix-up," Sarah said quickly, to smooth the situation over before it became too public. If word spread too far, it might spook her thief, even if it was the wrong quilt that seemed to be missing. "I'm very careful with the quilts, but it's possible it was simply misplaced. We've still got till tomorrow night to locate it."

Carolyn seemed to relax a bit at this. "Well, as long as we've got it by the time it needs to go up on the wall," she said. "Otherwise there's going to be an awfully big blank space." She lifted the entry tag on the first afghan and read the information. "In the meantime, I'll get these checked in."

As she did, Sarah's phone rang in her bag. When she lifted it out, the caller ID flashed the number from Maggie's store.

"Do you mind?" Sarah asked. "It's my daughter-in-law. I just want to make sure everything's all right."

This sounds way too harsh a response... "Do whatever you'd like!" Carolyn said, waving her away.

Sarah picked up the call. "Hello?"

"Sarah," Maggie said. "Are you still looking for that old quilt?"

Excitement thrilled through Sarah, but she tried to steady herself. "I am," she answered.

"Well, I just got one into my shop a few minutes ago," Maggie told her. "It looks old. And they told me it came from the fair."

"Can you hold on for just a second?" Sarah asked her. Then Sarah looked up at Carolyn. "Do you need anything else from me?"

Carolyn shook her head. "Just that grand-prize quilt," she said.

"That's exactly what I'm looking for," said Sarah. She waved silently to Gloria and Barbara, then slipped out the office door and down the stairs.

"Okay," Sarah said to Maggie when she reached the foot of the steps. "I'm sorry. I just had to finish something up."

"Oh, I understand," Maggie said. "How is everything going over there?"

"Well," Sarah said, "it's going. Now tell me about this quilt. How old is it?"

"I'm not sure how I'd tell that," Maggie said. "What do you look for, exactly?"

Sarah couldn't think of a quick way to break down the many intangibles she used when evaluating a quilt into a set of simple instructions, so she tried another tack. "Why don't you just try describing it to me?" she said.

"Okay," Maggie said. "Well, these don't look like regular fabrics."

"What do you mean by that?" Sarah prompted her gently.

"I've just never seen anything like this in a fabric shop," Maggie said. "The fabric doesn't have patterns on it. They're just plain colors. And they're not very bright. Mostly creams and browns and gray. The fabric even seems a little irregular in thickness, almost like it might have been handwoven."

Excitement bloomed into real hope in Sarah's chest. "What about the pattern?" Sarah asked. "How is it pieced?"

Maggie hesitated. "There aren't a lot of pieces," she said doubtfully. "I mean, not like a lot of the ones you work on. These are mostly big squares, with different pictures on them."

"Pictures?"

"Or ... shapes?" Maggie said. "I mean, you can tell they're meant to be something. This one's a tree," she said. "And this one's an animal."

There was definitely a tree on Helen's quilt, Sarah remembered: a regal-looking gray oak, devoid of leaves, with delicate branches that spread all the way to the edges of the square it had been appliquéd onto. And an animal sounded likely too. What else had been a distinguishing feature of Helen's quilt? The Pilgrim ship. "What about a boat?" Sarah asked.

"I'm not sure," Maggie said. "Here, let me unfold it on the counter. No ... nope ..."

After a series of rattles and thumps as she laid the quilt out and inspected it, Maggie let out a little yelp. "Here it is! I found a boat!"

Lord, thank you, Sarah prayed. *We found it just in time.*

"Can you hold it for me?" Sarah asked. "I'm coming right over."

"Are you kidding?" Maggie said. "Do you think I'd give this thing to anyone else now? I'd like to see them try to take it!"

Sarah smiled and ended the call. Then she headed down the midway to the meadow where her car was parked, trying to fit these new pieces into her old puzzle as she walked. The quilt was at Maggie's. That was an incredible relief. But how had it gotten there?

CHAPTER FOURTEEN

aggie's eyes sparkled as if she were about to announce the winner of the Miss America pageant. And Sarah's heart pounded just as if she were one of the finalists. Until now, she hadn't realized how deeply the loss of the quilt had upset her. But at the prospect of seeing it again, she was suddenly full of nerves, with even a few tears welling up in the back of her throat. She knew she would have been strong enough to face Allie, the fair board—even Helen, if that was what it came to. But she was indescribably relieved to have located the missing quilt, even if the mystery itself still remained to be solved.

Maggie set the simple cardboard box on the counter between them, flipped back the lid, and pushed aside the craft-brown tissue paper that surrounded the fabric, so Sarah could look in.

"There it is!" she said, her eyes dancing with delight over having helped solve Sarah's problem.

But with Sarah's first glance, her heart dropped. Her hand flew to her mouth, and to her surprise, tears came to her eyes. She blinked them back, hoping Maggie wouldn't notice.

"See?" Maggie was saying, tugging at one corner of the quilt to reveal a primitively pieced silhouette of a sailboat, nothing like the intricate Pilgrim ship on the quilt that had been passed down through Helen's family. "And I think the tree is around here somewhere too." She pulled a fold free to reveal another somewhat childish silhouette of a tree with a flannel cloud that loosely represented leaves. "You can see what I meant about the lack of color," she said. "But I guess that's what we were looking for, right?"

She looked up, her smile still bright.

It faded when she met Sarah's eyes.

"Oh, Sarah," she said, "this isn't it, is it? I'm so sorry."

"It's not your fault, honey," Sarah said, laying her hand over Maggie's on the glass counter. "You were just trying to help."

"But I got your hopes up!" Maggie said. "I was so sure it must be the one."

"Well, it sure sounded like it was," Sarah said. "So it had me fooled too."

Maggie let the fold drop back into the box in frustration. "So it's just some worthless old blanket."

Even in the midst of so much worry and frustration, Sarah couldn't bear to see a good quilt maligned. "No, no," she said. "Actually this is quite a nice piece, even though it's not the one I was looking for. How much did you pay for it?"

"One hundred," Maggie said.

"You got a good buy," Sarah told her. "It's worth quite a bit more. I'd be glad to appraise it for you, when the fair is over. But even now I can tell it's relatively rare, and these browns and grays you're not so crazy about actually indicate hand-dying, which is in demand with collectors these days."

Even as she switched into professional mode, worry and disappointment still filled her chest. *Lord,* she prayed, *please help me find this quilt. I know it might not seem important to you, but it means a lot to me.* She might not have any right, but she actually felt a little frustrated with God. Why would he let her think this was the right quilt, when it wasn't? Why would he have let something happen to Helen's quilt in the first place?

Despite everything she didn't understand, she felt some of the fear lift from her shoulders at the prayer. And as her mind cleared, she wondered about a new question. "Who brought this in?" she asked Maggie.

"Oh," Maggie said, "some woman from the fair."

"What did she look like?"

"Um . . ." Maggie looked up while she thought. "Blonde hair, nice haircut."

Allie Turnquist had blonde hair, Sarah thought.

"Not really short or tall," Maggie went on. "Kind of pretty. About my age. I feel like I've seen her around town."

All of that could apply to Allie Turnquist—or half a dozen people who had volunteered for the fair.

"How was she dressed?" Sarah asked. "Casual? Flashy?"

Maggie shook her head. "I'm sorry. I didn't really notice," she said. "As soon as she set the quilt down, I was focused on it."

Sarah smiled despite herself. She knew the feeling.

"But she was with the fair?" Sarah said. "Did she say that?"

Maggie nodded. "The fair board," she said. "She said she was working with them."

Sarah tried to fit these new pieces together. This quilt didn't appear to have been entered in the fair this year, so it hadn't been taken from the exhibit or the competition. But why would anyone associated with the board have brought it here to sell? Was someone at the fair operating some kind of trade in contraband quilts? The quilt could have fetched far more than Maggie had paid for it if they had taken it even an hour farther south and sold it to a more established antique shop. But maybe there was some advantage to Maggie's shop. Perhaps they had counted on Maggie not knowing the value, so that some other member of the scheme could easily come in and make an offer on it for far below cost.

"How is Grandpa William doing?" Maggie asked, interrupting Sarah's thoughts. "Jason said he hadn't been feeling well. What's going on?"

The question gave Sarah a sudden dose of perspective amid her anxious thoughts about the quilts. No matter what happened at the fair, or what trouble she had to go through, it paled in comparison with the question of her father's health. "I saw him this morning," she said. "They asked me to come in because he'd had trouble breathing. But by the time I got there, he was stabilized."

"That's good," Maggie said encouragingly.

Sarah thought back to her father's figure in the bed, sleeping with the help of powerful drugs, his breathing labored and his face drawn. It hadn't seemed exactly "good" to her. But she suspected it was a far prettier picture than the one she might have seen if she had arrived a few minutes earlier. She might not like seeing his health fail, but she could still find something to be grateful for. "I guess so," she said. "It's just hard to watch him struggle."

Maggie found Sarah's hand on the counter, and squeezed it. "I watched my grandfather go through the same thing," she said. "I know that's not the same as seeing your own dad go through it, but I know how hard it is not to be able to help someone you love."

"You just feel so helpless," Sarah murmured.

Maggie squeezed her hand again. "I know."

They hugged good-bye.

"I'm sorry it wasn't the right quilt," Maggie said again.

"It was worth a try," Sarah told her.

As she pulled out of the parking spot in front of Maggie's store, Sarah hesitated for a moment. Instead of turning left to go back to the fair, she turned right and headed into town. It was well past lunchtime. She was hungry, and maybe a break from the fair would give her some clarity about where to look next. She pulled up at The Spotted Dog, her favorite lunch spot, and went in. A crowd of women, all with various copies of the same book in their hands or poking out of their bags, were already in line, placing their orders, likely on a book club lunch date.

Leery of the crowd, Liam's corgi Murphy lurked in his dog bed, keeping an eye on the proceedings from a safe distance. When he saw Sarah come in, however, he pricked up his pointed copper-colored ears and trotted forward a few steps. Immediately, one of the women in line spotted him.

"Look at that!" she exclaimed. "Did you see this *cute* dog? Oh my goodness, honey! Well, come on over here!"

Instantly, half the ladies in line had crouched to their knees, their hands reaching for Murphy, cooing and calling.

Murphy stopped in his tracks, glanced at Sarah with the air of a long-suffering celebrity slightly exasperated by the antics of the local paparazzi, and retreated to his dog bed.

"Sarah," Liam said when she reached the front of the line. He gave her a broad smile, but she could tell he was a little overwhelmed by the group. "What can I get for you?"

Sarah glanced into the refrigerated case. Liam made any sandwich to order, but he also had a stash of standard favorites that he made fresh each morning, displayed alongside the desserts and sodas. "I'll just take the tuna sandwich," Sarah said, reading from the label.

"You sure about that?" Liam asked in his faint brogue. "You know I'm glad to make you something fresh."

"This is perfect," Sarah said.

"Well, it does take a bit of the pressure off," he said, handing her the sandwich. "Thanks for that."

Sarah pulled out her wallet.

"Chai?" he asked.

"Sure," Sarah said.

Liam started for the coffee machine, but Sarah stopped him. "Just whenever you're able," she said. "Take care of these ladies first. I'll have it for dessert."

Liam smiled gratefully and made change for her before turning back to the long line.

At her usual table in the corner, Sarah pulled her quilting notebook from her bag. If she had been trying to work through a problem with a quilt for a client, she realized, she would have been taking notes and organizing her thoughts all along. But she hadn't made notes since she discovered the quilt was missing. She had the sketch of the time line, but she hadn't even written down her suspects yet.

Lord, please help me make sense of this, she prayed. *If there's anything that I'm not seeing, please help me see it.*

She unwrapped her sandwich and took a few bites. Then she listed her suspects across the top of the page: Janet. Allie. Cherie. Earl. Shelly. Liam. Tentatively, she drew a line through Cherie's name. Everything Cherie had told her seemed to be true, and unless something came up to the contrary, Sarah was prepared to trust her. She also put a question mark beside Earl. If the girls were right that he had come in after Cherie, then the quilt had already been taken before he arrived. She still wanted to talk with him, but he couldn't have taken the quilt by himself.

Then she wrote clues and possible motive under each remaining name.

Janet. She hadn't returned Sarah's calls. What did she have to do with the strange man at the quilt exhibit?

In fact... Sarah thought, then added "man at exhibit" to the list. Below it, she wrote, "interest in quilt's value."

Allie. She had been vocal about her motive, she had certainly been there when Sarah left the building, and she knew her way around both the exhibit and the quilt office.

Shelly. Sarah wasn't sure why Shelly would have entered her knit work under multiple names, but she suspected it had something to do with the prize money. And if it was money Shelly was after, the quilt was worth a lot more than the fair prizes.

Finally, Liam. A few days ago, Sarah had been sure there must be a simple explanation for his presence in the quilt hall, but she had talked to him twice since then. He hadn't given her a straight answer either time.

She stared down at his name with a feeling she couldn't really explain. It went beyond simple curiosity or desire to find the quilt. She couldn't understand why he hadn't cleared up this misunderstanding right away. Liam had always gone out of his way to help her, and he wasn't the secretive type. But it wasn't just that. With surprise, she realized that she was hurt. Maybe she had grown to trust Liam's friendship more than she knew. In any case, it didn't feel good that he was keeping secrets from her.

At the bottom she wrote a list of clues that didn't fall under any one suspect yet: the hidden door, the rock that she had found just outside, the glitter under the table. And she changed the time line to reflect Cherie's memory of when she had visited the quilt, shrinking the window during which Helen's quilt had been switched with Janet's from forty minutes to about fifteen. She wished again that the girls had been able to remember the order people had come and gone, but instead, she wrote in the times that she did know above the names. Allie had still been there when Sarah left, at four forty. Cherie placed herself there around 4:45, and hadn't seen anyone until after she left, around 5:05. Liam said he had seen Allie there, which placed him early in the time line as well. But when had Shelly come and gone?

Sarah caught motion out of the corner of her eye and looked up. Liam had stepped out from behind the counter and was coming over, trailing steam from a hot cup of chai in his hands. Murphy slunk along behind him, sticking close to Liam's legs to avoid detection by the book club ladies. But when Murphy got in reach of Sarah, he lost all aplomb and turned into the wriggling ball of excitement Sarah knew so well.

She leaned down to scratch his pointed ears. He gave out a strangled little whimper of happiness.

"Hot chai," Liam said, setting it down beside her note-book on the table. "Thanks for being so patient."

Sarah looked up from his name on her list of suspects, nodded, and looked back down. "Thanks," she said.

Liam shuffled, unused to her curt response. Then he tried again. "What are you working on there?" he said. "Trying to identify another antique quilt?"

Sarah closed her notebook and looked up. "I know every-thing I need to know about this one," she told him, "except for where it is."

"Oh," Liam said, his expression slightly startled. "Well, I don't know that I can help you with that."

"Actually," Sarah said, "I think you're one of the only peo-ple who can."

"I don't understand."

Sarah pulled the chai closer to her. He certainly seemed eager to help, but some part of her hesitated to ask him about it again. It wasn't because she was worried she might upset him, she realized. It was because she didn't want to be upset herself if he refused to tell her.

She gave her head a little shake. She couldn't let her own hurt feelings keep her from doing everything she could to find the quilt. And, she realized, she had never explained her whole story to him either. He wasn't the only one who had been keeping secrets.

"That day at the fair," she began.

Right away, Liam's smile faded, but she pressed on. "I know you don't want to talk about it," she said, "and I don't know why. But you were one of the only people there when a very important quilt disappeared. I need to find it by tomorrow or I'm going to be in all kinds of trouble." Now that she had started, her words came in a rush. "I've been trying to find out everything I can from everyone who was in the area at that time," she told him. "But I still don't know why you were there, or what you were doing."

"Wait," Liam said, sinking into the chair across from her. "You don't think I had anything to do with the quilt's disappearance, do you?"

Sarah looked into his eyes for a long moment. Then she shook her head. "I don't," she answered truthfully.

"Well, if it will really help you," he said. "It's just such a silly story."

"What happened?" Sarah prompted.

"Well, you've seen those pastries I've got in the case, from the Sweet Sensations bakery, haven't you?" he asked.

Sarah nodded. He had just started carrying them in the past few months. They were baked by Katie Watson, a young mom in town, and the sweet potato cake with cream cheese frosting had quickly become one of Sarah's favorites.

"Well," Liam said, "I know how hard Katie's been working to get that business started. I see it every morning at six-thirty, when she comes in with a new basket of treats she's been up since four baking. But last week, I heard a couple of guys having coffee in the shop. They were from Murray's Baked Goods, up in Dexter. That's a big operation. But they were talking about the fair, how they were planning to enter their goods in some of the categories, to build their brand down here. Well, one of them said something about Katie's baking, and asked if the other guy was worried about the competition down here. The first guy said he knew someone at the fair and they didn't need to worry about any competition. I didn't like the way it sounded."

"What do you think he meant?" Sarah asked.

"I don't know!" Liam said. "But I got it into my head that Katie needed some kind of cowboy, to make sure everything was on the up and up. So I went charging over to the fair to police the baking entries, but...I got lost and wound up in your quilt exhibit instead of the baking hall."

Sarah suppressed a smile at the thought of Liam charging over to protect Katie Watson from the unsavory characters at Murray's Baked Goods.

"And the thing is, I didn't need to play policeman at all," he said. "When I did find the judge, she said Murray's had won a number of the runner-up prizes, because they'd put in so many entries. But they hadn't won any of the main prizes because Katie had taken the top prize in every category she entered."

"That'll be great for her business," Sarah said.

Liam nodded. "I hope so."

"I understand feeling a little silly, I guess," Sarah said. "But why did it take you so long to tell me?"

Now Liam looked sheepish again, although his eyes danced. "Well," he said, "you just seemed so interested in talking with me every time we ran into each other. I have to say, I liked it. So I guess I was just trying to stay mysterious for as long as I could."

It was Sarah's turn to look sheepish. "Well," she said, "hmm..."

Liam leaned forward and held her gaze. "I hope you'll forgive me," he said. "I never meant to stand in the way of your finding this quilt." He tapped on her notebook.

Relieved to be able to break Liam's searching expression, Sarah flipped the notebook open again. She drew a line through his name, and looked at the three that remained. Janet might be mixed up somehow with the strange man at the fair, but nobody had seen her at the scene when the quilt disappeared. Allie was still a strong suspect, but of the three of them only Shelly had managed to enter and leave the building without seeing anyone else. And Shelly had lied to Sarah about being at the fair. In fact, even if Shelly wasn't involved with the quilts at all, Sarah had to confront her about the blankets she had submitted under assumed names. And the kindest way to do that would be to give her a chance to explain herself, before embarrassing her before the fair board and the rest of the community. It might help to ask Martha to come along, since she had actually been the one to discover the deception. Still, Sarah didn't relish the idea of having that conversation. She sighed thinking about it.

Liam caught the gesture right away.

"Everything all right?" he asked.

Now it was a comfort to meet his eyes. "I think I know who I need to talk with next," Sarah told him. "I'm just not looking forward to it."

Liam nodded. "Sometimes the truth is hard," he said. "But you never go wrong in the end by looking for it."

"I know that's true," Sarah said. "Sometimes it's just easier to believe that than other times."

"Excuse me!" one of the book ladies called from the counter. "Is anyone serving here, please?"

"I'll be right with you," Liam called. Instantly, he was on his feet. "I'm sorry," he said, still hovering over Sarah's table.

Sarah waved her hand. "It's your customer!" she said. "Please."

"I'm really sorry for the confusion about the quilt exhibit," he told Sarah. "You'll have to let me make it up to you. The next chai is on me."

"That sounds like a deal," Sarah said.

"Brilliant," he said, his eyes dancing. "And it'll give me another excuse to talk with you."

CHAPTER FIFTEEN

When he answered Sarah's knock on the door this time, Shelly's son Adrian had undergone a transformation from pirate to scuba diver. He still wore the same swimming flippers he had been wearing the other evening, but now the ensemble was completed by a pair of blue jeans with an elastic waistband, and a diving mask and snorkel.

He raised the alarm about Sarah and Martha's arrival to the rest of his household by tooting something incomprehensible through the snorkel, then darted off into the dining room as if he were a fish taking cover from a shark behind a bank of coral.

"Adrian!" Shelly called from the back of the house. "Take the snorkel out of your mouth! What did you say?"

Adrian tooted something garbled from his hiding place beneath the dining room table. Shelly came around the corner and stopped at the sight of Sarah.

"I'm sorry," Shelly said, her voice rising, "this really isn't a good time."

At the sound of his mother's distress, Adrian burst from the dining room. He yanked the snorkel free from his mask and pointed it at Sarah and Martha as if it were a magic wand and he had just commanded them to vanish in thin air. When it didn't work, he dropped the snorkel and took his mother's hand.

Martha broke into her best smile. "Shelly," she said, "I'm so glad to see you. You've got some really beautiful pieces in the fair this year."

"Pieces?" Shelly said. "There must be some mistake. I only entered one."

"You know, I thought it must be a mistake too," Martha said, keeping her voice light. "But when I went to meet *Candace Drew*, it turned out your nephew lives at that address."

Shelly's expression froze. "Adrian," she said, "go on upstairs."

"I don't like her," Adrian said, glaring at Sarah.

"Upstairs," his mother repeated. Adrian scampered away.

"We haven't spoken to anyone at the fair about it," Sarah said. "We wanted to come to you first."

Shelly took a deep shaky breath. "Things have just been so tight around here," she said. "The baby's been sick ever since he was born, and no matter how much Mike works, we can't seem to catch up. He doesn't want me to go back to work, and I don't know if I even could, because someone's got to make sure the baby's all right, all the time. So when I saw how big the prizes were this year, I thought it would be a way I could make a little extra. I didn't mean to hurt anyone. Even winning one category would help with the bills."

"Well," Sarah said, "I'm probably not supposed to tell you this, but you did win. With all three of them."

"Really?" Shelly said, her eyes suddenly alight. "But will I have to give it back? When they find out?"

Sarah shook her head. "I don't know," she said. "You were at the fair that night I asked you about, weren't you?"

Shelly nodded. "I didn't want to bring all my pieces in person in case someone recognized they weren't all under the same name. So I waited until after hours and dropped them off at the textiles office."

"They were the last ones on the list," Martha remembered.

Shelly nodded.

Sarah watched Shelly, trying to gauge her reaction. Unless Shelly was a very good actor, she seemed so remorseful about the small lie she had told that Sarah had trouble believing she had planned and executed a major theft.

"Did you see anyone else while you were in the office?" Sarah asked.

"I did," Shelly nodded. "She almost scared me to death. Allie Turnquist."

"By herself?" Sarah said quickly. She couldn't quite imagine Allie stealing the quilt in front of Lily. Had this been the moment when Allie left Lily to make the switch out of her daughter's sight?

"Yes," Shelly said.

"Do you remember what time it was?"

"I timed it pretty carefully," Shelly said. "The submissions were due at 4:30, so I came right after they closed."

Early in the time line, Sarah thought. That would be about perfect, from what she knew. If Allie was already collecting the replacement quilt by then, it would have left her plenty of time to make the switch and escape with the antique quilt before Cherie showed up.

"Did she have anything with her?" Sarah asked. "Did you see her take anything out?"

"I'm sorry," Shelly said. "I was scared to death. I was just trying to complete my paperwork and get out of there as soon as I could, before someone recognized me. I barely saw anything. She didn't seem to pay much attention to me, though."

That sounded about par for the course with Allie.

"It would have been a big package," Sarah said, "hard to miss."

Shelly shook her head. "I—"

She stopped when Sarah held her hand up and said "Shh!" From Janet Stevens's yard, which backed onto Shelly's, Sarah had caught the sound of voices. And one of them sounded like Janet's.

"I'm sorry," Sarah said. "If you'll just give me a moment."

She raced around the house, into Janet's yard, Martha in hot pursuit. When they broke through the grape arbor between the yards, there was Janet, busily giving instructions to the handyman Sarah had met the other day. For a minute, the two women stood, eyes locked.

Then Janet turned tail and made a beeline for her house.

"Sarah?" Shelly called, crashing through the grapevines herself. "Martha?"

Without giving an answer, Sarah took off after Janet, Martha close behind.

When Sarah rounded the corner of Janet's house, into the front yard, she found Janet kneeling in the wood chips of her front garden, twisting a hissing faucet into the "off" position.

"Sarah! Martha!" Janet said, slightly out of breath. "I'm so sorry! But I had to turn off this faucet. My begonias were in danger of drowning. You know how temperamental they can be." She straightened up and stepped back onto the lawn. "At any rate, welcome to my garden. What there is of it. And Shelly! It's good to see you."

Sarah forced a smile. Maybe Janet hadn't been fleeing her after all. But if she was being this friendly to Sarah in person, why hadn't she responded to any of Sarah's calls?

As she wondered this, Janet smacked herself on the forehead, leaving a black smear of dirt. "I owe you a phone call, don't I?" she asked Sarah. "In fact, I think I owe you several. I'm *so* sorry. We went up north for the week after I dropped off the quilt, and we just got back today. I wanted to be home in time for the awards ceremony tomorrow night. After all that work, even if I don't win, I want to see anyone who beats me with my own eyes."

Sarah's smile faded at the mention of the awards ceremony, and Janet's own face grew solemn. "Oh, Sarah," she said, "it's nothing serious, is it?"

It didn't make sense for Sarah to contradict her current story: that it was Janet's quilt that had gone missing, not the priceless original. Perhaps Sarah could glean some clues to whether Janet had been involved or not by watching Janet's reaction to the news. Maybe Janet would even give her a clue about the man who had apparently called her from the fair.

"I hope not," Sarah said. "But we've had a small problem at the fair. One of the quilts has gone missing and …" Even though she was following her own plan, it was difficult for Sarah to give Janet the news. "I'm afraid it's yours."

Janet's eyes widened to what seemed like twice their size. "Mine?" she said, her voice high. "The quilt I made?" she asked, as if hoping someone might provide her with a different definition of "mine" that would explain the whole situation away.

Sarah nodded. "I'm so sorry," she said. "I judged it, and it did very well. But before we could hang it, it disappeared."

"*Disappeared?*" Janet repeated. Her voice quavered.

"We're doing absolutely everything we can to find it," Martha said.

"That's why I'm here, actually," said Sarah. "That's what I was calling you for, to see if you knew of anyone who might have had some interest in the quilt, or anything else that might help us to track it down."

"I do know someone who's interested in it!" Janet said. "That's the whole problem! You're sure it's gone?"

"We're looking," Sarah repeated. "Very hard. Can you think of anything that might help us?"

Janet shook her head and covered her eyes with her hands. Shelly reached out to pat her neighbor's back. Then Janet dropped her arms to her sides. "Sarah," she said, "this is a disaster. You have got to find that quilt."

"You said you know someone who's interested in the quilt," Martha said, pressing on gently. "Can you tell me who that is?"

"Only Jeff Walker," Janet said.

Martha looked at Sarah for an explanation. The name didn't mean anything to Martha but Sarah's own eyes widened. She had never met Jeff Walker, but she knew of him. He had a national reputation as a dealer in the finest antique quilts, and worked with exclusive clients on both coasts, including financial giants and Hollywood stars. In the past ten years, to keep up with the demands of clients who wanted exact replicas of quilts that had since gone off the market, he had begun to partner with a highly selective group of contemporary quilters, who were turning out some of the best homage quilt work anyone had ever seen.

Janet saw that Sarah understood the importance of the name, and nodded. "I met him at an exhibit almost a year ago," she said. "And ever since then, I've been trying to form a relationship with him. Working with his clients and copying the quilts he deals in would be a dream job. And he promised to come down and see this project. He wanted to see your exhibit, and he was going to compare it with my work when it goes up tomorrow. But how can he do that if we don't know where it is?"

Sarah's mind flashed back to the man with the cell phone in the exhibit the day before. "Has he been to the fair already?"

"Yes," Janet said. "He called me from the exhibit yesterday. He drives a hard bargain, but he's fair, and I could tell he was interested. He thinks Helen's quilt is one of the most beautiful examples of early hand-dyed quilting he's ever seen. But he said he couldn't make a decision until he sees my actual quilt."

Sarah bit her lip, unable to tell Janet that Jeff Walker already had. In fact, Janet's was the quilt he had been complimenting that day.

"How could someone have taken it?" Janet asked. "Wasn't there security? I mean, mine can't have been the only valuable quilt in that building. Not by a long shot. What about those expensive antiques you've got on display now?"

"Of course there's security!" Martha said, defending her friend.

"We have someone on duty constantly," Sarah assured her. "But this happened before the fair opened, while I was out of the building. I was only gone for a few minutes," she added, lamely. Even though there had been no reason to believe that the quilt wasn't safe when she left, the excuse still sounded hollow as she said it. She could only imagine how it would sound if she had to deliver it to the fair board—or to Helen.

Janet took a deep breath and folded her arms. "I'm sorry," she said. "I know this must be hard for you too. It's just that I've been looking forward to this for so long. It feels terrible to know I've gotten this far and now nothing might come of it."

Sarah actually knew this feeling well. It was exactly the way she felt about the exhibit and contest that she had planned for so long, that now seemed to be in danger of falling apart before the awards were even announced. But when she heard the defeat in Janet's voice, Sarah's own fighting spirit rose up again.

"Don't say that," Sarah said.

"We haven't given up," Martha added.

"There's a lot of time between now and the awards ceremony tomorrow night," Sarah continued. "I'm going to do absolutely everything I can."

"Thank you," Janet said. "I just can't believe someone would take my quilt. How much could it really be worth to anyone besides me? I mean, what kind of person would do a thing like that?"

"That's exactly what I'm going to find out," Sarah promised.

CHAPTER SIXTEEN

"W"ell, what have we here?" the bearded man asked. Sarah stepped closer, Martha crowding behind her.

"His tag says 'Earl,'" Martha murmured. "Just like Cherie said."

The young boy who squinted up at Earl was six or seven years old, in a blue and gold striped shirt. "Oliver," he said, and folded his arms over his chest.

Behind him, Oliver's mom took a few dollars out of her wallet and handed them to Earl. The bell and hammer game was one of several at the fair for younger kids where a prize was guaranteed simply for playing. But Earl pocketed the payment and swung into action as if this were, in fact, a high stakes battle with a game of skill and chance.

"All right, buddy!" he said, handing little Oliver a light wooden hammer that was almost as tall as he was. "Your job is just to hit this button. Hit it as hard as you can. You want that bell up there to ring. Got it?"

Oliver nodded, determination shining in his eyes. But his first swing was only powerful enough to send the bell-ringer halfway up to the winning bell. Oliver looked back at his mother, wondering what to do.

"Good try, honey!" his mom said encouragingly.

"Three tries!" Earl announced, although this was nowhere in the rules painted on the game's background.

"Go ahead, sweetie!" Oliver's mom said. "Hit it hard!"

This time, Oliver's swing was more powerful. But it only reached about two-thirds of the way to the bell.

Sarah adjusted her purse on her shoulder and shaded her eyes against the sun.

"Almost there!" Earl announced. "Give it one more swing."

Biting his lip in concentration, Oliver swung with all his might, then let his head drop back to watch the progress of the ringer as it shot up toward the bell. While he wasn't looking, Earl stepped lightly on the button Oliver had just thwacked. The ringer shot up the last few feet, and the bell pealed brightly.

Oliver's face broke into a wide grin.

"Wow, what an arm!" Earl bellowed. "All right! Pick a prize! Any one you want!"

Oliver abandoned the hammer in the grass and ran over to the array of inflatable toys. He selected a dolphin that was even taller than the hammer had been.

"This one?" Earl asked.

Oliver nodded and the man unclipped it from among the others. Oliver lurched over to show his mother.

"You want some help with that, honey?" his mom asked.

Oliver shook his head, renewed his grip on the dolphin's belly, and bore his prize off into the midway.

Sarah and Martha were now the only people at the booth. Earl grinned at them, then looked around for a child. When he didn't locate one, he looked back up at them, slightly confused.

"You like to play a round?" he asked, flipping the hammer up with his foot so he could catch the handle in his beefy hand.

Sarah shook her head. "No, thanks," she said. "I just had a few questions for you, if you've got a minute."

"Sure," Earl said. "At least until I have a customer. Shoot."

"I'm with the fair here in Maple Hill," Sarah told him. "And we had a little bit of trouble over in our quilt barn this year. I know you were over there on Tuesday around the time it happened, and I was hoping you might have seen something that would help us understand what went on."

"The quilt barn?" Earl repeated. "I don't know if I…I mean, there are a lot of barns on these fairgrounds, and…"

Beside Sarah, Martha crossed her arms impatiently. "Cherie saw you," she said. "Cherie? Over at the quick-sketch?"

The mention of Cherie seemed to rob Earl of his power of speech. His eyebrows shot up, and his mouth twisted into something that might have been either a smile or a grimace.

"Do you remember seeing anything unusual while you were there?" Sarah asked.

Earl shook his head.

"It's important," Sarah said. "I'm trying to locate something very valuable."

Earl spread his hands, dropped them, and then lifted them again, all without a word.

Sarah took a deep breath. "Can you tell me what you were doing there?" she asked.

Earl shrugged again.

Sarah had been won over at first by Earl's kindness with his young customer, but now she remembered him lurking in the twilight outside Cherie's trailer. Was there a darker side to him?

"What were you doing outside Cherie's trailer the other night?" Martha asked, her eyes narrowing.

Earl's eyes darted around the midway as if looking for an escape route. For an instant, Sarah thought he might actually make a break for it. Then he opened his mouth.

At first, nothing came out. He looked so miserable that Sarah began to take pity on him again.

"What is it?" she said, more gently.

"I just wanted...," he said, and then choked the words out, "...to talk."

"To talk?" Sarah asked.

Earl nodded.

"With Cherie?" Sarah guessed.

He nodded again. The mention of Cherie's name, which had made him tongue-tied before, seemed to break the spell now. "She always talks to everyone," he said. "But I never know what to say when she talks to me. So I thought, maybe, if no one else was around, I could think of what to say. I wanted to ask her if I could take her out on Monday before we open next week in Pennsylvania."

"So you followed her into the quilt barn," Martha said.

Earl shifted his weight from one foot to the other. "But she looked so interested in the quilts, she didn't even notice I was there. And once I saw her, I couldn't think what to say. So I just left."

"And then the next night...," Sarah prompted.

"I traded with a buddy so I could go over there just after she got off work," Earl said. "But—"

"She was already gone," Sarah finished for him.

Earl nodded, completely deflated.

"Did you see anything while you were at the quilt barn?" Sarah asked him. "Anything at all?"

"Just some kids hanging around," Earl said.

Audrey and Lexie, Sarah thought. They had seen him too. "Anything else?"

Earl shook his head.

"Mommy mommy mommy mommy mommy!" A little girl in pigtails tied with blue ribbons tore up to the booth. She stopped in front of the display of prizes and began to hop up and down. "Mommy! Mommy! Mommy!"

"I told her one game," her mother told Earl. "I guess it's this one."

"Well, we better make it a good one, then," Earl said heartily. "Excuse me," he said to Sarah and Martha.

"Thank you," Sarah said, and slipped away from the booth.

"You believe him?" she asked Martha.

Martha nodded. "A man doesn't lie about something like that," she said. "If he were making up a story, it'd be a lot more flattering to him."

Sarah looked up at the inscrutable faces of the giant lions that were being offered as prizes in the booth across the way.

"So where to next?" Martha asked.

"I don't know," Sarah said. "I think I better go back to the quilt office for a bit, and see if I can make some sense of all this."

"Fair enough," Martha said. "I think I'll get myself a candy apple before I go. I want to make sure I've got my strength up, for the road."

Sarah smiled at her. "Thanks for everything," she said.

"Anytime," Martha said. "And I'll be praying for your dad. And for you."

The two friends hugged.

"Thank you," Sarah said.

The quilt office was mercifully deserted when she returned to it. At her now empty desk, Sarah flipped open her quilt notebook again. She gazed at the list of suspects for a moment, and then drew lines through the names Janet, Shelly, Earl, and Liam.

Only one remained: Allie Turnquist.

Sarah looked down at the list of stray clues at the bottom of the page. The rock by the door, the time line—it all fit. Of all the suspects, Allie had always had the most motive and opportunity. Sarah just hadn't wanted to believe it.

As Sarah thought it over, though, other pieces began to drop into place. All summer long, each time she had seen Allie, Allie had pestered Sarah to put in a good word for her with Helen, in hopes that Helen might someday let Allie buy her quilt. Since the quilt had disappeared, Allie hadn't said one word about it.

All the interactions she'd had with Allie flowed through her mind, from Allie's first call announcing her donation to the exhibit and prize fund. The excitement she showed over bringing a world-class exhibit to Maple Hill and rewarding local quilters with even bigger prizes. The grandiose plans Sarah had had to talk her out of. The surprisingly good suggestions she'd had for potential quilts for the exhibit, including one of Sarah's favorite crazy quilts, on loan from one of Allie's private collector friends.

Allie hadn't always been easy to work with, but Sarah thought they had managed to maintain a kind of balance. Yet as she thought back, her heart dropped when she thought of all the times Allie had mentioned Helen's quilt. She had even mentioned Helen's quilt in that first conversation, Sarah realized. And Sarah couldn't even begin to count all the times it had come up since then, usually with a request that Sarah figure out some way to get it from Helen's hands into Allie's.

"Her children don't seem very interested in it," Allie loved to point out. "I know it's been in their family for years, but who's going to take care of it after she's gone? You'd be doing her a favor, really. Deep in her heart, she just wants it taken care of. Nobody in town would do that better than me. And that means it could stay right here in Maple Hill, where it's always been. Otherwise, who knows where it might end up!"

Sarah shook her head. Allie hadn't seemed guilty when Janet's quilt came up missing, but it was possible that Allie had talked herself into believing that taking the quilt was actually the right thing to do. She had certainly made that case to Sarah enough times.

And Sarah couldn't help thinking back on all the work she had done herself. She had been thinking about this exhibit for years, making little notes to herself whenever she saw wonderful quilts in other state displays: *this one would be perfect. Or, that one would fit right in.* The exhibit as it stood today was the result of an entire decade of dreaming. She had chosen and rechosen, arranged and rearranged a thousand times before she even knew the exhibit might ever become a reality.

And that had been only the beginning. Once Allie had made the donation that made the exhibit possible, Sarah's life had been almost entirely consumed by the planning.

When she wasn't solving one of her mysteries, or spending time with her granddaughters, or visiting her father, she had made hundreds of phone calls, called in countless favors, made all kinds of promises. The logistical work of organizing shipping and delivery from around the state, hiring a security company, dealing with press and advertising, and running interference with the fair board had sometimes been a full-time job. Not to mention organizing the quilt competition as she did every year, always a major task in itself, and even bigger this year due to the increase in the size of the prizes.

All that work had seemed worth it while she was doing it, since she was seeing her own vision come to life, and offering a gift to quilt lovers in Maple Hill and around the state. But now all that time and energy seemed tainted by Allie's betrayal. The idea that she had been a pawn in some plan of Allie's took all the hope and glow out of the long days of work. Now it just felt like hours of endless drudgery. Suddenly, Sarah was very tired. She let her head drop into her hands.

This was a dream come true for me, Lord, she prayed. *Why would you have let it happen if it was only going to turn out this way?*

Nothing seemed to answer her but the low clatter of rides spinning on the midway.

After a moment, she opened her eyes. Allie's name stood out starkly on the page in front of her.

Well, at least I know who I'm looking for now, she thought.

Once outside, she realized she had a good reason to be tired: twilight had begun to descend on the midway, and the lights of the rides were already starting to glow brighter in the dark. If Allie were even still at the fair, where would she be? Sarah slipped into the exhibition hall and took a quick look around, but Allie was nowhere to be found.

"Excuse me," she said to the guard—a new one now, probably on the evening shift. "Do you know Mrs. Turnquist?"

The guard shook his head.

"She's one of the organizers of the quilt exhibit this year," Sarah told him. "So she would have been in and out quite often. Blonde hair, well dressed…high heels?" she tried.

Apparently high heels were in short supply on the fair's uneven ground, and memorable enough to jog his recollection. Recognition lit up in the young man's eyes. He nodded. "Sure," he said. "But I haven't seen her in a few hours. Last I think I heard she was going over to the prize hall to help them hang the quilts."

Hanging the quilts, Sarah thought. That should have been her job, but she had been so busy looking for the missing antique that she had completely forgotten.

"Thank you," she said, and headed down the hill toward the prize barn.

The prize barn was kept locked for the first days of the fair, then thrown open on Friday night after the prize ceremonies, to draw visitors who had been there on a weeknight back to enjoy the weekend. But Sarah could see light under the door, and when she knocked, Gloria answered.

"Sarah!" she said. "It's good to see you! Come on in."

All around them, various award-winners were going up on display: winning cakes on their cake stands, gigantic pumpkins stacked in the corners, children's drawings tagged with blue, red, and purple ribbons. At the far end of the hall were the knits and quilts. Only about half of them were hung yet, but Sarah could see the gaping hole where the grand-prize quilt belonged.

"Does it look all right to you?" Gloria asked. "I know you usually direct the hanging, but Allie came down earlier, so we went along with her suggestions."

"It looks fine," Sarah said with a glance. Now wasn't the time to worry about details like which quilt hung where. Not while she was still missing the most important quilt at the fair. "Is Allie here?"

Gloria shook her head. "She left a little while ago," she said. "There really wasn't much for her to do, after she'd given her instructions."

"Did she say where she was going?"

"Home, I'd guess," Gloria said. "Most of us have been here all day."

If she had left only a little while ago, maybe Sarah could catch up with her. "Thanks," Sarah said, and hurried back out.

She followed the natural path between the prize barn and the fair exit, scanning the midway for Allie, but didn't catch sight of her. Finally she circled back to the textiles office, with the faint hope that Allie might have stopped in there at the end of the night.

It was just as empty as it had been when she left it, with the quilt and knit entries dozing on the wire racks in the dim light.

She sat back down at the desk, where her notebook still lay open, and looked down at the list of outstanding clues she had written neatly at the bottom. *There must be something I'm missing,* she thought. Then, painstakingly, she began to work her way back through the day. The conversation with Janet and Shelly. The late lunch with Liam. The visit to Maggie's shop. Her thoughts lingered over the last one.

A moment later, she scooped up her quilt book, locked up the little room, and headed for the fair office. Most of the lights were shut off for the evening, but Sarah could still see figures moving behind the glass. She tapped on the window.

Carolyn Johnson slid it open. "Sarah," she said. "How are you doing?"

"I know you're trying to close," Sarah said. "But I've got a quick question for you. I was down at my daughter-in-law Maggie's shop today, and she had a quilt come in from the fair. Do you know anything about that?"

"The missing quilt?" Carolyn asked.

Sarah felt a little pang of embarrassment. It seemed that the news was spreading through the fair board. She shook her head. "I wish it had been," she said. "That's why she called me, in hopes that it might be. But it was another quilt, one I hadn't seen before. I was just curious since the seller said they were from the fair, but I'd never seen the quilt."

"Did she say who brought it in?" Carolyn asked.

"Blonde hair," Sarah said. "Medium height. Middle-aged." As she spoke the words, she realized again that they perfectly described Allie Turnquist.

But Carolyn's eyes lit up at the description. "That sounds like Donna," she said, and turned away from the window. "Donna?" she called. She turned back to Sarah. "She's helping me close the office," she explained.

A moment later a pretty woman with a trim blonde haircut appeared in the window beside Carolyn. "Yep?" she said.

"Sarah wants to know about a quilt from the fair that turned up at the antique store," Carolyn said. "Was it in all that stuff you took down the other day?"

Donna nodded decisively. "Yep," she said again. "That and about a hundred other things we didn't need around here."

"Mostly grays and browns?" Sarah asked, checking. "Not too colorful?"

Carolyn nodded again. "It was my contribution to the office this year," she said. "I'm done stumbling through all the clutter that accumulates in here. You wouldn't believe it. Old calendars. Farm equipment. Prize entries nobody picked up five years ago. When I came in Wednesday morning, I had one of the Heller kids pack up everything that wasn't nailed down. Now the place is spotless. See?"

Donna waved at the small paneled office around her. She was right. It was cleaner than Sarah had ever seen it.

"I'm going to do it every year, now," Donna said. "That'll be my legacy on the fair board. No more office clutter."

"And some of it you took to Magpie's Antiques," Sarah prompted.

"Yeah, I never could bear to waste anything," Donna said. "A few boxes looked too nice to pitch. So I went down to see if they might be worth something. I came back with a couple hundred bucks for the fair's bank account!"

Sarah's hope that the quilt would prove some definitive link with Allie was fading, but she pressed ahead anyway.

"Do you have any idea where the quilt came from?" she asked. "Or when you first saw it?"

"That quilt's been in this office as long as I have," Donna declared. "And that's at least three years. Last winter when the heat went out, Harry Butler gave the financial report with it wrapped around his shoulders."

"My guess is that it was an antiques entry at some point," Carolyn said. "But no one ever came to pick it up. And no one could bear to throw it out."

Sarah nodded. She was well acquainted with the mess in the fair office.

"Well," she said, "thanks for your help."

"Oh my gosh!" Donna said. "I just realized. Why didn't I tell you about it? You're our resident quilt expert. Is that why you're asking?"

Sarah shook her head. "I was hoping it might help me find something else," she said.

Donna looked at her quizzically, then at Carolyn. Carolyn gave her a look that said "I'll tell you later." Sarah sighed. At this point, there was nothing she could do to keep the news from spreading.

"Well," Donna said, "good luck."

Her conscience smarting over the lost quilt, Sarah wasn't quite able to meet Donna's eyes. As her gaze wandered, she caught sight of tomorrow's fair schedule, pinned up neatly on the office wall. The Junior Homemaker's poise and interview competition was slated for tomorrow morning. The speaking element was an important factor, and the event was always well attended. Even if Allie hadn't given Lily much encouragement yet, she had to show up for that, Sarah thought. In fact, it was so public, she couldn't imagine Allie missing it. She hadn't managed to connect Allie directly with the missing quilt, but at least she knew a way to find Allie tomorrow.

"Thanks," she said again. Carolyn waved and slid the window shut.

On the way out of the fair, Sarah passed by Cherie's booth. At first glance, it seemed to be packed up and sealed shut for the night, but as Sarah slowed, Cherie slipped out from the shadow of the giant slide, swinging her portfolio at her side.

"Hey, stranger," she said, "you ever going to come back and let me finish your picture?"

Sarah smiled. "I wish I had time," she said. "I've just been so busy looking for this quilt."

Cherie's smile faded. "Wait," she said. "You're still looking?"

Sarah nodded. "You know, I talked with Earl today," Sarah told her.

"He help you any?" Cherie asked.

"He did his best," Sarah said. "But he told me he'd just been hoping to talk with you."

"Me?" Cherie said, surprise in her voice. "If I've tried to talk with him once, I've tried a dozen times. He's the quietest man in this carnival."

Sarah suppressed a smile, remembering how just the mention of Cherie's name had struck Earl speechless. "Well," she said. "That's what he told me. Maybe you should ask him."

"Maybe I will," Cherie said.

Now they had reached the end of the midway. Sarah paused at the turnoff for the parking meadow.

"Have a good night, honey," Cherie told her.

"You too."

CHAPTER SEVENTEEN

A ringing phone woke Sarah the next morning.

She lifted her head from the pillow, fumbled on the stand beside her bed, managed to push the "talk" button and put the phone to her ear without checking the caller ID.

"Hello?" she said, trying to keep the gravel out of her voice. What time was it, anyway?

"Sarah?" The voice was sweet, familiar, and crackly with age: Helen. "How are you doing, dear?"

Sarah sat up in bed, suddenly wide-awake. "Just fine, Helen," she said. "How are you doing?"

"It's not too early, is it?" Helen asked. "Oh dear, I didn't wake you?"

"What can I do for you, Helen?"

Helen gave a sheepish little laugh. "Oh, nothing," she said. "I'm actually calling to thank you for what you've already done. I thought I'd be so worried about the quilt all week that I wouldn't be able to enjoy anything. But do you know what actually happened?"

Unfortunately, Sarah did. But she still held out hope that she would be able to get things back in their proper places before she had to worry Helen. "What?" she asked.

"I was so *excited*!" Helen exclaimed. "Every time I thought of the quilt, I imagined it up on that wall, with all the people who have never seen it finally getting a chance to."

Sarah's stomach did a little flip over all the people she had let down by not taking better care of the quilt. It wasn't just Helen. As the older woman had inadvertently pointed out, the loss of the quilt was a kind of betrayal of all the people who had traveled from around the state to see it.

"I loved thinking about everyone who might go by," Helen said. "Mothers and their daughters. Other quilters like you. Whole families. I had the best time imagining them, all week. I was so happy and proud I could barely stand it. I don't know why it took me so long to let you put it on display. I should have done it years ago. It's not just part of my family's history, it's part of everyone's. So I wanted to thank you again for helping me see that."

Sarah could barely get the words "you're welcome" out, but she managed somehow.

"Well," Helen said, "I don't want to keep you. I know you must have lots to do. But I can't wait to see it all when my son takes me over!"

"Oh good," Sarah said in a strangled voice.

"I'll be looking for you!" Helen promised.

"I'll see you soon," Sarah responded, and hung up the phone.

An hour later, Sarah found her way to a spot on the bleachers as the audience filed in for the Junior Homemaker poise and interview event. She picked a spot high in the stands, where she would be sure to catch sight of Allie the instant she came in. But as person after person took their place on long aluminum seats, Allie never appeared. Finally the contestants filed out on stage, wearing carefully chosen day dresses, their hair and makeup precisely done despite the early hour.

Sarah took another close look around the judging arena to make sure she hadn't missed anyone, almost more alarmed for Lily's sake than for her own. Was Allie really going to miss her daughter's big event?

Up on stage, Lily was making her own inspection of the crowd, her eyes shining. But as she looked over each face without finding her mother's, her smile waned. Then, high in the bleachers, she caught sight of Sarah and her face lit up again. She raised her hand in a careful Junior Homemaker wave. Sarah waved back.

Now there was no way she could leave until the event had ended. Sarah sat through the program of questions with a mixture of amusement and impatience, as the teenage girls gravely gave their opinions on world politics, the importance of family, and their own personal dreams. Lily acquitted herself well, talking eloquently about how she believed old-fashioned homemaking techniques were still valuable in today's busy world. "I think they're important *because* they take so much time," Lily said. "They provide a way for a family just to be together. We're always so busy trying to get this or that done, but in the end just spending time with the people we love is the most important thing. Not to mention ..." she added with a hint of mischief, "the homemade stuff just tastes so good!"

The crowd broke into appreciative laughter.

Sarah did her best to be attentive to the whole program, nodding at Lily and smiling each time the girl looked to her for encouragement, but she couldn't help running through the list of all the things she should be accomplishing instead. *Lord,* she prayed, *you know everything else I could be doing right now. I hope you have a good reason for this.*

When Lily came down off the stage an hour and a half later, Sarah had part of her prayer answered. Lily made a beeline for her, clambering straight up the bleachers in her fifties-style day dress and a pair of high heeled shoes she had almost certainly borrowed from her mother. When she reached Sarah, she enveloped her in a giant hug.

"Thank you so much for coming," she said. "I didn't realize how nice it would be to have a friendly face in the crowd."

"But doesn't—" It took Sarah a moment to stop herself as she realized what Lily was saying. Was she really used to trying to celebrate the small achievements of her young life without a friendly face in the crowd?

Lily looked at her quizzically.

"You did a lovely job, dear," Sarah told her. "I was very impressed."

"I really think I might win this year," Lily said, her voice low and confidential. "I've got eight more entries in the fair than anyone else, and I think I did all right with my answers this morning."

Sarah nodded, refraining from her first impulse: to tell Lily not to worry so much about whether she won or not. She could see that it mattered to Lily a great deal, and she thought she knew why: not because Lily was so competitive herself, but because she hoped it might win her some affection from the always distracted Allie.

"My mom's going to be there tonight," Lily said eagerly, confirming Sarah's intuition. "She doesn't always come to …," she hesitated and gestured around at the crowd, "these things. But tonight the Junior Homemaker award will be given out at the same ceremony as the quilt prizes. She's going to explain the new judging system you helped her test, and the fair also wants to honor her for her donations to the exhibit and the contest."

Sarah desperately wanted to question Lily about where her mother might be right now, but she couldn't bring herself to do it. Lily was asking herself the same question, she was sure. Whatever the answer was, it wasn't worth hurting Lily's feelings to find out.

"So do you get to relax and enjoy the fair for the rest of the day?" Sarah asked. "Or do you have other events between now and tonight?"

Lily shook her head. "Nope, I'm free," she said. "I asked Mom if she wanted to look at some exhibits with me." And then she gave Sarah the answer to the question she had refrained from asking. "But I guess she must have gotten tied up at home. So I'm sure I'll figure out something."

"Lily!" one of the other contestants called from below.

Lily and Sarah looked down. The other girl waved a sheaf of papers and pointed to them. "We all need to fill one out!" she shouted.

"I'm sorry," Lily said, "I have to go. Thank you for coming!"

"Of course," Sarah called after her. "And you have some fun today!"

Lily smiled back over her shoulder and waved.

Sarah waited on the bleachers, watching as Lily filled out her form, handed it to the official judge, and drifted away with a pair of other girls. Then Sarah marched down the center aisle of the bleachers, her shoes thunking on the hollow aluminum, and headed for her car.

As she pulled up in front of Allie's house, she realized she didn't have a plan for what came next. She would charge up to the front door, knock, and then—and then what? Tell Allie about the missing antique and test her reaction? Accuse her of the theft and try to startle her into confessing? Sarah sat in the driver's seat for several minutes without coming to any conclusion. Finally, she popped her door open and got out anyway. The awards ceremony was approaching too fast. She didn't have any more time to waste.

Lord, she prayed as she went up the walk, *please help me find the words to say.*

But when she was at the door and rang the bell, she got the only response she hadn't expected: no response at all.

The front door was actually open behind the screen, but she waited for a count of twenty, then rang again. This time she could clearly hear chimes ringing deep inside the house. For good measure, she knocked. As she did, the screen door bumped back and forth on its hinge. It was open.

Sarah knocked again. "Hello?" she called. "Allie? It's Sarah!"

She counted her own breaths for another minute. Then she pulled the screen door open, and slipped in.

Allie's new house looked traditional from the curb, with old-fashioned shutters and white wood siding. But the interior floor plan was open and modern. The entryway led directly to a roomy living room with a cathedral ceiling that flowed naturally into a large kitchen full of shiny new appliances, separated from the dining area only by a small island of countertop. It took Sarah only a few moments to recognize that she was alone in the house.

She had been here before. Allie had thrown a giant party when the Turnquists first moved into the place, and invited anyone in Maple Hill who might be interested in quilts, and quite a few people who weren't, to a lavish spread designed to show off her collection. She had hung prize specimens around the living area from freestanding racks, but the real showpiece of the tour was her quilt room itself. Sarah knew exactly where it was: in the back of the house, just off the living room.

Sarah hesitated. She hadn't exactly meant to enter the house without permission, but now that she had, her heart began to beat fast at the prospect of investigating the area without Allie's knowledge. If Allie had, in fact, taken the quilt, the obvious place to start was her quilt room, where she hoarded and displayed all of her other prize possessions.

Sarah crept through the entryway to the threshold of the living room.

"Hello?" she called again. "Allie?"

No one answered.

Then, like a shot, Sarah scooted through the expensive leather furniture and past the blind eye of the giant plasma television, to the quilt room.

It was a gorgeous room, she had to admit. Allie had designed it herself, and she had spared no expense. "I wanted a Jacuzzi upstairs, and a balcony on the second floor, and this quilt room," she had told her guests at the open house, laughing. "Arthur said I could have the hot tub and the balcony, or the quilt room. Not all of them. I told him he didn't even need to bother to ask. There was no question!"

Sarah paused in the doorway of the custom-made room, wondering where to begin. Windows filled a sizable chunk of the back and side walls, carefully screened by archival shades designed to let light flow in without damaging the fabric. The ceiling was high, just like the one in the living room, but in the quilt room the dome led up to a skylight, again carefully tinted so as not to damage the precious fabrics inside. All the walls not taken up by windows had deep, wide shelves built into them, perfect for displaying and protecting Allie's collection of quilts. In the center of the room was a large rustic antique dining room table, shined to a high polish, surrounded by a dozen Quaker-style spindle chairs. It was the perfect surface for laying out the treasured quilts to enjoy all their unique beauty and hidden details.

Sarah had seen the space before, but it was still dazzling. Hundreds of quilts were displayed on the cream-painted shelves, little flashes of their patterns showing in their folds. The shelves started at the floor and were even built up around and above the windows. Several rows of them towered far above Sarah's head, and a neat rolling ladder had been installed, like in a private library, to reach them.

Sarah couldn't help it. Despite herself, the excitement and awe she felt each time she encountered a quilt from another time washed over her. All that work and thought. All that history and color. She stood in the doorway, one hand on the rich cream trim, drinking it all in.

Then, somewhere in the house, the air clunked on. Sarah jumped, sure she was about to be discovered. It took her a moment to recognize the familiar hum as cool air began to flow through the ducts. The sound brought her back to her senses. She wasn't a tourist in a new exhibit. She was here on a mission. And she was uninvited. She needed to move fast.

When she stepped into the room, she was all business. The quilt she was looking for was valuable precisely because of its differences from many other collectible quilts—its limited color palette, its unusual pattern. The shelves were so expertly organized that it would have been impossible to hide something among the neat rows, since each quilt was precisely folded, and pushed flush with the back of each shelf. Most of Allie's collection she could eliminate as possibilities at a glance.

She began on one side of the room, and worked her way around, following a zigzag pattern, from the bottom of one column up to the top, then from the top of the next column to the bottom. From time to time, if a quilt looked at all lumpy or bulky, she pulled it out and flipped it open to make sure nothing was hidden within. Nothing. A few times, items in Allie's collection were so enticing that Sarah had to force herself not to carry them over to the table to give them a full inspection. But the adrenaline that surged through her at the thought that Allie might return any minute kept her moving quickly around the room.

Finally, Sarah found herself in the far corner of the quilt collection, holding the last quilt. If Helen's quilt was here, it wasn't in the lower stacks. She had combed through over a hundred of Allie's quilts without finding it.

There was only one more place to look: in the upper shelves, which were too high for Sarah to see over the edge without help.

Gamely, Sarah climbed up the sturdy white rolling ladder. As soon as her eyes crested above the top shelf, she saw it.

Helen's quilt was the only one on the shelf that hadn't been carefully folded and stacked. Instead, it was wadded up as if a child had slept in it and then left without making the bed. No attempt had been made to camouflage or cover it.

Sarah rolled the ladder down to the spot where the quilt lay, climbed back up, and carried it down, her heart pounding in her chest. A quilt of this quality should never be wadded up the way it had been. Had anything worse happened to it?

She carried it down, laid it out on the giant table and went over it inch by inch. Her fears faded quickly. It was definitely Helen's quilt—Sarah recognized the loose stitching in several telltale places—and it was no worse for the wear for all its adventures, with the exception of a bit of mud, which she knew she could easily clean. In fact, it was in good enough shape to hang back up at the exhibit. Now all she needed to do was get it back where it belonged.

But as Sarah gently refolded the priceless quilt, she realized it wasn't quite that simple. If she returned it to the fair now, she wouldn't have any proof that Allie had stolen it. And if Allie went unpunished, Sarah worried something like this might happen again, if it hadn't happened already. *How many of these other quilts did she get through dishonest means?* Sarah wondered, looking around at the brimming shelves.

She couldn't ignore the possibility. She had found the quilt. Now it was time to involve the authorities.

She pulled her phone from her purse and dialed the number for the Maple Hill Police. "This is Sarah Hart," she told the dispatcher who answered. "I'd like to report a theft."

Chief Webber answered her call himself.

Sarah stood in Allie's entryway, watching him come up the walk. When he reached the foot of the steps, she opened the door. As soon as she had found the quilt, her fear about Allie coming home had vanished. Sarah might not have been invited in, but Allie's betrayal in stealing the quilt trumped all that. But Allie hadn't turned up in the few minutes since Sarah had called the police station.

"Sarah," Chief Webber said when he saw her. He pushed his police hat back. "This isn't your house."

"I'm afraid not," Sarah said. "It's Allie Turnquist's."

Chief Webber nodded. "That's what I thought." He climbed the steps. Sarah held the door open for him. "Somebody stole something of Allie's?" he asked.

Sarah shook her head. "No," Sarah said. "She took something of ours."

Chief Webber raised his eyebrows. "She's here?" he asked.

"No," Sarah said.

"Then how'd you get in?" Chief Webber asked.

Sarah felt a tinge of guilt. "The door was open. We've been working together at the fair," she added.

Chief Webber seemed to take that as a suitable explanation. "Well," he said, "would you like to show me what you're talking about?"

Sarah led him back to the quilt room, showed him Helen's quilt, and gave him a brief explanation of how it had gone missing, where she had found it, and its high value.

"That much?" the chief said, looking down at the muted colors on the aged fabric.

Sarah nodded.

"That makes this quite a crime," Chief Webber said. "Why didn't you report it to us when you first discovered it was gone?"

"I wasn't sure it was a crime," Sarah explained. "I was hoping it had just been mislaid, or that I'd made some kind of mistake—until I found it here today."

"Where'd you say you found it?" the chief asked, looking around the room.

Sarah climbed up the ladder again and pointed. "Up here," she said. "It wasn't even folded, just wadded up in a kind of ball."

Chief Webber frowned. "It's not a very good hiding place," he said. "Especially for something that valuable. You'd almost think she wanted to get caught."

Sarah climbed back down the ladder and gestured to the quilts displayed all around them. "Look at all this," she said. "Allie doesn't collect these quilts to hide them. It's important to her that people know she has nice things."

"More important than not getting caught?" the chief asked.

Sarah took a deep breath. Given what she had seen of Allie this week, she could believe it. "Maybe," she said.

Chief Webber looked down at the quilt doubtfully. "I hate to say this, Sarah," he began, "but all I've got to go on here is your word. I'd like to believe you, but we're talking about criminal charges here. What proof do you have that you didn't just plant the quilt here yourself?"

"And why would I do a thing like that?" Sarah asked.

"Why would Allie Turnquist steal a quilt from her own exhibit?" Chief Webber countered.

"We can ask her that," Sarah said, "just as soon as I get this quilt back to the fair, where it belongs."

"Not so fast," said Chief Webber. "If you're right that we're dealing with a crime here, that quilt is evidence. I can't just let you waltz out of here with it."

Sarah gathered the quilt up with a sinking feeling. She had spent all week looking for the missing quilt, and the instant she found it, someone was threatening to take it away again.

"Chief," she began, "I don't know much about the legal technicalities here. But I do know that thousands of people are going to come to Maple Hill tonight to see this quilt. Whether Allie took it or I put it here myself, this isn't where it belongs. I'll do anything I can to help you sort out the truth. You can even take me down to the station for questioning if you need to. But please let me get this back to the fair first. There'll be a guard posted on it. You can even post your own guard there. At this point, I'd be grateful for it."

Chief Webber gave her a long measuring look. Then he turned on his heel and stalked back through the house. Sarah hurried after him, clutching the quilt.

He didn't stop until he reached the front door. He swung it open, then looked closely at the latch and handle, both on the screen and interior doors.

Sarah watched him, curious and worried.

After a moment, he straightened up. "I don't see any evidence of forced entry," he said, "which speaks in your favor."

"Oh no," Sarah said. "The door was open. I thought someone was home."

"You say there's a guard over there at the fair?" he asked.

Sarah nodded. "Yes," she said. "I can have him stand right next to this quilt, if you'd like. It's professional security."

Chief Webber nodded. "All right," he said. "We'll sort out everything when we locate Allie. In the meantime, let's get this quilt back where it belongs. How would you like a police escort?"

CHAPTER EIGHTEEN

T hat's right," Sarah said, as Janet's quilt was finally lifted into its proper place, filling up the gigantic empty spot in the prize hall. "Careful!" she said as one of the fair volunteers wobbled on her ladder, temporarily allowing the edge of the quilt to drift dangerously close to the ground.

"I've got it!" the volunteer called. She righted herself on the ladder, and dropped her end of the tension bar into place. The volunteer on the other side of the quilt followed suit. The quilt swayed gently from the movement, then was still. The volunteers descended their ladders almost in unison.

"Thank you so much," Sarah told them. "It looks beautiful."

"Hanging it up is the easy part," one of the women called as she folded up her ladder. "It's making them that's hard."

Not to mention finding them when they're lost, Sarah thought. But her heart was full of satisfaction. She hadn't realized how much worry and responsibility she had been feeling over the lost quilt. As soon as she had held it in her hands again, she had felt a weight slip from her shoulders, and a sense of well-being steal over her. She'd had another jolt of fear when Chief Webber suggested he take the quilt in as evidence, but when she explained its importance at the fair, and promised that it would be under guard every moment until the fair closed, he agreed to let her put it back in its rightful place.

She had taken the quilt directly to the exhibit, corralling a couple of volunteers along the way and dispatching them to get ladders. When they returned, she'd had them carefully take down Janet's quilt from the place of honor in the exhibition hall. Then she had watched as Helen's quilt was lifted into place, for the second time that week.

The guard had stood next to her through the whole process. When the original quilt was safely hung, he shook his head. "I don't see any difference at all," he said.

"That's fine," Sarah told him. "As long as you can see it's here. And why don't you stand at this end of the hall for the rest of the fair?"

Then she had called Janet. "We found it," Sarah said.

Janet had been silent for so long that at first Sarah wondered if the connection was bad. "Janet?" she had asked.

When Janet spoke, Sarah could hear the emotion in her voice. "I'm here," she said. "I'm sorry. I'm just so glad. Jeff is coming to the house in a bit to pick me up. I hadn't had the heart to tell him yet that my quilt was missing. I didn't know what I was going to say if it wasn't there."

"Well, it's not missing anymore," Sarah told her. "I'm about to supervise putting it on display. It'll be up before you two get here."

"You don't know what this means to me, Sarah," Janet said. "Thank you."

"It's nothing," Sarah said gently. "I just wish we'd never had to worry you in the first place."

Now Sarah stood in the prize hall, surrounded by giant pumpkins and toddlers' art projects, looking up at the complete array of winning quilts. They represented a dizzying depth of talent and vision, and of work—by the quilters, the fair board who kept the gates of the fair open, and Sarah, who had organized and judged the contest for so many years.

Thank you, Lord, she prayed. *I still don't understand why this had to happen, but I'm so grateful to have everything back where it belongs.*

Except Allie, she realized. For the last several days, Sarah hadn't seemed to be able to escape Allie, but when Chief Webber and one of his patrolmen had searched the fair for her, she was nowhere to be found. They had located Lily, though, who said she had spoken to her mother earlier in the day, and that Allie was still planning to take her place on stage for the prize ceremony as planned. Sarah was supposed to meet Chief Webber over there before the ceremony began.

"Sarah."

Sarah turned around to find herself engulfed in a hug from Janet. When Janet released her she stepped back. The well-dressed man Sarah had seen on the phone in the exhibit a few days before stood beside Janet. But now he was smiling.

"This is Jeff Walker," Janet said.

Jeff put out his hand. "Sarah Hart," he said. "It's a pleasure to meet you."

Sarah smiled back. "You too," she said as she shook his hand. "I've heard so much about you."

"Not as much as I've heard about you," he said. "Congratulations on the exhibit. It's a gem. Better than I've seen in some museums."

"Thank you," Sarah said.

"I hope you'll forgive my brusqueness the other day," he said. "I was deep in negotiations, as you may have heard."

Sarah nodded.

"We've just come from looking at the original again," he told her. "It's exquisite. Now I just need to see Janet's homage."

"Well," Sarah said, "that's the interesting part. You've actually already seen this quilt."

"I have?" Jeff asked. Janet looked at Sarah, waiting for an explanation.

Sarah nodded again. "It turns out there was a mix-up between the homage and the original in the quilt office," she said. "Janet's quilt hung in the exhibit hall for most of the fair as the antique. We just switched it back this afternoon."

"So you're saying…," Jeff started, his mind working to follow the thread of the story, "the quilt I saw before was actually Janet's?"

"Yes," Sarah said.

"But it was *perfect*," Jeff said. "I've been working in the antique quilt market for decades, and I had no idea I was looking at a copy."

Janet's face lit up. Sarah smiled. "Janet's very talented," she said. "And she uses all the old techniques."

"So the one we just came from," Jeff said, "that was the original?"

"Yes," Sarah said. "It's been back on display for a few hours now. And we just hung Janet's up here, where it belongs, so it'll be in place when the prize hall opens after the prize ceremony."

"Do you mind if I…?" Jeff began, gesturing toward the quilt.

"Don't let me stand in your way. It's what you're here to see. Please," Sarah said.

As Jeff stepped forward, Janet slipped her arm through Sarah's and gave Sarah's hand a squeeze. Sarah squeezed back.

Jeff gave the quilt a thorough inspection, stepping in close to pick up details, standing back to take in the whole scope. Then he turned to Janet and Sarah, shaking his head.

"It's wonderful," he said to Janet. "Indistinguishable from the original, except for a few wear marks on the antique. You and I have some work to do together."

Because Sarah was standing next to her, she could hear Janet give the tiniest of excited squeals. But Janet kept her cool in answering Jeff. "I'd like that," she said. "Very much."

"My only question is if you'll be able to keep up with all the projects I'll have for you," Jeff said, smiling. "I imagine demand will be quite high for work of this quality."

"I'll take anything you can throw at me," Janet said.

Jeff nodded. "I'm sure you will," he said. "Well, wonderful."

Outside the doors of the prize hall, the din of the crowd was starting to grow as families, children, and teenagers streamed past, starting to find their seats for the awards ceremony. Between friends and relatives, with all the connections in a town as small as Maple Hill, almost everyone knew someone who had entered something in the fair. Jeff glanced at the passing traffic.

"They're going to the judging arena," Sarah said. "We'll be giving out the prizes soon. I guess we've spoiled the surprise for Janet this year, by letting her know she's the grand-prizewinner. But would you like to stick around and see her receive the award?"

Jeff shook his head. "Congratulations," he told Janet. "But I'm afraid I've got a plane to catch. It's a little early, but it was the only one I could get. And I've got what I came here for," he added, glancing up at the quilt. "I think this is the beginning of a great partnership."

He held out his hand again and both Sarah and Janet shook it. Then he slipped out of the prize hall, heading against the foot traffic.

Janet squeezed Sarah's arm again. "I can't believe it!" she breathed. "He liked it!"

"Because it's wonderful!" Sarah said. "Anyone with half a mind can see how talented you are."

Janet let her head drop onto Sarah's shoulder in relief. "My only question now is how I'll do all that work for him!" she said. "He does get a lot of it, I know. I don't want to let him down."

"Well, you can always hire your own help," Sarah said. "I know Shelly Andrews actually has been looking for work. And she's right around the corner from you."

Janet's eyes lit up. "You're right! She does such beautiful work with color and yarn. Have you seen it?"

Sarah nodded. "There's some of it up here," she said, pointing to the knit display nearby.

"That would be perfect," Janet said. "Do you think she'd really do it?"

"I think you should ask her," Sarah said. "But I suspect she'll say yes."

"I will," Janet said, all the worry gone from her eyes. She glanced out at the passing crowd, which grew bigger by the minute. "It's getting time to start," she said. "I just want to go brush my hair before I go on stage. You don't mind, do you?"

"Get out of here!" Sarah said, giving her one last hug. "And Janet," she called.

Janet turned back.

"Congratulations," Sarah said.

Janet answered with a giant grin, and was off again.

Sarah checked her watch. It was still twenty minutes before the awards ceremony was scheduled to start. She was supposed to meet Chief Webber in five minutes. She went out the door and joined the crowd, which quickly swept her into the judging hall. But instead of letting it carry her into the bleachers, she broke free, finding a small square of real estate just inside the door. Across the hall, at the other exit, she saw the patrolman Chief Webber had called into service. It took her another minute to realize that Chief Webber stood only a few feet away from her, doing his best to keep from being jostled by the crowd.

"Any sign of her?" he shouted over the roar.

Sarah shook her head, scanning the familiar faces for a glimpse of Allie, and wondered about Allie's long absence from the fair that day. Had Allie just been off somewhere, doing something she thought was more important? Had she come home, and discovered that the quilt was gone? Was she still blissfully ignorant that the theft had been uncovered? Would she show up at this ceremony at all?

Allie was nowhere in sight, but Sarah did spot Lily, already in place, waiting quietly with the other Junior

Homemaker contenders in the front row of the audience. Suddenly, Sarah realized what Allie's arrest would mean to Lily. Lily had been so hopeful that this would be her moment, for a change. Now her mother had managed to steal the attention from her again.

Sarah leaned closer to Chief Webber, still watching Lily. "You'll do this discreetly, won't you?" she said. "There are so many people here."

"You think I want to bust up the whole ceremony?" Chief Webber answered. His answer was brusque, but Sarah knew he would do his best to keep things quiet.

Lord, please take care of Lily, she prayed, for what seemed like the hundredth time that week. *Be with her. Make this moment be hers.*

The stands continued to fill steadily until, just before the program began, there was standing room only in the back. Then the speakers overhead crackled to life and Harry Butler, the fair board member, welcomed the crowd. As they clapped, a dozen other board members and local notables filed out. There was Allie Turnquist, happy as a clam, not a hair out of place, her expensive heels higher than ever.

Sarah glanced at Chief Webber, whose lips had pulled into a thin line. "Well, I can't interrupt the ceremony now," he said. "We'll have to get her when she comes off."

A minute later, he glanced at Sarah again.

"You have any idea how she even got up there?" he asked.

Carolyn Johnson bustled up and took a standing spot near them. "She got there from the trailer parked behind the stage," she said. "She had the bright idea this year we'd use it as a dressing room, not that any of us ever had to dress for this kind of thing before."

"Aren't you supposed to be up there?" Sarah said, nudging her. "You're on the board."

"I'm strictly backstage this time around," Carolyn said, holding her hands up. "I don't have to face the crowd again till next year."

"Shh!" Chief Webber insisted.

Sarah and Carolyn fell silent. The program was beginning.

CHAPTER NINETEEN

The crowd roared with applause. Harry Butler had warmed them up well, with an enthusiastic introduction about how Allie Turnquist's donations had changed the character of the fair that year, drawing a bigger pool of entrants to the quilt contest, and allowing Sarah to mount a nationally recognized exhibition of regional quilts.

There was a special little roar of appreciation at the mention of this, and Carolyn had nudged Sarah. "That was for you, I think," she whispered.

"No," Sarah said, "people just love quilts."

Carolyn laughed.

"These generous donations haven't just expanded our quilt and knits programs," Harry had said in closing. "They've given new vitality and energy to the whole fair. New visitors have come through our gates this year. National reporters have given attention to our events. People have seen everything that Maple Hill has to offer. And for that, we all have to thank...Allie Turnquist."

The crowd had come ready to cheer—for their friends, for their relatives, and for the whole crazy project of the fair, bringing together an entire town's livestock and domestic talents along with the delightful nonsense of the midway and the demolition derby. They were ready to celebrate. The response was thunderous.

Allie basked in it, smiling and waving as if she had been accustomed to this kind of treatment all her life. "Thank you. Thank you so much," she said.

Sarah glanced at Lily in the front row. Lily looked up at her mother, her face inscrutable.

"Well, this is really wonderful," Allie said as the crowd simmered down. "I so appreciate you all coming out to enjoy the fair and celebrate the prizewinners with us. If you ask me, the increased awards we offered this year were only what our talented fair entrants have always deserved."

There was another burst of applause. Allie waited it out, smiling beatifically.

"But before we get on to the awards program, I'd like to tell you a little bit about some innovations we've made in our judging this year. In the past, the judging hasn't been exactly...scientific." She gave a little laugh, but nobody laughed with her. Undaunted, Allie went on.

"This year," she said, "I invented a new system, to help bring us into the next century. It uses a group of special metrics to establish which quilts stand out from the rest in a way that's truly fair and consistent. And I hope that this, as much as any other kind of gift, will really be my legacy to the Maple Hill Fair this year."

Sarah watched Allie in amazement as the crowd broke into another round of applause. She didn't know if she had ever seen anyone quite so shameless. By stealing the prized quilt, Allie had done more than anyone that year to destroy the legacy of trust and respect Sarah had built over the past decades. Now Allie was up there talking as if she had curated the exhibit and judged the quilts all by herself. The next thing they knew, Sarah thought, she would be taking credit for building the Ferris wheel and spinning all the cotton candy too.

Sarah didn't mind not getting the credit herself. She was much happier working in the background and found it was usually a lot easier to get things done there. What she really couldn't believe was how untroubled Allie seemed to be by the theft she had perpetrated. She must have been planning it for weeks, if not months. She had betrayed Sarah, and Helen, and the entire town's trust. Didn't she feel even a tiny twinge of guilt?

Harry Butler was making his way to the front now, with a large brass plaque. "In honor of Allie's generous contributions this year, the fair board would like to give her this small token as a memento," he said, his voice warbling over the cheap sound system in the arena. "It can't really express our gratitude, but it's a start."

"Oh, thank you!" Allie exclaimed. She took his hand and they both glanced down at a photographer who knelt just below the front row. His flash exploded, and Allie took possession of the plaque. "Thank you so much!"

Another smattering of applause.

"All right," Harry said, turning to the crowd. "Are we ready to learn who this year's Maple Hill Fair prizewinners are?"

The crowd roared.

Allie navigated down the rickety steps from the makeshift stage, the plaque in the crook of one elbow, her other hand on the railing to balance herself in her towering heels. Chief Webber reached her just a few steps from the foot of the stairs.

"Mrs. Turnquist," he said, "I have a few questions for you."

"Can it wait?" Allie said, gesturing back at the stage. "I was just about to sit down. This is the Junior Homemaker portion."

On stage, the girls in the competition were filing up the opposite set of stairs to form an awkward row. Some of them smiled brightly at some fixed spot out in the crowd. Some of them fidgeted with their dresses. A few stared blankly, as if they were still trying to figure out where they were or how they had gotten there.

". . . not just lovely," Harry Butler was saying, "but talented!"

Sarah stepped up behind Chief Webber. Allie glanced at her.

"I'm sorry," he said. "It can't."

Allie drew the plaque to her chest and crossed her arms over it as if it were the breastplate on a suit of armor. "What's this about?" she demanded.

"I'd like to talk to you about the antique quilt that was stolen," Chief Webber said. He made an unsuccessful attempt to take Allie's arm and steer her away from the foot of the stage. She shook his hand free.

"Stolen?" she said, her voice rising.

A few people in the front rows glanced over at the sound. An older woman in a Maple Hill High School sweatshirt gave them a scowl that would have silenced even the unruliest child. It had no effect at all on Allie.

"Nothing's been stolen," she insisted. "We did have a quilt that was *lost*," she said, looking pointedly at Sarah. "But it wasn't one of the antiques. And all that is Sarah's business, anyhow. She made all the arrangements and checked everything in. If you're having a problem with something that's missing, she's the one who's responsible."

It was interesting, Sarah noted, how quick Allie was to give Sarah credit for everything now that she was no longer on stage.

"I've talked with Mrs. Hart," Chief Webber continued doggedly. "That's why I'd like to talk with you."

For the first time, Allie gave Sarah more than a passing glance. Her eyes narrowed.

"Canning!" Harry Butler exclaimed from the stage, working through the list of all the categories in which this year's Junior Homemaking contestants had participated.

"Needlework! Swine showing!" After each category came a little burst of applause. Harry waited for it to fade, and then went on. "Horsemanship!" he added.

From the stage, Lily glanced over at the policeman deep in conversation with her mother. Allie didn't notice, but Sarah did. A sharp pang shot through her heart. *Lord,* she prayed, *this is going to be hard for Lily. Please help her.*

"Oh," Allie said. "I understand." Her voice finally dropped, if only slightly. "You don't have to tell me what this is about. Sarah Hart has been trying to prevent this quilt program from moving forward ever since I got involved. She thought I didn't notice," Allie said, glaring straight into Sarah's eyes. "But I noticed. She dragged her feet at every step. She just wants things to be her way, whether they work or not. All that matters to her is that she gets to run everything, so no one else can take her credit. Isn't that right, Sarah?"

Sarah just looked at Allie, silent. It was amazing how well Allie's accusations about Sarah fit Allie's own behavior. For a moment Sarah caught a glimpse of how hard it would be to live in a world that was a constant battle over who was in charge, and where favors were exchanged only on the strict basis of tit for tat, never out of simple friendship or a desire to serve. It seemed like a very cold world. For the first time since they had begun working together, Sarah felt pity for Allie Turnquist.

"Jams and jellies!" Harry Butler announced from the stage. "Carpentry!"

"So if you're looking for a quilt, ask her," Allie said, jerking her head toward Sarah. "She didn't let anyone get near her precious quilts. Did you, Sarah?"

Again, Sarah didn't answer.

But Chief Webber did. "Then maybe you can explain," he said to Allie, "how a valuable antique from this fair came to be part of your quilt collection?"

"My collection?" Allie repeated. The disbelief in her voice was so real that Sarah glanced closely at her face. Was she an incredible actress? Or did this accusation really come as a surprise? Still, Sarah had seen the quilt in Allie's quilt room with her own eyes.

"Helen Baxter's quilt," Sarah said. "We found it in your collection this afternoon."

The crowd burst into its biggest roar of applause yet. One of the girls stepped forward from the line with a wide smile to receive her second runner-up trophy. The glitter on her Junior Homemaker sash glinted in the hot arena lights. Something stirred in the back of Sarah's mind.

Allie gave a harsh laugh. "I should be so lucky!" she said. Then she looked at Chief Webber. "Helen Baxter has turned down my offers to buy that quilt more times than I can count."

Chief Webber was unmoved. "Then perhaps you can explain to me why I saw it with my own eyes in your home today."

Allie's smile faded. "You're serious about this?" she said. "It was in my house?"

"Yes," Chief Webber said.

"And how did you happen to find it there?" Allie asked.

Sarah took a step forward. "I found it," she said.

Allie gave another brittle laugh. "Why am I not surprised? I won't even ask how you got in," she said.

Sarah flushed. "The door was—" she began.

Allie cut her off. "Maybe you could do some detective work of your own," she said to Chief Webber. "Did you ever think that she might have been the one who planted it there? She's the one who had access to the quilts. She's the one who had them all locked up in her little room."

Another shower of applause rained down around the first runner-up as she stepped forward to claim her prize.

"Mrs. Turnquist," Chief Webber said, "I'd be glad to discuss all these theories with you if you'll just come with me."

"And now," Harry Butler intoned. "The moment we've all been waiting for—this year's Maple Hill Fair Junior Homemaker."

The crowd grew hushed.

"I'm not going anywhere!" Allie hissed.

"Lily Turnquist!" Harry Butler exclaimed.

Lily stepped forward from the line with a brilliant smile, scanning the crowd for a glimpse of her mom. Sarah watched as Lily's eyes locked on Allie, just as Chief Webber took her arm to lead her away.

Harry Butler smiled warmly at Lily as she charged toward him, but his smile faded as she breezed right by and rattled down the stairs and off the stage.

The crowd let out a collective gasp. Suddenly, all eyes were on the little group of Sarah, Lily, Allie, and the police chief.

"What's happening?" Lily demanded. "Mom? Are you all right?"

"Let's move this discussion out of the way," Chief Webber said, hustling Allie around the corner of the stage, out of sight of the crowd.

"Mrs. Hart?" Lily asked Sarah, her eyes wide. "What's going on?"

Sarah put her arm around Lily's shoulders and the two of them followed Allie and the chief as he led them behind the trailer that formed the back of the stage.

"Well," Harry Butler said, trying to make the best of the situation, "there you have it. It's the fair, where anything can happen! Let's have a round of applause for all of our accomplished young ladies."

Grateful for some direction, the crowd broke into cautious applause.

"Mom?" Lily asked, catching up to Allie. "What's happening?"

"It's totally ridiculous, honey," Allie began.

"I apologize for this timing," Chief Webber said, "But you see—"

Both of them stopped and looked at each other.

"They've got a crazy idea that I took a quilt," Allie burst out. "It's totally ridiculous, of course."

"Except for the fact that the quilt was, in fact, found in your home," Chief Webber pointed out.

Lily looked stricken.

"Because *Sarah Hart* planted it there," Allie insisted again.

Lily glanced at Sarah, her eyes full of worry. "No!" she said. "Mrs. Hart didn't do that!"

All the adults stopped to look at Lily. She seemed to shrink under the attention. "I mean, it doesn't make sense," Lily said. "Why would she ruin her own exhibit?"

Sarah glanced closely at Lily. Nobody had mentioned anything about the exhibit yet. As far as Lily knew, the only quilt that was missing was Janet Stevens's. Why would she leap immediately to the conclusion that it was an *antique* that was missing?

"Well, then who do *you* think did it, Lily?" Allie demanded. "You're not pointing a finger at me, are you?"

Lily shook her head vigorously. "No, no," she said. "I guess it was just some kind of mistake. Maybe it wasn't really...," she seemed to struggle to say the word, "stolen."

Suddenly, all the clues that Sarah had collected over the previous week fell into a perfect pattern in her mind. The thief had to have had knowledge of both quilts, access to the exhibit during the time Sarah was gone, enough familiarity with the fair to know about the hidden doors in the exhibit halls, and the opportunity to place the missing quilt in Allie's home. Allie fit all the criteria—but so did Lily.

In fact, Sarah realized, thinking back, it had been *Lily* who spent time alone in the exhibit hall after her mother left. Sarah had assumed that Lily had been with Allie when Lexie and Audrey saw Allie leave, but the girls had never mentioned Lily, not even under all Sarah's questioning. Perhaps because she hadn't left by the main door, but by the secret side entrance. And when Shelly had seen Allie in the quilt office, where had Lily been? Likely in the exhibit hall—alone.

"Well, that'd be just great, if it was all some kind of mistake," Allie said impatiently. "There's only one little problem. Who do you think did it, if it wasn't Sarah or me?"

Lily looked back and forth between the police chief, her mother, and Sarah. The girl's eyes filled with tears.

"Lily," Sarah said gently. "Do you have something you'd like to tell us?"

CHAPTER TWENTY

Lily dropped her gaze to the ground. "I'm sorry," she murmured.

"Lily?" Allie asked. Her voice had suddenly lost all of its edge. "What are you talking about?"

Chief Webber shifted uncomfortably from foot to foot.

Sarah laid a hand on Lily's back, and Lily let out a little sob.

"I didn't mean to hurt you, Mrs. Hart!" Lily said. "I know how hard you worked!"

"Lily," Allie said, her voice measured, "what are you talking about?"

Now Lily looked up at the chief. Her gaze faltered for a moment, but then she faced him. "I took the quilt," she said. "It was me."

"Lily!" Allie breathed. To Sarah, she suddenly looked like a completely different woman. Her high heels were sunk deep in the soft dirt of the arena, leaving her slightly off-kilter. Her shoulders, normally so perfectly squared, were hunched. She looked like a blow-up toy that had begun to leak air, and lean, and slump. "Why would you do a thing like that?" Allie asked her daughter.

"I didn't mean to," Lily said again. "But I was just so mad."

Whatever the incident had been, it clearly hadn't made much of an impression on Allie. "When?" she said. "I don't remember that."

Lily gave a strange little exasperated laugh. "You didn't realize it," she said. "It was right after the quilt tour."

Sarah nodded. That would fit the time line she had constructed.

"I was trying to tell you about a shirt I'd sewn," Lily said. "I'd just turned it in, and I only finished it an hour before the deadline, and it was the first time I'd ever used pin tucks before, but they came out perfectly. It actually won first prize in its category. I think it's one of the things that helped me win all this," she gestured back at the stage beside them. "I was hoping it would, and I wanted to tell you all about it. But all you could talk about was that stupid quilt. So I told you I didn't want to talk about the stupid quilt. And you said, 'Lily, I'm not interested in talking with you about anything if you're going to act like a child.'"

Now Allie remembered. She nodded, her eyes still wide. Lily had her full attention.

"And then," Lily said, "you left." Her voice broke slightly when she said it, and she paused to collect herself.

Allie looked from Sarah to Chief Webber and back to Lily again.

"I didn't even know what I was doing," Lily said. "As soon as you went out of the room, I just went over to the quilt and yanked it. I don't know why. But when I did, it all came crashing down on my head. And it fell in the mud that people had tracked in on the tour. I knew I couldn't hang it back up like that. And I knew Mrs. Stevens had been working on the copy quilt and it was still in the quilt office. So I wadded up Mrs. Baxter's quilt—"

Involuntarily, Sarah winced. Allie flinched with her. If they shared nothing else, they did share a deep respect for the preciousness of the old quilts.

"I know!" Lily said, catching the gestures. "But I was so scared. So I waited by the side door until I saw you come out of the quilt office, and then I ran in and hid Mrs. Baxter's quilt and found the other one."

"And you hung it up all by yourself?" Chief Webber asked, sounding doubtful.

Lily nodded. "I've helped mom hang quilts a hundred times," she said. "It's harder with one person, but I can do it."

Sarah calculated. Lily was right—someone who knew what she was doing could have accomplished the switch in almost no time at all. Sarah had actually ordered special slide-lock display hangers that year with Allie's extra donation, to make hanging the quilts faster and easier.

"And then what did you do with it?" Allie said, her voice still slightly dumbstruck.

"I put it in a garment bag I brought," Lily said, "with the clothes for the different events. And I took it to the car."

"You brought it home in that *garment bag*?" Allie said. Sarah hadn't thought it was possible for Allie's eyes to get any wider, but they did. "On top of the *dry cleaning*?"

Lily nodded miserably.

"And then ...," Allie struggled to complete the thought, and the sentence. "What?"

"Then I realized," Lily said, "that I'd done what you always wanted. I got you Mrs. Baxter's quilt."

"You stole it?" Allie asked, dumbstruck. "For me?"

Lily dropped her eyes. "I don't know," she said. "I mean, I knew I couldn't give it to you. But I also knew how much you wanted it. So I thought where could I put a quilt that nobody would notice? I realized the quilt room was perfect. There were already so many, no one would notice one more. Especially not if I put it up on those high shelves."

"Helen Baxter's quilt was in my quilt room," Allie asked, "all this week?"

Lily nodded. All of Allie's attention was now focused on her daughter. Lily looked at her mother with apprehension, but there was no anger in Allie's face, just a kind of wonder, as if she was seeing Lily clearly, perhaps for the first time in years.

"I am just so sorry," she said, turning to Chief Webber. "I had no idea any of this had happened. I'm shocked. What do we need to do about this?"

Chief Webber cleared his throat. "Well," he said, "considering the story that Lily here tells, I imagine our first step would be to explain the situation to Mrs. Baxter. If she's not interested in pressing charges, then we can decide how to deal with the situation without something permanent going on Lily's record."

"Her record," Allie repeated, sounding dazed.

Lily looked frightened. She glanced at her mother, then at Sarah. "My record?" she said. "Mom? What does that mean?"

Allie didn't answer. Instead, she enveloped her daughter in a hug, wrinkling her carefully chosen suit, and wobbling on her expensive heels. When they let go, Sarah could see that Lily's face was wet with tears.

"Is it all right if I take her home?" Allie asked Chief Webber.

The chief nodded. "I'll release you on your own recognizance," he said.

"Helen's here tonight," Sarah told them. "I'll talk with her."

Allie nodded, her expression still a little vague from the shock. Then she and Lily slipped out through the back of the arena, Allie's arm around Lily's shoulders, and Lily's arm around her mother's waist.

Sarah and Chief Webber waited in the shadows of the stage for the ceremony to wind down. When the last applause died, they came around the corner, scanning the passing faces for a sight of Helen.

Sarah spotted her first, being helped down the bleachers by her son, a husky man in his fifties in a work jacket with a corduroy collar. When Helen glimpsed Sarah, she waved enthusiastically, then hurried down the remaining stairs to reach her, her son at her side. "Sarah!" she said. "I was hoping I'd have the chance to see you! We just went by your exhibit before the awards ceremony. It was stunning. I'm so proud our quilt played its little part."

"I'm not sure I'd call it little," Sarah said with a smile. "It was the focus of the whole exhibit. In fact, that's what I was hoping to talk with you about."

"Oh?" Helen said, her eyebrows rising.

Quickly, Sarah explained the events of the past week: the missing quilt, the lengths she had gone to in order to recover it, and the final revelation of Lily as the culprit. "What Lily did was wrong," Sarah said. "And it put your quilt in danger, which I feel sick about. She needs to learn her lesson, but Chief Webber and I aren't sure this is a case that really belongs in the legal system."

Helen shook her head thoughtfully. "No," she said. "That doesn't sound quite right, does it?" Then her eyes lit up. "And there's more than one way to learn a lesson, isn't there?" she said. "I bet you and I could think of something good, don't you, Sarah?"

Sarah smiled and nodded.

Chief Webber gave a brief smile of his own. "Then I think I'll leave you two ladies to it," he said. "If you'll excuse me."

"Thank you, Chief Webber," Sarah said.

Chief Webber nodded at the woman and her son, who returned his greeting. Then the chief walked off.

"I have to apologize to you, as well," Sarah said to Helen. "If I'd been taking better care of your quilt, none of this could ever have happened."

"You know what I think?" Helen said.

Sarah shook her head.

"That's just nonsense!" said Helen, patting Sarah's hand. "I'm sure you did the best you could. In fact, it sounds to me like you went quite a bit above and beyond. These kinds of things can happen to anyone. And this one turned out all right in the end, thanks to you."

"I'm so glad you feel that way," Sarah said.

"No, this whole experience has been wonderful," Helen said. "Seeing that quilt up there tonight, and watching the way people stared when they looked up at it, I realized how selfish I've been all these years not to let anyone see it. I think that was a mistake. Nobody but you could have helped me see that, but now that I do, I might not be so quick to say no the next time somebody asks."

Sarah smiled. "I'm sure there are lots more people who would love to see it," she said.

Helen took a deep breath. "Well, honey, if you don't mind, this has been a lot of excitement for me. I'd like to go home now."

"That's what I'm here for," her son said gamely.

"It was so good to see you," Sarah told Helen. "And thank you again."

"No," Helen said as she started off, "thank *you*."

As Helen moved away, Shelly Andrews stepped up from behind her. "I know you're probably so busy," she said. "I just wanted to talk with you for a minute before you have to go."

"Sure," Sarah said. "Is everything all right?"

Shelly nodded. "It is," she said. "And I only wanted to thank you for it. I went to the fair board this morning and told them about my entries."

Sarah put her hand on Shelly's arm. "That must have been hard," she said.

Shelly nodded. "Yes," she said. "But I decided, no matter what happened, I didn't need money badly enough to lie about who I really am."

"And what did they say?" Sarah asked gently.

Shelly gave a rueful laugh. "Well," she said, "they looked it up. And it turns out that it's not actually against any rules to enter things under different names—or to enter things more than once. I should have read the rules myself to begin with. I could have saved us all a lot of trouble."

"So you get to keep the prizes?" Sarah said.

Shelly nodded. "Yes," she told Sarah. "But I've already decided I'm going to give a hundred dollars of it to a charity that sends blankets to needy kids. I need to do that, to remind myself that money's just not as important as so many other things."

Sarah smiled. "That sounds like a good idea," she said. "Have you seen Janet Stevens around the fair yet?"

"Janet?" Shelly asked. "I don't think so. Why?"

"She has some good news," Sarah told her. "You should ask her about it."

"I will," Shelly promised. She leaned in to give Sarah a quick hug good-bye. "Thank you again," she said. "I had gotten really mixed up about what mattered most, until you called me on it."

"I'm not sure I did anything special," Sarah said, "but I'm glad if it helped."

"It did," Shelly said. She smiled again and joined the throng coursing out the arena doors.

Sarah felt a tap on her shoulder. She turned around to see Lexie and Audrey, both beaming.

"Good job, Grandma!" Audrey said, and wrapped her in a tight hug. "Everyone loves your exhibit."

"The prize quilts look great!" Lexie chimed in. "And I don't even like quilts."

"Just like your grandmother, eh?" Sarah teased.

Lexie grinned.

"Did you ever find that thing you were looking for?" Audrey asked. "It sounded like it was really important."

"The thing you had all those questions about?" Lexie added.

"Well, I did find it," Sarah said, "due to your help, in part. So thank you both."

"All I did was stand there and watch the calf get his bath," Audrey said. "And that's going to come in handy when I bring home Zeus for a pet."

"You can't have a sheep for a pet!" Lexie squealed.

"Come on," Audrey said, heading for the door. "Let's go see him again!"

Sarah smiled as the girls disappeared into the crowd, Audrey's words ringing in her ears: *it sounded like it was really important.*

Sarah hadn't been able to think about anything but the missing quilt for most of the fair. And it *had* been important. But looking back over the week now, finding the quilt hardly seemed like the most important thing that had happened. What had been more important was watching Janet's eyes light up when Jeff Walker admitted that her copy had fooled him. Seeing the confidence return to Shelly Andrews when she decided not to lie any longer about who she was, no matter what the circumstances. And the moment when Allie's harshness and bravado had left her, as she began to see—really see—how much Lily needed her.

Why had God let all this happen? Sarah hadn't been able to understand it all week. But now she had a few more clues. Looking for the quilt, she had discovered she wasn't the only person in Maple Hill trying to solve a difficult puzzle. Hers wasn't the only life in which God was working gently to lead her to his solution. And amazingly, he had pieced the pattern together so that her struggles had helped other people discover their own answers. She had been looking for the quilt for herself, but what she had thought of as her troubles had helped the people around her find confidence, and communication, and hope.

Thank you for helping me find the quilt, she prayed as the crowd flowed by, laughing and talking. *Thank you for giving me a little glimpse of everything else you're doing. And thank you for using me, even when I couldn't see the whole pattern of what you're creating.*

When she finished, she looked up at the metal rafters of the arena. She couldn't see God, of course, but she had a sense that if she could, he might be smiling.

CHAPTER TWENTY-ONE

"W ould you like another one, Dad?" Sarah asked, holding out the plate of raspberry oatmeal bars she had made that morning.

Tiffany had been right about the swings an older person's health can take. Sarah's father had been frighteningly sick this past week, but this morning he was sitting up, his color close to normal, munching happily on the sweets Sarah had brought him.

"I guess I will," William said, choosing one of the golden squares from the tower of treats that Sarah had made for him.

"We had the fair parade yesterday," Sarah told him. Her father had always loved taking her down to watch the floats and fire engines and horses march through town when she was a girl, and even after she had grown up, he had never stopped going down to see the parade himself. Eventually he had begun to take Jason and Jenna when they were small. They had loved scrabbling around in the street to pick up the candy from the floats. They would carry it back to him and he would hide it away safely in his pockets. When they walked back to the house, he would turn his pockets inside out and pour out all the candy they had collected on the dining room table, to their great delight.

She could never be sure what her father would and wouldn't remember, but now his eyes lit up. "Oh yeah?" he said. "Jim Barry still have those big black dray horses with the old carriage?"

Jim Barry had passed away a few years ago, but her father had forgotten. Sarah didn't correct him. Instead, she offered him another detail that might tickle his fancy. "Art Callendar drove his 1965 Mustang," she told him. "Factory red. He's the original owner. Never let it get out of mint condition."

This bit of math seemed to confuse her father, but he let it pass.

Sarah set the plate of cookies down on his bedside table and covered them carefully with plastic wrap. Then she leaned forward to take her father's hand.

"I'm so glad to see your feeling better, Dad," she said.

"Better?" he repeated.

Sarah squeezed his hand gently. Apparently he had already forgotten how sick he had been that week: the infection and the fever, the medicines they had tried, her worried visits, his labored breathing. That was a mercy, she guessed, to balance all the other precious things that his memory loss had taken away from him. At least the bad moments were erased along with the good ones.

"Yep," she said. "You weren't feeling very well."

"Is that right?" he asked.

Sarah glanced at her watch. "It's time for me to go, Dad," she said. "But I'll be back to see you soon."

"Sounds good," he said gamely. Sarah kissed his forehead and went out to the front desk.

Tiffany waved as Sarah approached.

"He seems so much better," Sarah said. "It's wonderful to see the change."

Tiffany's smile was guarded. "Well," she said, "that's how it is with older folks. They do make these fast recoveries sometimes. But you have to remember, sometimes they slip just as quickly."

"I guess that's what we saw this week," Sarah mused.

Tiffany nodded. "At this time of life," she said, "it's really impossible to know."

"Well," Sarah said, "I know I'm glad he has you to take care of him."

"We're glad to have him," Tiffany said. "And it's good to see you around here from time to time too."

Sarah smiled and went out.

Allie and Lily Turnquist were already on her doorstep when she pulled up to her house. As she walked up to the front door, Lily gave Sarah a big smile.

"Hello, Mrs. Hart!" she said.

Allie was uncharacteristically quiet.

"Hi, Lily," Sarah said, opening the door to let them pass in. "Allie. Good to see you."

Allie nodded.

"The quilt room is back here," Sarah said, leading the way. When they stepped into her familiar haven, Sarah realized how different it was from the pristine showcase where she had found Helen's quilt hidden in Allie's house. In place of Allie's vast array of valuable quilts, Sarah's quilt room boasted mixed quarters and bolts of fabric, both antique and brand-new, a small library of quilt books, her own machine and workstation, boxes of tools and gadgets. The only valuable antiques in the place weren't hers—they were projects that she was repairing and restoring to return to clients for their enjoyment. It wasn't perfect like Allie's sun-drenched, custom-made room, but to Sarah it still felt like home.

She tapped her fingers briskly on the work island in the center of the room, where Helen Baxter's quilt was carefully folded. "Here's where we'll start," she said. "Let's take a look at what we're dealing with."

"I hope it's not too bad," Lily said, worry in her voice. "I'm really sorry about all this."

"Well," Sarah said, rolling the quilt out to inspect the damage, "we've got several things going for us already. Helen's family has taken excellent care of this quilt, so we're not dealing with tears, or stains, or dye migration."

"What's that?" Lily asked.

"If quilts are left folded for a long time," Allie told her, "sometimes the dyes will seep through from one piece of fabric to another."

"Have I seen that?" Lily asked.

"Maybe at a few shows," Allie said. "The quilts I collect don't usually have that problem."

Sarah suppressed a smile. Allie was subdued today, but she couldn't help being herself.

Now the quilt was laid full-length on the workstation. Lily winced and pointed at a splash of chalky brown in the bottom corner. "There," she said. "Is it bad?"

"I'm sure it looked a lot worse when the mud was wet," Sarah said.

"It did," Lily said quietly.

"There are gloves in the bucket," Sarah said, nodding at the little steel pail where she kept latex gloves for working on the quilts. Allie and Lily both reached for a pair.

"Luckily, I've got a very special tool for removing this kind of thing," Sarah said.

"There's a quilt-mud-removal tool?" Allie asked. Sarah could hear her voice rise with the anticipation of some new thing to own. "Where did you get it?"

"I don't remember," Sarah said. "I've had it for a long time."

She went to the closet and pulled out her decades-old vacuum cleaner.

"It's just a vacuum cleaner," Lily said, surprised.

"It does the job," Sarah said. She knelt down and rooted around among her quilt books until she found the square of mesh screen she had sandwiched between two books for safekeeping. She laid it down on the stain.

"Now your job," she said, looking at Lily, "is to hold that in place. Just don't put your hands over the stain, so I can reach it with the vacuum. The screen will let the dirt through, and keep the vacuum from damaging the fabric or disturbing any stitching."

Lily's and Allie's hands settled into place on each side of the screen. Sarah flipped the vacuum cleaner on and gently sucked the loose fragments of mud into the vacuum. When she was done, only a dusty shadow of the mud remained.

"Now the back," she said.

Working together, the three women flipped the quilt over and used the vacuum and screen on the more serious stains on the backing fabric.

"I guess it looks better," Lily said doubtfully as they flipped it right side up again.

"Well, we're not done yet," Sarah told her.

"This won't hurt the value," Allie assured her daughter. "Helen won't even have to mention it in the quilt's history. It's just a little cleaning."

It was just like Allie—more concerned with the quilt's cost than its meaning. But she was doing her best to make Lily feel better, Sarah knew. And Lily looked at her mom gratefully.

"How do we get the rest of it out?" Lily asked.

"The same way you get clean when you're dirty," Sarah told her.

"Soap?" Lily guessed.

Sarah nodded. "That's right!" Sarah said. "We're just a little more careful about how we apply the soap and water mixture."

Over the next hour, she and Lily and Allie worked carefully on the quilt, daubing at the muddied portions, rinsing their rags, and then daubing again until all traces of the mud were gone. Then they carried the quilt out to the backyard and hung it up to air dry in the bright summer sun.

"That was nice," Allie said. "I don't usually get to spend time really getting to know a quilt like that."

Sarah nodded. "I love learning about quilts by working on them," she said. "I almost don't mind when I have to give them back."

"I don't know if I'd ever feel quite like that," Allie said.

They laughed.

"It looks just like it did before," Lily said quietly. "I can't believe it."

Sarah put her arm around Lily and gave her a little hug. "Good job," she said.

When Sarah let go, Allie put her own arm around her daughter's shoulder. "Good job, honey," she said. The words didn't sound natural coming from her, but Lily didn't seem to mind. She wrapped her arms around her mother's waist, and held on.

Sarah watched the two of them as the quilt swung gently in the breeze. Somehow, even though she had turned her life upside down searching for the quilt, it seemed like the least important thing that had happened.

ABOUT THE AUTHOR

Vera Dodge is a writer and avid sewer who is delighted to blend both her passions in the Patchwork Mysteries series. She grew up in small towns in the Midwest.

A QUILT OF MEMORIES

BY KRISTIN ECKHARDT

 CHAPTER ONE

A blast of chilly air met Sarah as she walked into The Spotted Dog Café and Bookstore on Thursday afternoon. The cooled atmosphere was a welcome reprieve from the August heat and she took a moment to enjoy it while Murphy, the canine doorman, ran up to greet her with a sloppy kiss on her bare ankle.

"Hello there," she said, reaching down to pet the scruffy corgi. "It's a hot one out there. I'd stay inside if I were you."

Murphy rolled onto his back for a tummy rub and Sarah obliged for a moment, then straightened up to look for Martha. They had agreed to meet here for a late lunch and Sarah was starving.

She saw Martha seated in the far corner of the café, her crochet hook making quick work of the ball of soft pink yarn in her lap.

"Sorry I'm late," Sarah said, taking the chair opposite.

"You're not late, I was early." Martha held up the crochet hook, a tiny baby bootie dangling from it. "My niece just found out she's having a little girl."

"That's adorable."

"Wait until you see the sweater and bonnet that I'm going to make to go with it. She's not due until December, so I'll have plenty of time to make a full layette."

Sarah leaned back in her chair. "A Christmas baby. That will be nice. I can't believe summer is almost over, although it sure doesn't seem that way with this heat."

"School starts next week." Martha tucked her crochet supplies into her bag. "Fall will be here before we know it."

Fall was Sarah's favorite season. The days were still warm enough to enjoy time outdoors but the evenings were nice and cool. Best of all, the autumn foliage in the Berkshires was breathtaking. The rich palette of colors always inspired her to start a new quilting project.

Karen Bancroft, a waitress at The Spotted Dog, approached their table. "Good afternoon, ladies. Our special today is cucumber soup served with an Italian grilled cheese and tomato sandwich."

"That sounds perfect," Sarah said. "I'll have that and a glass of iced tea, too, please."

Sarah's cell phone rang before Martha could order. The cell phone screen identified the caller as the Bradford Manor Nursing Home, where Sarah's father lived.

"Excuse me for a moment," Sarah said, slipping out of her chair and walking a few steps away before answering the call. "Hello?"

"Sarah, this is Tiffany Henderson at Bradford Manor. I'm calling about your father."

Tiffany was one of her dad's nurses and her tone made Sarah uneasy. "Is he all right?"

"The doctor's here with him now," Tiffany explained. "He'd like you to come over if you're available."

"What's wrong?"

Tiffany hesitated. "It's not an emergency, but you need to talk to the doctor."

"I'll be right there." Sarah hung up the phone then walked back to the table, her mind searching for an explanation. *Had Dad fallen or gotten an infection? He had been fighting a cold, perhaps it had turned into pneumonia.*

Tiffany's evasiveness certainly hadn't stopped her from worrying.

"I have to go," Sarah said abruptly, reaching for her purse.

Martha leaned forward. "What's wrong?"

"I don't know. That was Dad's nurse at Bradford Manor and she said his doctor wants to see me."

Martha started to rise from her chair. "Do you want me to go with you?"

"No, please stay here and have lunch," Sarah said, trying to remain calm. "I'm sure everything is fine. Tiffany assured me it wasn't an emergency. If it was serious, Dad would be on his way to the hospital."

Martha hesitated, then sat back down. "All right, but call me and let me know what's happening."

"I will."

Sarah passed Liam as she headed for the door.

"Hello, Sarah," Liam said, greeting her with a wide smile. "I didn't see you come in."

Any other time, she would stop to chat with him, but she didn't know how long the doctor would wait for her. "I'm sorry, Liam, I've got to go," she said pulling the door open. "I'll talk to you later."

He began to say something to her but the words were lost as the door closed behind her. She hurried to her car, her eyes squinting against the bright sun. A light sheen of sweat gathered at the back of her neck.

With each step, fear and uncertainty niggled their way into her mind. Her father had seemed tired during her last visit. She had blamed it on his cold, but maybe she should have been more concerned. At the time, she had been in a hurry to get home and put the finishing touches on her latest quilting project. Now she was kicking herself for not contacting his doctor or, at least, speaking to one of the nurses.

"Live in faith, not fear," Sarah said aloud as she drove toward Bradford Manor. It was one of her father's favorite mantras, one he used to repeat when she was a young girl caught up in one worry or another. She still found that advice comforting, a gentle reminder that God is in charge of our lives.

Sarah parked her silver Grand Prix in front of Bradford Manor, then hurried into the building. A few of the residents sat in wheelchairs outside their rooms and she gave them a tight smile as she made her way toward her father's room at the end of the hallway.

Tiffany Henderson met her at the door.

"Hi, Sarah." Tiffany tucked her stethoscope into a pocket of her navy blue scrubs. "Dr. Canaday is in with your father now."

"Is he...okay?" Sarah asked, unable to contain the tremor in her voice.

Tiffany reached out to gently pat her arm. "He seems fine, now. Dr. Canaday will explain everything to you."

Sarah nodded, and then walked into the room. Her father lay in his bed, his eyes closed and an unusual pallor on his lined face.

Dr. Canaday stood on the other side of the bed, writing in a chart. He looked up when he heard Sarah approach. "Hello, Sarah. I was hoping to see you before I left today."

"Hi, Dr. Canaday. What's wrong with Dad?" Sarah stood next to the bed rail waiting for her father to open his blue eyes. But he just lay there, his breathing soft and even, undisturbed by the sound of their voices.

"It looks like your father suffered a TIA, which is short for a transient ischemic attack." Dr. Canaday set down the chart. "It's a type of ministroke and the symptoms usually last for a few minutes or sometimes up to an hour. I was notified that he was experiencing some weakness on the left side of his body. I did some preliminary tests as soon as I arrived and he seems to have recovered now."

"Does that mean he'll be all right?"

Dr. Canaday hesitated. "I wish I could say for sure, Sarah. A TIA can be a warning sign of an impending stroke."

William opened his eyes, his gaze unfocused for a moment. Then he turned his head just far enough to see her. "Sarah?"

"I'm here, Dad," she said, taking his right hand in hers and leaning closer to him. "Everything's all right." She looked up at the doctor, hoping he would confirm her words.

The doctor gave a short nod. "He's fine at the moment, but I want to admit him to the hospital for a few days to run some tests. We can monitor his condition there and—"

"No," William interjected, his gaze still fixed on Sarah. "I like it . . . here."

His dementia made it difficult for him to adjust to new situations. She knew a hospital stay would confuse and frighten him. "He doesn't want to go to the hospital," Sarah told the doctor. "Is there any way you could treat him here?"

Dr. Canaday hesitated. "At the very least, he needs a CAT scan and that can only be done at Maple Hill Medical Center."

"Sarah," William breathed again, giving her hand a weak squeeze.

She was torn between following her father's wishes and doing what was best for him.

"Is it possible to take him to the hospital for a CAT scan and bring him back the same day?" Sarah asked. "I know he'll be much more comfortable here and I'll stay with him day and night if necessary."

Dr. Canaday's face relaxed into a smile. "Okay, you two win. I'll schedule the test for tomorrow morning. He should be back at Bradford Manor in time for lunch."

Sarah leaned closer to her father. "Did you hear that, Dad? You don't have to stay in the hospital."

"Okay," William said on a yawn.

She reached up one hand to gently brush his sparse white hair into place. "Go ahead and sleep now. I'll stay here as long as you need me."

Dr. Canaday picked up the chart and tucked it under his arm. "I think he'll be all right, Sarah. You don't need to camp out here either. We'll know more about his condition when we get the test results back."

"Thank you."

Dr. Canaday headed for the door. "I'll see you two tomorrow."

After the doctor left, Sarah tucked the blanket more snugly around her father, then pulled a chair close to his bed and sat down. It wasn't the best news, but it certainly wasn't the worst. She closed her eyes and whispered a prayer.

"Thank you, Lord, for my wonderful father. I should thank you every day for having him in my life, but sometimes I get too busy to count all my blessings. Be with him, Lord, comfort and keep him close to you. Help me to be a blessing in his life as he goes to the hospital for tests tomorrow." She sucked in a deep breath. "Please let him be all right."

Sarah leaned back against the chair, her head tilted slightly so she could watch him sleep. It always surprised her how quickly life could change. She had awakened today with plans to meet Martha for lunch, followed by a trip to Wild Goose Chase to check out the new fall fabrics.

She closed her eyes. One phone call had changed all that. But there was nowhere else she wanted to be at this moment.

"Sarah?"

She opened her eyes, her neck stiff. "Hm?"

"You fell asleep in the chair." Tiffany set William's supper tray on the rolling bedside table.

"Oh dear." Sarah straightened, rubbing one hand over the back of her sore neck. "What time is it?"

"Almost five." Tiffany walked over to the other side of the bed and gave Sarah's father a gentle shake on the shoulder. "It's time for supper, Mr. Drayton."

He opened his eyes, and then smiled. "Hey, that smells pretty good."

Sarah agreed, her mouth watering as the nurse lifted the plate cover to reveal tender roast beef, mashed potatoes with gravy, and a dish of applesauce. That's when she realized she hadn't eaten a thing since breakfast.

"You get to eat in your room tonight," Tiffany said, then looked over at Sarah. "Would you like a tray too?"

"That would be wonderful." Sarah stood up, trying to work the stiffness out of her muscles. "I'll just run to the dining room and purchase a tray for myself. Do you mind staying with him until I get back?"

Tiffany smiled. "Of course not. Mr. Drayton is one of my favorite residents."

Sarah watched her father dig into his dinner, happy to see that he had a healthy appetite.

She walked out into the hallway and headed toward the dining room, still trying to clear the cobwebs from her head.

She could hear the clink of silverware and the low murmur of voices as she reached the center of the nursing home.

"Sarah?"

She turned at the sound of her name and saw Rebecca Gillespie, Bradford Manor's financial director, emerge from her office.

"Hello, Rebecca."

Rebecca was in her midthirties and a lifetime resident of Maple Hill. Sarah remembered when little Becky Gillespie used to come to her door selling Girl Scout cookies, intent on winning the prize for the most sales. Now she went by Rebecca and had traded her unruly blonde pigtails for a neat French braid.

"I know this isn't the best time." Rebecca stood in the doorway, looking picture-perfect in her teal blue silk suit. "But I really need to talk to you. Do you have a few minutes?"

"Of course." Sarah walked into the spacious office, a little surprised when the woman closed the door behind her.

"Please have a seat," Rebecca rounded her desk and sat down in her black leather chair. "First things first. How is your father doing?"

"I think he's doing pretty well. He slept most of the afternoon and seems to have a good appetite."

"I'm happy to hear it," Rebecca replied, shuffling thorough the papers on her desk. Then she placed her hands in her lap and met Sarah's gaze. "I need to talk to you about Mr. Drayton's account. His last monthly payment was rejected due to insufficient funds."

Sarah blinked. "There must be some mistake."

"I'm afraid not. I called the bank when I received the notice and they verified that he didn't have the funds to cover the payment." Rebecca cleared her throat. "I realize you have other things to worry about right now, but the directors are really cracking down. If Mr. Drayton's payment is not made in the next two weeks, he won't be able to continue staying at Bradford Manor."

Sarah rose to her feet, unable to believe her ears. After all the years he had spent here, they would kick him out? "I'll get it straightened out."

"I know this seems…cold," Rebecca stood up. "It's the part of my job I hate the most. But we have bills to pay too and an obligation to all our residents to keep this place up and running."

"I understand," Sarah said, although she still thought the timing was awful. But no matter. She would head to the bank tomorrow and make sure the payment was made. She certainly wouldn't allow her father to be evicted from the place he had called home for the last ten years.

"Thank you, Sarah," Rebecca said as she walked her to the door. "Please let me know if there's anything I can do to help."

"I will."

Sarah left Rebecca's office, telling herself she would feel better when she got some food into her stomach. This day had been full of surprises, none of them pleasant.

She headed to the dining room and purchased a supper tray, then returned to her father's room. He had finished his meal and was now sipping a cup of coffee.

"More food?" he asked, eyeing the tray in her hands.

Sarah chuckled. "This is for me but I'll share if you're still hungry." She set her tray down on the table, then leaned over to kiss his forehead.

"I'm not hungry but Jimmy is probably starving." He set his coffee cup on his tray. "Is he home from the lake yet?"

Her brother James hadn't been home for a very long time. He lived with his wife Lucia in Livorno, Italy. "Not yet."

"Well, tell him to hurry," William said, settling back against his pillow. "I need to talk to him."

"I will, Dad," Sarah replied, determined to call her brother as soon as she got home tonight. She needed to talk to him about their father's health and the condition of his bank account. Maybe she could finally convince James that it was time to come home.

A NOTE FROM THE EDITORS

We hope you enjoy Patchwork Mysteries, created by the Books and Inspirational Media Division of Guideposts, a nonprofit organization that touches millions of lives every day through products and services that inspire, encourage, help you grow in your faith, and celebrate God's love in every aspect of your daily life.

Thank you for making a difference with your purchase of this book, which helps fund our many outreach programs to military personnel, prisons, hospitals, nursing homes, and educational institutions. To learn more, visit GuidepostsFoundation.org.

We also maintain many useful and uplifting online resources. Visit Guideposts.org to read true stories of hope and inspiration, access OurPrayer network, sign up for free newsletters, download free e-books, join our Facebook community, and follow our stimulating blogs.

To learn about other Guideposts publications, including the best-selling devotional *Daily Guideposts,* go to ShopGuideposts.org, call (800) 932–2145, or write to Guideposts, PO Box 5815, Harlan, Iowa 51593.